RAGNARÖK UNWOUND

IKEPELA IVES
BOOK ONE

KRISTIN JACQUES

Midnight Tide
PUBLISHING

RAGNARÖK UNWOUND

KRISTIN JACQUES

CONTENTS

To my mom and her electric typewriter.
What magic we wove.

ONE

A VALKYRIE WALKS INTO A BAR

IVES NURSED A DOUBLE-SHOT MAI TAI, swiping through Tinder's Friday night hopefuls when the Valkyrie plunked down on the barstool next to her.

She was pretty sure it was a Valkyrie. She ran through the mental checklist of mythical beings as she pointedly ignored the six-foot blonde boring holes into her skull with laser-focused baby blues. Definitely immortal, the woman gave off enough heat to melt the ice cubes in her Mai Tai. There were a few creatures that fit those physical parameters, but the Nordic runes tattooed around her biceps sealed the deal.

In a place like Johnny Ho's Tiki Lounge, the blonde stood out. Aside from the glitzy name, Johnny Ho's was more of a local watering hole than the tourist hotspot it aspired to be. Compared to the bronzed and burnt skin tones of Johnny's native clientele, the Valkyrie practically glowed like a moonflower.

That was Ives's sucktastic luck. Being sought out at her favorite hangout by an immortal bombshell was the appropriate end to this shitstorm of a day. Determined not to let the shieldmaiden interfere with her current sob fest, Ives ducked her head and sipped her now watered-down drink. She swiped her thumb against the phone screen with a little too much vigor, sending a string of potentials to the virtual waste bin as she fought not to grind her teeth. *Damn.* She hated being stared at, and immortals were the worst for it. Most of them didn't need to blink.

"Ikepela Ives," said the Valkyrie.

Hearing her full name made Ives jump, sloshing her drink onto her hand. She swore softly, and the blonde noted her reaction with a satisfied nod.

The Valkyrie leaned in with a muted clink of concealed metal, far too close for comfort, and stage-whispered, "I have come to secure your services."

Ives briefly closed her eyes to keep from rolling them. *No shit, Sherlock.*

The bartender paused before them, quirking an eyebrow at the blonde as he placed a tumbler in front of her. "Here is your scotch neat, miss."

The Valkyrie pulled back and beamed at the man. "Ah, thank you, good sir!" She slapped a handful of old, *old* coins on the bar as she threw back the drink in one swallow. "Another, if you please," she said, belching into her fist.

The bartender blinked at her. His eyes went unfocused, the same glazed-over expression most mortals got when they stared too long at a divine being. The Valkyrie frowned at him as the staring continued, waving a hand in front of his face.

"Nick, the lady asked for another," said Ives, snapping him out of it with the sound of her voice.

The bartender shook himself; some of the glassiness in his eyes subsided. "Be right up," he mumbled, shuffling away.

The Valkyrie turned to her. "What was wrong with that man?"

"IT grad, tattoos, and makes a mean grilled cheese," Ives murmured, keeping her eyes on the Tinder profile screen as she ignored the persistent woman. "What girl can say no to grilled cheese?"

The Valkyrie drummed her fingers on the bar hard enough to rattle the tiny Tiki statue decor. "Ikepela Ives—"

"Treat me like a pirate and gimme that booty? Oh, that is too corny even for me," said Ives.

Nick placed another scotch in front of the Valkyrie, scurrying off when he caught the thunderous expression on her face. Sparks of electricity crackled through her golden locks. That made Ives tense. Immortals who sucked at keeping a low profile were ones who didn't care about collateral damage, which meant it was time to abandon Johnny Ho's before things got ugly. Ives made a call without the aid of her cell. *Jules, time for 'One Too Many'.*

"Ikepela Ives," said the Valkyrie, at the end of her fuse, judging by the tone of her voice. "I demand an audience."

Time to stall.

"You call me by my first name one more time, and I will break your fingers," said Ives. She slurped the rest of her watery Mai Tai and slammed the glass down.

The woman snorted. "Where I come from, that is merely flirting."

Ives squinted at her, fishing a rum-soaked cherry from the bottom of her glass. The sudden infusion of alcohol sent a warm flush through her cheeks and fuzzed her sense of self-preservation. "How about a broken arm?"

The woman grinned, revealing absurdly perfect teeth. "Foreplay."

"Yeah, well, you aren't my type blondie, so fu—"

"Ives!" A petite brunette popped up at Ives's elbow, wrapping slender fingers around her forearm. Her new companion stared up at the Valkyrie with wide eyes. "I think it's time we get you home." Her stature might be small, but her grip was iron, and she yanked Ives off the barstool before she could insult the shieldmaiden further.

"I haven't paid my tab," Ives whined. She leaned heavily on her companion.

"I took care of it," squeaked the tiny lady, steadying Ives when she tripped over the half step at the entrance. "How many shots of rum did Nick put in there?"

"Three," said Ives and held up four fingers. She giggled.

Tall, blonde, and sparky watched as they stumbled off, tracing a finger along the rim of her tumbler. She didn't move to stop them, though she was unhappy about Ives's departure judging by the sparks that skittered across her fingertips. Another insult Ives would no doubt pay for later when the Valkyrie caught up with her.

All she wanted from the evening was to drink away her good judgment while browsing for a possible playmate to cancel out an abysmal pisser of a day. Instead, here she was, making her 'drunken' escape with a Valkyrie's glare burning her backside.

The two made it to the parking lot before Ives pressed her mouth to the smaller woman's ear. "Are we in the clear, Jules?"

"Gigantor hasn't followed us yet, but I doubt she'll wait long." Jules nibbled her lip, eyeing Ives from beneath a mop of glossy brown curls. "I know it makes you a bit woozy, but we should take the express route home."

Ives's stomach flopped at the very mention of it. That Valkyrie was nothing but bad news. "Do it."

Jules wrapped her thin arms around Ives's waist. She felt a tug in her bowels and straight up through her spinal cord as the world wobbled at the edges. The next second, she blinked in her darkened apartment. Jules released her as reality caught up, squeezing her insides.

"Ugh!" Ives rushed for the bathroom and emptied the contents of her stomach. Jules paid good money for that Mai Tai too, well, Ives did since they shared her bank account. Another grievance she could throw in the Valkyrie's face. With a groan, she straightened to find her roommate waiting in the doorway with a fizzing glass of Alka-Seltzer. Ives took it with a grateful nod and drained its contents. The couch looked damned inviting, but she was fooling herself if she thought the Valkyrie wouldn't track her here. Jules flit about the room, tidying nervously. After the tiny woman's third circuit rearranging the same stack of books, Ives came to a decision.

"We can't stay here tonight," she said, heading for her bedroom to snag her overnight bag. "We'll head over to Dad's. He won't mind us crashing for the night."

Jules squealed, clapping her hands together. "He's *so messy*," she said with a dreamy look.

Ives rolled her eyes. "You know you have an open invitation to stay at his house whenever the urge hits." She regretted opening her mouth when Jules's expression turned somber.

"You need me more," said Jules softly.

Ives flapped her hand at their apartment. "Hogwash. This place is spotless."

Jules *did* have a gift for decluttering.

"You know what I mean," said Jules, a sad smile lifting the corners of her mouth.

Ives braced herself on the bed, her bag open and waiting. She knew exactly what Jules meant. There were reasons left unspoken, that *couldn't* be spoken. It was safer to consider their situation a mutual need. Jules had nowhere else to go. Ives had no other friends. She anchored Jules while Jules always had her back.

Ives tossed in a few random articles of clothing and

gathered her toiletries, ignoring Jules as she reorganized the bag with matching outfits. Her roommate's eye twitched when Ives dumped damp bottles of shampoo and conditioner on top of everything. Ives snapped her bag shut, throwing an arm around Jules's shoulder as they exited their shared apartment.

"Just promise me—organize, no rearranging. The last time, I thought he was going to have an aneurysm when you cleaned the workshop," said Ives.

Jules pouted. "I simply put all his tools in their proper places."

"It took him a week to find his socket wrenches."

That made Jules giggle, though her expression swung back to worried. "What about the shieldmaiden?"

Ives could feel a headache forming. The Valkyrie would catch up to them sooner rather than later, and what she represented made Ives's skin crawl.

I'm not ready to do this.

Chill sweat dripped down her back despite the evening heat. She forced a smile for her companion. "We'll burn that bridge when we come to it."

🪦🪦🪦

The Valkyrie watched their departure from a nearby balcony. Hildr preferred high places, seeing the world from an aerial vantage point. She always saw so much more than she did from the ground level. She pursed her lips as she watched the mightily sober Ives and her fae companion clamber into a miserable excuse for a vehicle, a rust-mottled jeep with peeling seats. It didn't start the first time, causing Ives to shout and bang on the dashboard until it grudgingly rumbled to life. Hildr kept her eyes trained on them until the jeep's red brake lights were glowing dots zipping away into the night.

A crow landed on the balcony railing, dancing from foot to foot.

"Are we sure she is the one? She doesn't look like much," said Hildr.

The crow tilted its sleek black head, cawing in a rather derisive tone for a carrion eater.

She made a face. "No need to be so rude about it."

Hildr required a tool. Her awareness spread until it narrowed on a creature padding along the side of the road.

During his brief life, Chester was a good dog.

Born on the streets, he spent his formative years scrounging food from the trash bins of local restaurants, a diet consisting of gristle, bones, and spam. It was a hard living. His skin clung tight to his ribs; his frame was lean and wiry from chasing off rival dogs and his mortal enemy —cars.

Those brightly colored chrome monsters plagued his existence. They spooked the tasty pigeons and seagulls, emitted blasts of sound that assaulted his sensitive ears, and zipped past at unforgivable speeds. Crossing the pitted black tar from the row of restaurants to his sleeping place each day was a task fraught with danger. It was only a matter of time when one of those cars would prove too fast and crush him against the road like he'd seen happen to other unfortunate animals.

The thruway was quiet this time of night except for the occasional eighteen-wheeler or questionably sober local. The last car, a battered jeep driven by a woman who reeked of salty stress and bitter ashes, passed some time ago.

Time was a strange concept to Chester. Humans believed dogs had no concept of time, of life or death, but that wasn't entirely true. Chester was quite aware of death and how it stalked the street dogs. He felt the passage of time keenly from one scavenged meal to the next by the hollow pit in his belly. It was the idea of food that drove him, the air pungent with the scent of slightly turned ham. He never understood how humans could throw out a perfectly delicious ham.

It was all he could think about as he darted across the thruway. He didn't see the sleek red car until it was too late. It didn't even slow down as it rammed into him. The initial impact blazed through his body before the blessed numbness as his nerve endings stopped working. Death took him, sparing him the agony of a body shredded between tire and road. His spirit was done. It should have departed to the next world—except it lingered, waiting for *what*, he did not know.

The Valkyrie emerged from the shadows.

Chester watched as she approached what was once his body. She pressed her lips tight, anger apparent in her narrowed gaze as flashes of light played over the surface of her pale skin.

"You will have justice," she murmured. The words confused Chester, but there was little time for pondering their meaning. The pull of the other side beckoned to him, tempting him with the unexplored scents and hidden things in an endless field of windswept high grass. Still, he waited.

The Valkyrie squatted next to the carcass.

"I know I am pushing the bounds of technicalities, All-Father, but the trail grows cold," she said. "As long as Ikepela Ives travels in the company of that person, my skills are inadequate to track her. I need someone whose senses bypass natural glamour." The Valkyrie bit her lip as she held out a hand over Chester's body. He wondered who she spoke to. What did this strange sparkly woman intend to do?

"Rise, noble creature, warrior of your race, and become one with the Pack." The Valkyrie tensed her shoulders. Chester felt a tug within the core of his soul, a surge of power that yanked tight, like an invisible leash. His spirit shot forward, following the newly formed tether as light and energy filled his broken body. Bones cracked and snapped back into place. Shredded tissue, muscle, and skin knit itself together. Old scars faded from his pelt as an ethereal glow wove into his fur, making it thicker, more lustrous than it had been in life. His body filled out with a pulse of vitality, bulking slabs of muscle and fat.

"Attend, Hound of the Pack. I require your aid."

Chester, the newly made Hound, rose to his feet, his spirit meshed to his new stronger form. His tail thumped against her legs as he danced, giddy at the life coursing through him. The Valkyrie he now knew as Hildr held out her hand to him, which he licked with enthusiasm, grateful for the new life he'd been given.

"Yes, yes, I know," she said. "I need you to focus on our task. Find me the one who carries this scent." She held out a crumpled tee-shirt. "Ikepela Ives will give me an audience. It is the Fate Cipher's Duty."

The Valkyrie smelled of storms. Chester breathed in the scent from the shirt, a hint of bitter ashes and salty stress. There was still a tease of the scent trailing through the air. He barked, taking off like a shot down the thruway.

Two

A NOT-SO-SUCCESSFUL ESCAPE

THE JEEP GROANED to a halt outside a small bungalow-style home nestled amid the palm trees and tropical blooms like a weathered crown jewel. Ives sighed at the sight. Lavi Ives insisted the unkempt look had more to do with feeling attuned to nature than with his abhorrence for yard work. Either way, the mechanic let the encroaching plants run wild. Eventually, she suspected, the house would be reclaimed by the forest and her father would simply live in the trees. He was not big on material possessions. The only things he treasured were his tools and one framed picture beside his bed.

Ives blew out a breath through puffed lips, nudging Jules awake. A gentle evening rain was setting in, slapping against fat green fronds with a crescendo of 'pat, pat, pats.' There was one definite advantage to the overgrowth; both girls were still dry when they made it to the porch. The wood creaked in greeting beneath her feet as Ives fished out her house key. The hour was late, but she doubted her father was asleep. He was a night owl, like her. She also knew better than to try and capture his attention by knock-ing. There was only one place her father would be this time of night. If she listened hard enough she could hear the muffled tang of a hammer to metal through the workshop door.

It took an extra shove to open the front door, the wood swollen from the constant damp of the wet season. Jules danced in behind her, clapping her hands gleefully at the chaotic disarray that met them in the hall. Ives bit her lip to keep from laughing. Ever since she'd 'acquired' Jules, her father's housekeeping went from bad to worse. She suspected her father purposefully let the mess pile up to keep Jules occupied when she visited. If Jules wasn't cleaning something, she started organizing and her father's reaction to the workshop incident was fresh in Ives's memory.

"Have fun," she said, squeezing Jules's thin shoulder as she passed. She followed the sound of hammering, cutting through the path left in the piles of clutter and garbage.

She paused outside the master bedroom, the only room her father kept clean and Jules was not allowed to touch. Moonlight caught the silver picture frame on the nightstand. Shadows obscured the figures in the photo but she'd long memorized their faces. Three figures, her father, herself as a newborn, and the face she'd traced over and over during her childhood to commit it to memory. Ives sighed. She didn't need to think of crap like this right now. She continued to the back of the house, opening the door into the familiar sweltering heat of her father's workshop.

By day, Lavi Ives was a regular mechanic at Mikey Cutter's Garage. At night, he went home to his true passion. Working the forge, be it through metal sculpture, welding, and other such hobbies, her father was driven to the blistering heat of forge and fire, bending and twisting molten hot metal to whatever took his fancy. He had acquired many skills over the years, knew how to craft everything from chain mail to wind chimes of curlicue wire strips.

Ives entered as he dunked his latest project in a cooling tank of water. Her father looked up through a cloud of steam, tracks of sweat running down his grease streaked face. He wore his usual apparel of torn jeans and a dingy sleeveless shirt, covered from his knees to his chest by a scorched leather apron. Her father left his project to cool as he moved toward her. He wasn't all that tall, topping out at five foot ten, but he made up for it in width. Lavi Ives had the muscles of a blacksmith and the burns to match, but in his mid-forties, he had a full head of black hair with only a hint of salt. When he wasn't covered in grease, there was little evidence of his age in his smooth features. He was a man in his prime, but he hadn't had a date in years, no matter how much Ives nudged. The reason sat on his night-stand, in that cursed picture frame.

Her father enveloped her in a bear hug, filling her nostrils with the scent of machine grease and Old Spice. It was her father's signature smell and it eased the tightness in her shoulders.

No matter how dire the situation, she felt safe here. Her father always made her feel safe, even if he couldn't protect her from her 'calling'. For a second, she could imagine she was a little girl again, without a care in the world, blissfully unaware of her birthright.

"It's late, Ike," said her father against the top of her head. "Trouble brewing?" Her father was the only one she allowed to call her by any variation of her first name.

"I don't know yet, but I think it's a doozy," she said. If the freaking Valkyrie on her tail was any indication.

Her father was silent for a moment, letting her regain her calm. "And you aren't ready." He sighed when she stiffened. "It was bound to happen sooner or later, Ike. It's part of your nature. They are drawn to you the same as your mother." Ives extricated herself from her father's hold, biting down a sharp retort. Her father always looked so wounded when she insulted the woman. She'd vent to Jules later. Speaking of which...

"I brought Jules with me," said Ives. Her father grinned, letting the subject change slide.

"Well, as you saw, I have been anticipating your friend's visit," he jerked his head back to the scattered bits of metal on his work station. "Why don't I clean this up and make you some breakfast?"

"It's the middle of the night," said Ives, catching sight of the clock on the wall. Scratch that, it was four-thirty in the morning. Where had the night gone?

"Did you want to crash in your room then?"

"Have you been up all night?" Ives accused, folding her arms.

"Mikey is doing inventory in the shop. I have the next few days off so my time is my own, little miss. Now are you going to let me coax what is bothering you with an omelet, or do I have to break out the thumbscrews?"

Her father nudged her shoulder as he passed, hanging his apron by the door.

Ives scrunched up her face. "There better be cheese. Lots of cheese. Oozy levels of cheese!"

The two exited the shop to a spotless house. Jules was alone, maybe, fifteen minutes. Her father whistled, shaking his head at the sight of polished wooden floors.

"You should visit more often, Ike," he said, making his way to the bathroom to wash up. Ives shook her head, searching for Jules.

She found her roomie in the kitchen, cupping a mug of honey and warm milk. Her father kept a stock of such things just for their visits.

"You outdid yourself," said Ives, sliding next to the petite girl. The night was indeed waning, the quick spat of rain already gone as the lingering clouds took on the gray light of predawn through the sink window. Jules sat in the soft glow of the kitchen lights, a blissful expression on her face as she sipped her libations.

"He remembered how much I like clover honey," she said in a sing-song voice.

"Dad's good with the details," said Ives, glancing through the window. Across the road, through a copse of palm trees, the Pacific Ocean tumbled against the shore. The proximity of the sea was one of the many perks that made her father's home such a sanctuary. Perhaps after breakfast, she could run out for a dip. It was so peaceful here. She could hear the wind whispering through the palms leaves and overgrown fronds. There was a dog barking, though their closest neighbors were a mile away. The island birds were waking. They would start up a racket in an hour.

Her father emerged from the bathroom, his ruddy bronze complexion mostly free of machine grease. He leaned over the counter to plant an affectionate kiss on Jules's cheek before starting on breakfast.

"Care for an omelet, Jules," he said, grabbing the frying pan off the wall hook.

"No, thank you, sir, I am good with this." She toasted her mug to him, blushing at his raised eyebrow. Her father knew a great deal about the truth. Perhaps more than Ives knew herself. He knew what Jules was, or at least what Ives deduced she might be, though there were times his hospitable tendencies butted heads with her roommate's nature.

Jules ducked her head down. "I'll take a bit of toast though," she mumbled.

"Good enough," her father winked at the flustered

woman and turned to on the stove. The kitchen soon filled with the sound of sizzling butter and whisking eggs. Ives got up once to make coffee, settling down with a steaming cup as her father slid a plate of perfectly oozy cheesy eggs in front of her.

"All right, little miss, spill," he said, settling down with his meal. Jules kept her head down nibbling on her toast. "What sent you scurrying to my door?"

Ives dug into her meal. Her father was more correct than he knew. A run-in with a Valkyrie, no matter how unwelcome, wouldn't be quite enough to send her fleeing home. "I saw Mordred today."

Her father spat out a few choice words. "What did that punk want now?"

"He needed a favor. And he's not a punk, dad," said Ives, poking at her eggs. "It's more complicated than that."

Her father snorted, nothing buying it. He might be more enlightened than the average person but there were some things she couldn't share. She couldn't tell him Mordred broke her heart because she refused to use the skills she'd inherited. Suffice it to say, a run-in with her ex was the tipping point of her day. She thought she was finally over the pain of seeing him until he showed up on her doorstep, pushing her, *again*, to use the powers she'd avoided for the last three years. The Valkyrie was just the cherry on top of the shit sundae.

While the shieldmaiden wasn't the only reason she'd run to her father's house, she couldn't ignore that problem for long. Nor could she shake the feeling that whatever the Valkyrie wanted her for, it was much, much bigger than Mordred's problems. Possibly bigger than anything she'd been asked to handle before. Not that she'd handled much, but that was her decision. It had been her only choice, stubborn as it was when her role had been thrust on her. Ives sighed.

"I'd rather not talk about him. Um, dad, what do you know about Valkyries?"

Her father set down his fork, his expression unreadable. "Did you encounter one recently?"

She opened her mouth to answer when the front door blew off its hinges.

A rangy dog with silvery gray fur raced inside, circling the table with a chorus of booming barks. Jules squealed, clambering onto the tabletop. Ives and her father stood puzzled until the tall, statuesque blonde filled the doorway. The Valkyrie stomped forward in a pair of black steel-toed boots, the air crackling with her presence. Flickers of static sparked off her pale skin, dancing through her long, loose hair. Lightning flashed in her icy blue eyes as she drew close to Ives. She stopped a few feet away, her face set with grim determination.

"Ikepela Ives, I demand an audience in the name of Odin All-Father."

THREE

SANDALS ARE NOT WINTER FRIENDLY

HER FATHER REACTED FIRST. Lavi rolled out to a crouch in front of Ives and flung a hammer with surprising accuracy at the Valkyrie. If the blonde hadn't whipped a naked sword out of the air, it would have smacked her square in the throat. Where had her father pulled a hammer from? He already had another small club in his hand when the Valkyrie lowered her weapon, extending an open palm toward him.

"Peace, Lavi Ives. Your bravery is noteworthy but unnecessary." The Valkyrie made the sword vanish, holding up her empty hands. Her gaze moved to Ives, and her expression fell. Desperation drew lines in her flawless face. "Please, Ikepela Ives, I need your help."

Ives swallowed, the weight of the moment settling on her and slowly cutting off her air. Running away was no longer an option, not when she'd led the Valkyrie right to her childhood home. Fleeing the apartment was a huge mistake. "All right, fine. Lay it on me."

Her sense of doom and gloom heightened as the Valkyrie dropped to one knee. Something about it screamed wrong.

"I seek your aid to prevent the reckoning, Fate Cipher."

Ives flinched as her official title dropped from the Valkyrie's lips.

"Ragnarök has begun."

Ives sat down hard on the kitchen stool, clinging to her kneecaps to keep from falling right out of the chair. "*The* Ragnarök?" she said faintly. Her brain refused to process it. They told Ives she would be sought out, that beings of myth and legend would beseech her to untangle prophecies cast for spite, power, or punishment. They told her she would save the world from the arrogance of the gods.

They told her all of this on her eighteenth birthday. Though, considering how many bombshells were dropped that day, it was no surprise it hadn't exactly sunk in till now. Maybe if she hadn't spent the last three years largely avoiding her new reality, she wouldn't feel ready to sink in the earth right now.

"I-I..." she sputtered. "Shit."

A tremor of panic slithered up her ankles, knocking her knees together. This was too much. She should have taken on more minor entreaties. Now, she was expected to tackle the Norse Armageddon. Fixing minor destinies or even Mordred's tangled fate would have been a far better trial run. Instead, she'd ignored her abilities. Run from them. Her one 'successful' use of power was an unconscious one, and the result of that incident was watching her from the top of the kitchen table.

Jules saw her floundering. She jumped off the table, placing herself between the kneeling blonde and her frightened roomie. "She's not ready. Find someone else." She folded her arms to hide her shaking.

The gesture was not lost on Ives. It was a jolt to her system to see her diminutive companion protecting her from the big bad Valkyrie. Her father squeezed her shoulder, strengthening her through his presence. She took a deep breath and stood, gently pulling Jules behind her.

The Valkyrie rose to her feet, giving Ives a speculative once over. "Unfortunately, I agree with you, small fae person, but I'm afraid there is no choice in the matter," she said. She kept her expressive face carefully masked, but her words alone told Ives how much the Valkyrie found her lacking.

Her father made a sound. Ives cringed. She knew what was coming and doubly regretted her decision to run home at the first sign of serious trouble.

"What do you mean no choice? What about..." His voice trailed off.

Ives swallowed. This was the worst time and place to tell her father this particular piece of information, one she'd kept to herself for a dozen ill-conceived reasons.

Ives closed her eyes. "Because there isn't anyone else." She peeked at her father's stunned expression through her eyelashes. "Not at the moment."

His face darkened. "Ike?"

A tremor shook the ground. The dog whipped toward the shattered front door with a vicious snarl that made the hairs on the back of her neck rise.

The Valkyrie's eyes widened. "Ikepela Ives, we must leave this place." She seized Ives's arm faster than she could blink.

Jules had a firm hold of her other arm.

"Wait!" said Ives. She could sense what the Valkyrie intended. The hurt in her father's expression threw her off balance. She couldn't leave him like this. What he must be thinking, of her, of what happened to the woman he loved and lost.

The Valkyrie hissed in her ear. "There is no time to

soothe his feelings, Ikepela Ives. The enemy has found you."

"Enemy?" Another tremor shook the ground beneath her feet, a moment before a roar vibrated through the floorboards, like the rumble of an eruption. "What the hell was that?"

"The enemy," said the Valkyrie, her mouth set in a grim line. "Unless you wish to endanger your father, we must go."

That got through to her. She bit her lip and turned to her father. "I'll explain later. I promise."

Her father nodded. "You better, young lady."

"Hound!" The Valkyrie yelled. "Guard the father of Ikepela Ives to your last breath, by order of the All-Father!"

The dog barked in acknowledgment and continued watching the front door. The ground bucked beneath their feet. Whatever was causing it drew closer.

"Time to go," said the Valkyrie. She scooped up Ives in her arms.

Jules refused to be left behind, slipping up and over to hang off the blonde's shoulder.

The Valkyrie scowled at her but didn't try to dislodge the small woman. "Brunhilda will never let me hear the end of this," she growled as the air buzzed around them. She stepped forward.

And set Ives down on a snowy patch of ground.

As she was dressed for a very different climate in sandals, t-shirt, and shorts, she yelped. Snow licked her bare toes. The chill wind nipped her exposed skin and set her teeth chattering.

"Du-u-u-ude, not cool," Ives said through clicking teeth.

The Valkyrie frowned. "Nay, Ikepela Ives. It is very cool."

Ives would have rolled her eyes if her eye sockets hadn't immediately frozen. *Immortals.*

Jules tumbled off the Valkyrie's shoulder with a squeak. "She's mortal, you enormous bimbo! They do not adapt to sudden climate changes well!"

The Valkyrie squinted. "Do not insult me, tiny fae person. I did not realize Ikepela Ives was of such fragile stock."

"That's it," Ives said. She scooped up a handful of snow and lobbed it right at the Valkyrie's face. "One, stop using my full name. It's freaking me out. Two, what the hell was coming after me, and how is that dog going to be enough to protect my father? Three, you couldn't port us to a ski lodge or something?"

Jules wrapped her arms around Ives, but the cold was unrelenting and her clothes were far too skimpy to cope with this middle-of-nowhere destination the Valkyrie transported them to. The blonde sported the same pinstripe power suit and combat boots she wore in the bar, though Ives assumed it was a glamour, necessary when immortals moved through the human population. If Ives looked at the Valkyrie just right, the suit wavered in the corner of her vision to studded leather armor and fur-lined cape. At least one of them was dressed for the cold.

The Valkyrie surprised her. In a blink, the glamour fell away as she reached up to unlatch the cape from her back, wrapping it around Ives's shoulders. "My apologies for your discomfort, Fate Cipher, but I needed to hide your scent trail from the Jotunn."

Ives gratefully pulled the cape around her, exhaling at the rush of warmth across her frost-numbed skin. "Thank you," she said, with a small smile. "I do prefer Ives."

The blonde bowed her head. "And I am the Valkyrie Hildr. Now that we have exchanged formal greetings, allow me to bring you to a warmer location and brief you on the situation."

Ives hesitated and glanced at Jules. "What about my father?"

Hildr puffed up at the question. Her expansive chest lifted even further as she sniffed in disdain. "The Hound is a personally chosen warrior. He will be more than adequate in protecting your father. Now come, or do you wish to lose your toes to frostbite, mortal?"

Ives's grumbled as the Valkyrie led them out of the snowy wood, though she swore she spied a trickle of nervous sweat that slid down the Hildr's brow.

🪅🪅🪅

Despite the Valkyrie's precautions to vacate Ives from the premise, Ives had lived in the house for twenty years. Her essence, ingrained into the wood, was quite strong. Even if she hadn't driven to her father's home that night, it was likely the Jotunn would have tracked her scent there first. A cascade of booming footsteps trekked across the island shore and caused the whole house to shiver.

Luckily for the errant Valkyrie, Lavi's home was under guard by more than a single Hound of Asgard. Another presence stirred at the invasion of such ilk on their territory, observing the matter from a cautionary distance. However, it didn't do to interfere in mortal affairs when they were perfectly capable of taking care of themselves. The presence settled in, watching the scene unfold just beyond the plane of mortal perception.

Lavi stood his ground in his emptied kitchen, a troubled look on his face as he flipped a hammer from one hand to the other. The Hound barked a warning. A massive blue foot wedged through the entrance of his home.

Lavi cursed and rushed forward with the hammer raised and ready. The observing presence focused on that glaringly massive blue foot. *Why was this beast even here? What trouble was stirring in the currents of the world?* Hound or not, if Lavi didn't do something he was going to lose more than his roof. The Hound scrambled after him with a string of warning barks far louder than a normal animal, like cracks of thunder. The Hound nipped at the back of Lavi's shirt, trying to perform its duty to "rescue" him. It might have been an adequate protector in other circumstances, but Lavi Ives was a Child of the Island.

He unleashed a war cry as he brought the hammer down on the giant's big toe. Heat flared through his veins, gilding his bronze skin, the blessing of his goddess. Power slammed through the giant's foot. It shattered bone and tore flesh, as it drummed straight through to the crust of the earth until the power touched its brethren. Heat answered the call of heat. Magma bubbled up, spurting forth through the ground to answer the call of Lavi Ives.

The giant fell back, howling in pain, and cradled his injured foot. He barely had the presence of mind to scuttle backward as lava erupted in front of him. The glow of molten earth outlined the demon of a man behind it as he shook his hammer at the giant.

"Tell your masters to stay the hell away from my daughter!" Lavi snarled. He glared as the giant continued a crooked crab-walk backward until it hit the Pacific. It dissolved in a heap of icy slush and rushed away through the ocean currents.

The observing presence gloated at the fleeing beastie. *Giants—cowards the second you stood up to them.*

Lavi inhaled, a look of intense concentration creasing his face as he sealed the crack in the earth. The lava rapidly cooled. Messy, but it'd keep his house from burning down.

He slid the hammer through his belt, ignoring the bewildered Hound.

"I know you're listening, Auntie," he said. The surrounding trees were still too quiet as if nature held its breath.

The presence paused. Lavi's tone spoke volumes. Tentative bird song sputtered back on as the presence pulled back.

Lavi shrugged his shoulders and turned. Man and dog considered one another. The Hound whined, clearly out of its depth. Its tail gave an uncertain wag.

"Here, boy. Want some bacon?'

She observed as the two vanished through the shattered entrance. Her mortal brethren would visit her shrine sooner than expected. What trouble had Lavi's daughter landed herself in this time?

🜛🜛🜛

Valkyries traveled in style. As soon as Ives acquiesced to follow Hildr the Brusque, Hildr clapped her hands—a boom that echoed through the forest, chased by a cheery jingle of sleigh bells. An ornate wooden sled pulled by two stags the size of Clydesdales halted in front of the trio. Ives settled on one side, Hildr on the other, while Jules fidgeted in between them, an energetic buffer that allowed Ives to stare over the side and contemplate her life choices.

Ives had wanted to be an engineer. Her father gave her a love of all things metal and she had a deep-seated fascination with mechanics. Toward the end of high school, she had an early acceptance and noteworthy scholarship for the University of California, Berkeley. Her eighteenth birthday changed that.

In a single day, her dreams were shot, her future locked to a thankless task.

The same day she met her mother, a woman she remembered only from a bedside photo.

And the goddess responsible for destroying her life.

Ives left her house that morning, following routine. Her father kissed her goodbye and warned her to be careful. It was the same warning he gave every morning. The last normal morning of her life. The Gods are nothing if not exact in their timing, so at 10:21 AM., in the middle of Advanced Physics and the very moment of her birth eighteen years ago, Ives was ripped from reality.

She remembered the heat first—the rough rub of it against her skin, how it pulled at the moisture in her veins so that great streams of sweat poured down her back. This wasn't the familiar warmth of her father's workshop. It was Hell breathing down her neck. The air wavered, creating a heat mirage that obscured her classmates. The desk vanished beneath her. She fell and landed on smooth obsidian.

Ives sat on a large shard of black rock surrounded by magma. She shrieked as the heat flushed over her, smothering, searing the air in her lungs. She might have screamed and screamed until the heat ate her alive, but a hand clapped over her mouth, cool against her scorched lips.

"Hush, sweetheart." It was a woman's voice, one she dreamed about often as a child, yet one she was certain she was far too young to remember. It was a voice that was supposed to sing her songs and chase away her nightmares, a role unfulfilled.

Ives blinked up into a face she recognized, the very face that stared out from the picture frame on her father's nightstand. It was more shocking than her current surroundings since she hadn't 'seen' her mother in person since she'd been a baby. Sadness creased a perfect, unchanged face, her dark brown eyes wet with unshed tears.

"Oh, my beautiful girl. You are perfect," she said. Her hand cupped Ives's cheek.

Ives didn't know whether to laugh or cry or scream in her mother's face. She had so many questions, too many, but before she could voice one, the magma bubbled up around them.

Her mother grabbed her and held her close as a column rose from the surface, up and up until the magma crested. It fell away from the figure, flowing over her skin like water. The woman stood nearly ten feet tall. Fire dripped from her dark curls and licked along her naked bronze skin. Her eyes snapped open, the same black obsidian as the rock Ives cowered on, gleaming with terrible power. Her gaze fell on mother and daughter.

Ives felt stripped bare, her entire life laid out for the woman's black gaze. She swallowed and trembled in the arms of the mother she barely knew as the goddess approached them. That was all she could be—a goddess. Her mind couldn't comprehend anything else.

"You're scaring her," her mother snapped.

The goddess paused and considered them. Ives was certain she was about to toss a fireball at them when she ran her hands down her body. The flames settled into drapes of red cloth covering her. She continued walking toward them, leaving footprints of solidified stone on top of the magma that slowly sank below the surface. Her body shrank to more reasonable proportions as she approached until she stood before them, much more human in size. The facade of normality did nothing to stifle her presence. Her obsidian eyes perused Ives.

"So, this is the child?" The goddess folded her arms. She pursed her lips. "I granted your request for an eighteen-year reprieve, Keawe. Are you prepared to pass the mantle to your offspring and accept your punishment?"

"This is hardly the place for such matters!" her mother protested.

The goddess's expression darkened. "I could make the rock smaller."

"She is Lavi's daughter, too."

The goddess's expression softened. She sighed, pinching the bridge of her nose in an oddly human gesture. With another wave of her hand, the heat and magma vanished. Ives sat across from her mother at a low, black stone table on a cushion of red velvet. The room they occupied was comfortably warm and cozy, an office sized windowless cube lit up by some unseen red-orange light source, adorned in shades of black and red.

The goddess was thankfully absent.

"Mom?" Ives breathed. She still shook from her encounter.

Her mother reached across the table. Tears spilled down her face as she clasped Ives's hands tight.

"I don't have much time, darling one, but I wanted you to know I am so proud of you. I love you and your father very much, but my duties have kept me from you both."

Ives shook her head, unable to comprehend the situation. "Who was that woman? Where have you been? What—"

Her mother put a finger to her lips. "So many questions." Her gaze hungrily scanned her daughter's face, drank in the details. "You have your father's eyes." She smiled and gently pinched Ives's chin. "But my mouth."

She sat back, their hands locked together. "You, my daughter, have a very important role in this world."

"We're here," said Hildr.

Ives shot back to the present, disoriented by the memory, so fresh it could have been yesterday. The Valkyrie had brought them to a picturesque lodge, constructed of logs at the base of a snowcapped mountain.

Ives exhaled a steaming breath and stared up in wonder. "Where in the world are we?"

"By my account, Iceland," chirped Jules as she pranced through the snow.

Hildr leaned toward Ives. "How did you acquire your fae companion?"

"Long story," said Ives. She didn't want to explain how Jules was a fluke, a one-in-a-million encounter. They had more pressing concerns than the origins of her roommate.

The trio headed into the stately lodge, greeted by a blissful rush of heat. The source was the massive fire taking up an entire wall of the common room. Hildr gestured for them to make themselves comfortable on a set of fur-covered couches. Ives settled on one and crossed her legs so the cape tented around her. She luxuriated in the warmth. Feeling crept back into her toes as the Valkyrie returned and pushed a mug of hot golden liquid into her hands.

"Heated mead," she said, handing another one to the excited Jules. She took a seat across from Ives. "Now to business. I formally petition the aid of the Fate Cipher on behalf of the All-Father and his council."

Ives took a cautious sip of her drink to delay her answer, pleasantly surprised by the sweet, hot liquid. She took another deep gulp to shore up her courage. "Now, what exactly does that entail, Hildr?"

The Valkyrie paused. She opened and closed her mouth a few times. She gnawed on one knuckle, clearly at a loss for words.

Ives took pity on her. She tried to recall her sorely

lacking studies in myths and legends. She had had a rough adjustment period to the whole Fate Cipher business, and the world was chock-full of more ancient religions than it knew what to do with, not to mention the myriad of immortal beasts and beings lurking about. It was hard enough coming to terms with her new status quo, and she spent the last few years keeping a low profile. Aside from her random encounter with Jules, the supernatural world, with a few exceptions, left her alone to the point where her mother's instructions and warnings lost their urgency.

Until now.

She strained to recall what she could. One rather unpleasant Norse myth came to mind since it gave her nightmares for days after reading it.

"Ragnarök," she said. The word rolled over with her tongue. Yes, that gruesome legend did mention it. The details flowed from the murky depths of memory. "Isn't there a very specific series of events that kicks off the whole business?"

Hildr squirmed. "Well, *some* events happened while others did not."

Ives narrowed her eyes and took another sip of her drink. "Explain."

Hildr puffed out her cheeks. "You are correct. There is a very specific course of events that must take place as dictated by the Norns. Certain beings are meant to rise and challenge the gods, culminating in the release of the Betrayer. He is the one who leads the armies of the Jotunn against the All-Father, the one who heralds the unleashing of chaos and the ruination of the world in a storm of fire and ash. Verily, this never sat right with the All-Father. The Betrayer was like a brother to him and his actions... What he did was out of character even for him."

Ives pinched and tugged on her bottom lip. "Are we

talking about the same god? The evil one? The father of lies?"

"He wasn't always a liar," said Hildr softly. She stared at the low flames in the hearth.

"Yes, she's talking about Loki," said Jules into her mug.

The name made Ives shiver. "Okay, so you don't believe he's evil."

"They punished him nonetheless." Hildr sighed. "We all have our parts to play in the end."

Ives nodded. "Okay, but what I remember of the story—his punishment was pretty brutal. He is going to be mighty pissed when he breaks free. You want me to stop the angry god of lies from slipping his leash and tearing you guys a new one?"

There was a beat of silence as Ives realized several things at once. Such as why a Jotunn monster dude would come after her. Or why the Valkyrie would bring her to a secluded wilderness lodge in the middle of Iceland.

So she couldn't run.

"He's already slipped his leash," said Ives. The hot mead turned to sludge in her stomach.

Hildr sat up, her expression was sheepish. "Unfortunately, yes. Loki, God of Fire, the Trickster, appears to have broken free."

Ives sputtered a bit. "What do you mean 'appears to'? Where the hell is he now?"

Hildr couldn't meet her gaze. "That is the problem. Not even the All-Father can find him."

FOUR

VEGAS, BABY

New York held the title as the city that never slept, but Vegas was the city where the party never stopped. The air was constantly aglow from the flashing lights of casinos, beckoning the tourists with the scent of stale smoke, sweet perfumed sweat, and the lulling laughter of women with lipstick-stained teeth. The desert heat was equally effective in driving the patrons into the waiting air-conditioned mouth of the casinos, where it chewed them up with thrown dice and slot-machine levers.

There were fewer tourists in the waning hours of the night, whittled down to a scattered drunken number determined to live out as many shameful fantasies as possible before they returned to their button-down lives. Most of the patrons in the wee hours of the morning were the regulars, the lean, hungry ones. They permeated the air with their cloying unwashed scent, spiked with desperation and greed. Even these twisted souls could sense the predator in their midst.

They twitched as he passed them, clad in a shredded long-coat and top hat. Forgotten finery of a century long since passed. Hair like an open flame shot through with copper filaments fell to his shoulders. Steam or smoke appeared to rise off his broad shoulders, dismissed as a trick of the light. Their bloodshot eyes followed his every movement as he settled down at the blackjack table.

The female dealer looked up, disgusted by the tattered state of his clothes, prepared to chase another bum away from her table when her dismissive glance-over reached his face. She stilled, lips parting, stunned.

Coppery stubble dusted the sharp, chiseled angles of his face, mostly concealing the faint scars that dotted his sensual lips. His hat cast a short shadow over his features but couldn't hide the beauty. His irises winked like emeralds from beneath the brim, set above a slightly crooked patrician's nose. The flaws should have marred his appeal but only seemed to enhance it. The dealer wondered if he was a celebrity in disguise until those jewel-toned eyes snapped to hers.

"Care to start the game, love?" he said in a smoky voice of honey and heat.

The dealer swallowed, grateful she'd recently gone to the bathroom for fear she would wet herself. The wild madness in his gaze snapped at the primitive core of her mind with sharp white teeth.

The man seemed to catch himself, casting his gaze down to the green-felted tabletop. The dealer shook herself with a shudder. Why did she feel so off? She cast an appreciative eye on the beautiful man before her, noting the chips he passed from hand to hand.

"Right away, sir. Care for a drink? I can summon a waitress."

A sinful smile curled his lips. Her heart fluttered in her chest. "That would be wonderful. What would you recommend?"

The dealer swallowed hard for a very different reason now. Her skin tingled. She could imagine that voice bringing her to orgasm if he just leaned over to whisper naughty things in her ear.

She snagged a tired passing waitress before she started rubbing against the table. "Polly, could you bring the gentleman a scotch on the rocks?"

Polly turned, the exhausted sneer falling from her face as she caught sight of the man. "Right, away, Mel." She fanned herself as she hurried off.

When the morning shift came to relieve her, they encountered the ragged man with the downcast gaze. He nursed a sweating scotch, picking up and dropping his sizable stack of chips with a constant clatter clack that immediately set the new male dealer's teeth on edge. So did the fact that Mel, the ice queen, bent to kiss the stranger's cheek as she left and slipped her phone number between his fingers.

The new dealer eyed the stranger with a sour expression. He tapped the tabletop with impatient fingers. Guy probably didn't even tip. "You done yet, buddy?"

The man glanced up at him as he emptied his glass in one long swallow. Unlike Mel, the new dealer hadn't relieved himself recently. A trickle of urine slid down the leg of his black pants. He stared, unable to break contact with that mad green gaze.

The stranger blinked first, setting his empty glass on the table. "I would like another scotch, hold the ice."

"Sh-sh-sure thing, Mister," said the dealer. He flagged down another waitress with a shaking hand. "Anything else I can get you, sir?"

The man smiled and handed off his empty glass to the new waitress so that he casually brushed her wrist. She left in a flurry of giggles. He turned his attention back to the quivering dealer and kept the open, friendly smile on his scarred lips.

"Oh, no. I'm just here to kill some time."

FIVE

DRAG ME TO HELL

IVES CAREFULLY SET down her mug of mead so she didn't throw it at the Valkyrie. It wasn't Hildr's fault they'd lost the god who started their apocalypse. It wasn't her fault the All-Father, their freaking head honcho, couldn't find said lynchpin of catastrophe. And it certainly wasn't the Valkyrie's fault the only operational Fate Cipher was supremely ill-equipped to handle an apocalypse level disaster.

She set her fingertips in a steeple and pressed them firmly to her lips for a full minute before she trusted herself to speak.

"Hildr, how much do you know about me?" she said, her voice as flat and quiet as possible.

Jules still sensed the coming storm and snuggled closer to her. She would forever be grateful for the fae's presence. It was a reminder she'd succeeded once.

"I know you are the only mortal of your kind to exist, to *ever* exist. I fear I am ignorant of how such an aberration came to pass, but it was difficult enough to track you down." Hildr's face was marked with concern. Her eyes kept darting to the door of the lodge as if she were afraid Ives would bolt on her. That wasn't too far from the truth.

"I've... I've never really used my powers. On purpose," Ives said faintly. She was *so* out of her wheelhouse here. How was she supposed to even begin to tackle something utterly massive? Was the Valkyrie certain this whole Ragnarök business was truly grinding forward?

There is a way you can tell, you know, whispered a part of her brain.

She wanted to scream at it to shut up. That little niggling voice was correct, but it meant opening up that door in her head, one she hadn't worked up the nerve to open more than a crack, not since that day.

She dug her nails into her palms. The power, her mother's power, terrified her, like trying to leash living lightning. As much as she hated the sensation, she couldn't run from this, because if Ragnarök was truly kicking off, there would be *nowhere* to hide. She released a slow breath from deep in her diaphragm, and she kept releasing it after her air ran out, pushing down and out until her head began to spin. She sank into that spinning sensation. An internal door jarred open, allowing the first intangible mental threads to snake through. She snagged a loose end and pulled it forward until she drew out the tangled mess inside her core. Every fine hair on her body stood on end.

Ives opened her eyes. The world around her was overlaid with glowing threads—threads that pulsed with unconscious dreams, coarse dull threads of regret that hung like chains, bright shining threads that represented a creature's life span. Immortal threads were a shimmering dark gold, strong as steel cables, tangible as spider silk, while mortal threads held a pearly luminescence that slowly faded with time.

And then there were threads of destiny.

Everyone had them. Everyone, down to the most average of human beings you could think of, held a thread of fate. For the majority of people, the threads of their fate were a healthy robin-egg blue, interwoven with strands of violet freewill. The choices of a lifetime spiked those blue threads with shots of purple, weaving the story of a life. For most mortals, their fate was their own, untouched by divine influence.

Immortal destinies were different. They did not carry the threads of their fate with them as humans did. Their fates found them. Ives turned her gaze to Hildr and beheld the thread of the Norse doomsday.

Ragnarök wasn't just one thread, but a knotted coil that pulsed a scarlet red, like fresh blood. The thread was buried into the Valkyrie's skin and wrapped around her throat, spilling across her neck like an open wound. Ives swallowed at the sight of it. Hildr was not meant to survive the apocalypse. The grisly sight teased a memory forth.

She remembered the story now. The god of fire, Loki, chained in the earth. The venom of a serpent dripped poison into his eyes until the twilight of the gods. His children would be pitted against their immortal foes. He would rally the ice giants against Odin and his ranks. The story gave her nightmares, not the event of Ragnarök but the Trickster's punishment. She couldn't imagine such pain, both physical and mental. They'd bound him in the entrails of one of his children. The serpent's venom was so potent it made him writhe hard enough to shake the earth. It was the sort of punishment that would drive anyone mad, especially if they had to endure it for centuries.

"Why such a cruel torment?" She looked at the Valkyrie.

For a moment Hildr's immortal glow dimmed. There was a lost expression on her face, gone in a flash. Her voice was full of long carried sorrow. "He killed the Beloved One." She sighed. "At least that is what the elders say."

So the Trickster was a murderer, except the Valkyrie seemed doubtful. Elders? "Wait. What?"

Hildr blushed to the roots of her hair.

"You mean, you weren't there?"

Hildr leaned in close, eyeing the door once again. "This is not so common knowledge, but that first generation of Valkyries was wiped from the annals of history. We are the All-Father's eyes and ears. We are trusted with conscripting the fallen, those proven noble and brave, into Odin's armies. I think one of the original Valkyries knew something, a secret that went against what we were told. It is a piece of our history that remains unresolved. The All-Father never speaks of it, as if they never existed, but there are whispers, rumors among us. And his actions betray his fears." As she held Ives's gaze, her ice-blue eyes sparkled in the firelight. "He sent me alone to find you, Ives. No matter your past, or your abilities, he believes you can help us."

So, only the entire Norse pantheon relied on her, a lone mortal. *No pressure.* Ives inhaled deep, sucking in air until her lungs twinged. Part of her wanted to scream and scream. It was the all-too-human part of her, one she squelched as she peered down at her lap. She may not have the experience, but this was her world, too, and an apocalypse tended to ruin everyone's day.

There was something else, another motivation that spurred Ives to meet the Valkyrie's gaze. The memory of the red and black room tickled the back of her thoughts. There were other reasons Loki's story gave her nightmares. Her mother could be suffering a similarly cruel punishment, somewhere, in a prison of divine making. Looking into Loki's fate might give her a true hint at finally finding out what happened to Keawe Ives.

"How do we find a trickster?"

"Well, there are a few individuals we could press, but I doubt we will find them very cooperative." Hildr looked at her sideways. "Your best chance is to appeal to Lady Hel."

"That sounds ominous," said Ives, rising to her feet.

Jules bounced up, her face a mask of shock. "You can't be serious! Ives can't go there!"

Hildr's expression turned cagey. "Of all his children, she is the most receptive to the call of the gods. The All-Father bequeathed her the realm of the dead."

"The realm of *the dead*!" Jules stomped her foot. "Which you can only go to if you *are dead*!"

Ives raised a hand. "Hey, can I have some input here?"

Hildr shifted uncomfortably. "It's only temporary, tiny fae, and I am uniquely suited to this task. Once she's there, the Fate Cipher's capable of a bit of reconnaissance on her own."

A chill crept over Ives. She didn't like the turn this conversation was taking.

"I refuse to let you send her in alone," snapped Jules.

"That is the nature of death," countered Hildr, fishing for something between the couch cushions behind her.

"Uh, hold on a second. No one said anything about dying," said Ives. She backed away from the arguing pair.

"Calm yourself, Ives. Death is merely a temporary state for a warrior of Asgard. Aha," said Hildr as she yanked a dagger from the cushions. "Catch."

She tossed it to Ives, and, like a sucker, she caught it. As if she couldn't help herself.

"What am I supposed to do with this? Threaten to cut her?"

Hildr snorted. "As amusing as that would be, no, Fate Cipher. The dagger is merely a technicality. Think of it as your tug line to reality."

Jules yelped and froze. "Ives, don't let go of it. No matter what happens." She glared at the Valkyrie. "Don't do this. What if Hel won't let her go?"

"Have more faith in your mistress, little one!" Hildr stood, drawing a bow and arrow from a ripple in the air. The arrow was strange—not metal, but carved crystal that reflected shards of light from the fire. "This will sever your soul from your physical body. From there, you must convince the Lady of Death to help you find Loki."

"But you haven't given me enough info—" Ives cut her words off with a shriek as the Valkyrie shot her. The crystal arrowhead struck her chest and slid right between her ribs to pierce her heart. There was no pain to accompany her mortal wound. None at all. Ives gaped at the arrow protruding from her rib cage. Her gaze flicked to Jules, the fae's hands clapped over her mouth in shock, and then to Hildr. Hildr lowered the bow, lifting a nearly invisible thread between her fingers.

Panic sank its claws deep across her shoulders, her body was too heavy. Ives didn't know how to find the Lady of Death! What would happen to her once she reached the realm of the dead? How was she expected to succeed with a measly dagger? No sound came from her mouth as she tried to shout at the Valkyrie. Her vision grayed and went dark as her body slid downward, down, down, straight into the earth.

♀ ♀ ♀

Jules rounded on the behemoth blonde. Fury crackled through her veins. She'd watched Ives get skewered and shoved between realms and hadn't lifted a finger. The floor shivered beneath her feet, but she focused on the idiot Valkyrie.

"How dare you?" she hissed and stomped forward.

Small cracks appeared under Jules's feet, which Hildr noted with a puzzled frown.

"You barely gave her enough information to survive down there," Jules said.

"The Fate Cipher is fully capable of maneuvering through Hel's realm," said Hildr, sounding a tad defensive.

"She knows *nothing* of your world!" Jules snapped, close enough to give the Valkyrie a resounding kick in the shins. It didn't accomplish much other than hurting her toes.

Hildr went still. "Explain, small fae creature."

"She told you she had no experience, that she was mortal," said Jules. She paced despite her sore toes.

"Yes, she said she hadn't attempted such a massive undertaking before."

Jules wanted to tear her hair out, or, more accurately, the impatient Valkyrie's hair. "She's barely used her powers! And not just inexperienced, untrained. The duty, the abilities—all of it was dumped in her lap three years ago."

Hildr still looked puzzled. "Surely that is enough time for her to acclimate to her new position?"

That earned the Valkyrie another useless kick to the shin. Jules hopped up on the couch, holding her toes. "I think I broke something." She looked up at Hildr. "There was no training, no teacher. She was alone and scared. She barely touched the power inside her. I vowed I would never let her handle this burden alone again." She swallowed the lump in her throat. A tear slipped down her cheek. "I failed her."

She hiccupped a sob and buried her face in her hands. Hildr settled next to her, clearly uncomfortable with tiny crying females. She gave the fae a hard pat between the shoulder blades that sent the small woman sprawling across the couch.

"Peace, small fae. Training or not, I can sense the strength in your mistress. I admit I, too, was dubious at first, but she has mustered her courage in this very room."

Jules lifted her tear-stained face. "You think so?"

"Truly," Hildr said and puffed out her chest. The effect was rather frightening. "Fear not, Jules. I assure you I will retrieve your mistress from Hel's clutches once she retrieves the information we need."

Jules tilted her head, dubiously eyeing the near-invisible thread. "But what if—"

The door slammed open with a swirl of snow. Hildr jumped to her feet, sword in one hand, thread firmly clutched in the other. A hooded figure filled the doorway. Faster than even immortals eyes could follow, the figure lifted a loaded crossbow. The bolt loosed and zipped through the air. Hildr swung her sword only for the blade to pass right through the intangible bolt, which continued on its path and vanished into the wall.

Hildr recovered her balance and faced their attacker, but the doorway was empty.

"What the heck just happened?" Jules stared at the entrance wide-eyed. It was Hildr's silence that made her look back.

The color had drained from Hildr's face, and she held the severed end of the gossamer thread in her fist.

SIX

LADY DEATH IS A LEVEL-60 MAGE

Ives's senses kicked back online with a sudden gut-wrenching snap. Not so much a feeling of someone treading over her grave as *steamrolling* over it. Her descent to the Underworld lurched to a halt. She hung suspended over an abyss, aware of the yawning mouth to the realm of death beneath her, but blind to it. Something whistled past her as the tug in her gut returned. She released an inaudible scream before her body—as if it was really here— plummeted through the abyss.

The free fall scrambled her thoughts. She tumbled end over end, grabbing for anything to break her fall. Her fingers brushed the arrow shaft piercing her chest, the first solid thing in her grasp. Her knowledge of magical objects was sorely lacking, but her abilities were working just fine. Those rarely used senses told her the fine thread the Valkyrie used to tether her to the above world was severed. She could see the sliced end in her mind's eye.

Oh, damn. Ives was on her own. Gritting her teeth, she yanked the arrow free. Being shot hadn't hurt, but ripping the arrow out was pure agony. With no air to scream, she crumpled inward in silent pain, pressing her hand to her chest. Despite the lack of a physical wound, pain radiated from the area. She pushed it aside, as much as she could, feeling for the thread tied to the shaft. It was thicker now, nearly as wide as her palm. It would have to be enough. She wasn't sure this would work, but she forced herself to concentrate, pushing her mystical senses to open wide. Possible or not, she would damn well will it to happen.

The darkness melted away as strands of glowing thread coalesced around her. There were billions, finely strung together, all aglow with the pearly luminescence of life. Humans were naturally tethered to the underworld for the length of their lives; death was inevitable. Billions of lives dangled at her fingertips. They illuminated her surroundings. It wasn't an abyss she fell through but a trench in the earth. She caught a hint of a faint, distant light below. This pit had a bottom, which she would hit at a very high velocity sooner or later. That was not a pleasant option, since she'd possibly undone whatever magic Hildr had done to send her down here. Her body certainly *felt* solid, definitely not severed from her physical form.

There had to be a way to slow her descent. Not a lot of options presented themselves. She glanced at the glimmering web of threads she fell through. What would happen if she grabbed one? She'd probably kill some poor bastard in the real world. What if she snagged somebody's child? The thought horrified her.

Concentrate!

She stared at the threads, timing herself, ignoring the ever-growing source of light below her. A wrong move would kill someone before their time, but if she missed, she'd splatter when she finally hit the ground below.

There! Her hand snapped out, wrapping around a nearly opaque gray thread. Her descent slowed as she hitchhiked on the thread of a dying soul. For a moment, the life she touched flared in her mind, flooding her with memories, harsh and sweet, and the entirety of the human experience in a flash. Ives barely maintained her sense of self but had the presence of mind to tie the Valkyrie's rope to the dead thread, releasing it before the memories overwhelmed her. The moment she did so, she found she could breathe again.

Ives gulped great mouthfuls of air. She clung to the arrow that shot her, letting the anchor of the dead soul carry her the rest of the way down.

Her feet touched a solid surface in a great hall of glossy, black marble. Ives unhooked her rope so the soul could continue its journey unhindered before she sank to her knees, wrapping her arms around her middle. She'd succeeded in spelunking safely into the underworld. Even as she wondered what the hell went wrong up top, she knew she could do this. All she had to do was find the Lady of Death and convince her to give up the location of Loki. Easy peasy lemon squeezy. What had Hildr called her? Hel? *Hel of Hell.* She bit back a nervous giggle as she took in her surroundings.

Ives raised a brow at the decor. The floor beneath her was polished to a mirror finish, but the walls were non-existent. Instead, there was a forest, the trees in varying shades of black. Their thick trunks lined the corridor with a natural canopy of woven branches above her. Intermittent torches set into the stone floor lit the way, an eerie corridor of shadow and flame. Whoever designed this place ran with the theme.

As she climbed to her feet, she debated the wisdom of calling out Hel's name in the sketchy hall, when she heard a cluster of noises.

A string of ear-blistering curses carried through the dark in a distinctly female, albeit raspy, voice. Ives froze as a toddler-sized plushie flew through the trees, landing with a defeated high-pitched wheeze about twenty feet in front of her. She padded up to it and prodded it with her toe to get a better look at it. The plushie was a stuffed Cthulhu, staring up at her with wide wobbly eyes. It was also bright pink.

"Heals! For the love of the gods, where the frack are my heals?!"

Ives followed the voice. A twitch built up behind her left eye. A sudden gap in the tree trunks revealed the opening to a bedroom. This day was rapidly growing more and more surreal.

The contrast between the black-on-black hallway and the room before her was like comparing apples to cupcakes with confetti sprinkles. The walls were plastered from top to bottom with posters, most were from films of the past century, though there was one distracting poster of a kitten dangling from a branch with the phrase, "Hang in there," in the middle of the far wall.

A black marble ceiling capped the space strung with dozens of strands of white Christmas lights in the shape of icicles. A princess-style four-poster bed occupied the center of the room, complete with draping black canopies and silken black sheets. The effect was ruined by the pile of odd plushies occupying nearly half of the king-sized mattress, most of them an eye-watering shade of pink. The whole set up came together with the crumpled Strawberry Shortcake comforter bunched at the end of the bed.

Ives turned toward the clack of keys.

"Crap, crappity, crap, crap. Decurse, Buzzbirdy. Decurse! Well, you're a damn druid, aren't you?"

Ives couldn't register what she was seeing at first—other than the Underworld must have great Wi-Fi. The computer rig was a gamer's wet dream, placed atop a dark wooden desk. A massive oak chest was open beside it, displaying an obscene amount of candy, including every variant of Skittles under the sun. A figure sat in a luxurious leather swivel chair, black leather, of course. Though the figure faced the doorway, their attention was firmly fixated on the screen. The flickering computer screen illuminated a face straight out of a nightmare. Flashes of green, red, and blue glinted off exposed bones. A skeletal hand dipped into a bowl of Skittles perched precariously on the edge of the desk, plucking out a cherry red. Ives watched, mesmerized as the skeleton popped the Skittle between her teeth. A small noise escaped Ives's lips, thankfully eclipsed by the furious clicking of bony fingertips against the plastic keys.

"Oh, come on! There are only so many fireballs I can throw here. That wipe is on you ass-hats. Oh, yeah? Well, you know what, Buzz? Go choke on a pizza roll. Pathetic overgrown mama's boy, still living in his basement." Her bony fist slammed down on the desk, making the bowl of Skittles bounce with a clatter. The skeleton stood and tried to yank off her headset, hindered by how thoroughly tangled it was in her full head of dark hair. She cussed and stumbled away from the desk as she tried to free herself, revealing Care Bear pajama bottoms to complement her AC/DC t-shirt. The rest of her face came into view.

Ives sucked in a breath.

The woman heard *that* one, freezing in place. She cautiously looked up through strands of midnight silk, her single green eye focusing on her visitor.

"Oh, shit."

SEVEN

A HEART-TO-HEART

HUMANS WERE FLAWED CREATURES. Their greatest flaw was mortal memory. The islands had mostly forgotten their gods and goddesses. Many of her divine siblings now slept, no longer tethered to their mortal children. Not her, she of flame and rock, rooted in the endless flow and ebb of magma, never quite at rest. They didn't forget her, her name still whispered, a myth of raw elements and dangerous beauty. She'd watched the islanders shed their queens like wilted blooms, the age of technology sweeping through with the force of a monsoon. Never once did she feel threatened as she did now.

What foolery had her mortal brethren become tangled in now?

She scented foreign fire on the air. It worried her. Old forces were stirring, beings that no longer had a place in this modern world. Not that *that* would stop them from mucking it all up. The very idea sent her scurrying to the realm between. She ignored the scathing looks she received from those three biddies as she left sizzling footprints in her wake. This was *their* fault anyway. She made her way down the whispering hall, through the hanging tapestries until she reached the one she sought. She contemplated her current choices as she watched the figure pace within the woven prison. This unfolding prophecy tasted like ruin that would reach even her remote corner of the world, and for the first time, she felt a pull to interfere with 'foreign affairs.'

"Oh, great Pele, I seek your counsel."

The goddess sighed. Her focus shifted to the mortal kneeling at her physical altar. Lavi Ives. Surprise, surprise. She supposed she owed him an audience and she intended to make her entrance as a goddess.

First, she evoked heat. The temperature climbed rapidly. The sweltering air beat against his skin. Sweat poured down his back, sliding over his temples and into his eyes. Lavi didn't twitch, not even to blink. A true child of fire, that one. She sighed as she stepped through the shimmering heat. She sat in the same style, facing him. She kept her expression carefully aloof as she cocked her head to the side.

"Why have you summoned me here, child of fire?" Her voice rumbled as she spoke with the fury of the quaking earth.

"You filched on our deal." Lavi's nostrils flared.

Her proximity made it difficult to maintain his temper. Her very presence tugged at the chaotic energy that ran in his veins. She sensed the pain in his voice and bowed her head. She felt something appallingly close to regret—his pain *was* her doing.

"Did you want me to break her completely, Lavi?" Her dark gaze locked with his. "After learning about her mother? About herself?"

"After you dragged her mother to who knows where?"

Lavi's hands curled into fists. He inhaled a ragged breath, trying to hold his calm. He knew better than to insult a goddess, no matter whose blood ran through his veins. "I don't suppose you will tell me where she is?"

"Your lover or your daughter?"

He glared at her.

A sad smile tugged at Pele's lips. "You know I cannot. Just as I could not hide her from the seers. They demanded justice for her...indiscretion."

Lavi's shoulders slumped. "I refuse to regret Ike."

Her immortal heart ached at his words. She curled her fingers under his jaw, forcing him to meet her gaze. Centuries and dozens of generations separated them, but Lavi Ives looked at her with Ka'ohelo's eyes. "Never. Whatever heritage flows through her veins, she is yours. Therefore she is one of mine." She looked over his shoulder, her mind's eye far away from the small cave.

"I worry for her, Auntie," said Lavi.

A smile creased her dark eyes. "True strength is forged in fire. Your daughter has already tasted more flame than she realizes. I think she will surprise those snow-dusted gods."

A frantic bark sounded from outside. Pele frowned. The Hound companion stood guard outside the volcanic cave containing her altar. His booming barks echoed through her obsidian halls.

"What is it?" Lavi started to his feet.

The goddess rose with him. A scowl twisted her features. "Someone who should not be here," she said.

A bellow permeated the hot air of the cave with a sharp taste of foreign fire.

"Island goddess!"

It was a voice of flames that raged out of control and consumed all in their path. It held the same promise of destruction as Pele herself, but there was a discordant undertone she did not possess. Where her wrath brought renewal and fertility to the earth, this voice promised the oblivion of cinders and darkness. It was a voice of silken chaos, attempting the rouse the goddess to war.

"Come, join the army of Surt, Lord of Muspell."

Eight

MOMENTOUS MOMENTS

THOUSANDS OF MILES AWAY, on an island of ice and snow, the booming echo of a ragged howl carried on the harsh north wind. The wolf had occupied the island for hundreds of years. It was his sentence, the fate of his birth, of his father's sordid past. He waited for the end, for the release of Ragnarök. A simple set of tasks lay before him: escape the island, seek the All-father, and devour him. Three little tasks before the gods put him out of his misery. Before the Lord of Muspell reduced the world to ash and shadow. He'd waited so long he remembered nothing of who he'd once been. Was he was once an honorable creature? Had he once wore another skin? The constant agony of the chain digging into his neck leeched his memories away for centuries until he was nothing but a creature of destruction and madness. In the endless storm, he waited...

The hooded one approached the wolf, a strung crossbow at rest on his wrist. His footsteps crunched through the snow, long before his figure appeared through the sleeted wind. The wolf watched him, wary. This was not how the end unfolded.

The hooded man lifted his weapon. It revealed a strange

arrowhead of spun crystal. It seemed like such a fragile construct, incapable of doing its set task.

The bow triggered. The arrow shrieked through the air and struck the chain that fettered the wolf's neck.

Coils of metal snaked to the ground and gathered at the feet of the stunned wolf. For a moment, it was too shocked to react to its sudden freedom. The figure disappeared back into the storm, and a glint of gold winked from the recesses of his hood.

The wolf's black lips pulled back over his teeth. Freedom. Now to leave this island and begin the razing of the world.

The great wolf Fenrir's howl rose once again. It overpowered the storm in its frenzy.

* * *

Across the world, in the smoky pits of Vegas, the scarred stranger clutched the blackjack table in front of him. The weight on his chest had doubled and left him gasping.

"Hey, buddy, you okay?" The male dealer reached for him. There was no good answer to such a question. Only one individual in the world would be able to see what was happening to the man, but the Fate Cipher was not there to see the threads of fate tighten around the Trickster.

* * *

"You shouldn't be here." *Tug, tug, scrabble, scrabble.* "Balls. Hang on a tick."

Hel, the goddess of the Norse underworld, was not what Ives expected. Sure, the skeletal portion of her face seemed appropriate for a goddess of death, but aside from that? As Hel wrestled unceremoniously with the headset tangled in her wild hair, Ives studied the other half of her face and decided the beings who designed the gods were jerks.

While one side of Hel's complexion was a nightmare come to life, the other side had to be the most beautiful woman Ives had ever seen. The intact half had smooth pale skin like polished porcelain and a perfect arch in her dark brow. Her features consisted of lovingly sculpted angles and a lush mouth that poets would have written verses about if it didn't give way to a leering skull. The goddess was a walking contradiction of beauty and horror. Ives felt she had been royally boned in a very literal sense.

"Oh, for the love of— Let me," Ives said, reaching for the goddess's hands.

Hel froze as Ives gently worked her hair free. She laid the freed headset in Hel's slack grip, a bit worried by the flabbergasted expression on the goddess's face.

"Uh?"

"Um, er, you aren't dead," said the goddess, her one eye blinking rapidly.

"No?" Ives patted herself down, reassured to find she was still solid. "I don't think so, anyway."

"You *touched* me?"

Odd, Hel acted like it was an unusual instance to be touched. Sure, the half-skull face was a bit off-putting, but Ives had seen quite a few monstrous beasties lurking about in her short time as a Fate Cipher. They were quiet and kept to themselves, afraid of humans. Most monstrous things were, in fact, not very monstrous at all. Ives had been in the company of the goddess for all of two minutes and couldn't shake the feeling Hel wasn't monstrous either.

"How else was I supposed to get this infernal thing free from your hair? You know, they make a much better wireless version now." Ives nodded to the goddess gaming station.

"UPS takes ages to deliver down here, and the delivery charge is outrageous," said Hel. Her gaze fixated on Ives, who was on the verge of fidgeting when Hel reached out and gently poked the tip of her nose. "How did you even get down here? I mean, no offense, but I don't receive many visitors, and usually, they're whiny dead people."

Ives cleared her throat. She'd thrown herself off-task. "Truth is, I'm here to ask for your help."

"Oh?"

It was the tone that made Ives pause. Hel's fleshy half was expressive. Ives watched the curiosity slip from the goddess's face at her words and settle into a blank mask.

"Why don't you get many visitors?" It wasn't what Ives intended to say, but there was something about Hel's expression that reminded her of herself. Such as when certain ex-boyfriends showed up on her doorstep asking for help with nary a care about *her* feelings. Ives recognized that pain.

Hel blinked and looked away. She made an intense study of the floor, rolling the hem of her t-shirt between her bony fingers. "I understand I am rather unsettling to look at."

It was Ives's turn to stare at the glum goddess. How the heck did a divine being end up with self-esteem issues? This was the ruler of the Norse underworld. Her moniker was Lady Death, but her lone eye shimmered with deep shadows.

"It's not that bad," said Ives.

The goddess's gaze snapped up, rife with suspicion.

Ives held up her hands. "Take my word for it. There was this undead fae beastie I stumbled on in the suburbs once. He liked to dumpster dive and scared the dickens out of the local cats. His skin kept shedding off in these god-awful clumps of gore, but the guy was a sweetheart once you got to know him."

"You are a very strange person," said Hel.

Ives sighed. "So I've been told."

Hel folded her hands in front of her. "You know, Strange One, once you're in the realm of the dead, it is nigh impossible to leave."

Ives tried not to think how the arrow's line broke midway down. She hoped the Valkyrie had a backup plan. "Ah, but not completely impossible."

The goddess smirked, a rather frightening gesture when half her face lacked lips. "Ask your question. Though I doubt I will be very helpful to you. As you can see, I don't get out much." She leaned against the desk, planting her hands on either side of her hips so the skeletal tips of her bony hand clicked against the wood.

"Well, I need your help to find Loki."

Hel snorted. "Looking for dear old Dad? I can give you a map to the mountain, but surely there were easier ways of obtaining that little nugget of information than asking me. I mean, it's not exactly a big secret." She stopped talking when Ives blanched. "Did I miss something?"

"I take it you don't know he, uh, slipped his bonds, then?"

Ives winced as the goddess's hands slid off the desk. Hel went crashing chin-first in a graceless heap that sent the bowl of Skittles flying. Multicolored candies rained down on the marble floor. Ives watched a few pieces roll to a stop by her toes before looking back to the goddess.

Hel was back on her feet, hugging herself. Her one eye was wide with panic. "Shit. I'm dead. *More* dead. So freaking dead. The deadest!" She sputtered, her teeth chattering between syllables.

"What are you talking about?" Ives sucked in a sharp breath at the bleak expression on Hel's fleshed-out half.

"This doesn't make sense. How did it go so far and no one noticed? How did I not sense it rising? I'm not ready! I haven't completed my tier-nine oblivion mage set!" The goddess spouted gibberish and showed no signs of stopping.

"This is going nowhere fast," Ives muttered. If Hel couldn't help her, then it was time to find an exit. There was no hint of the Valkyrie, though honestly, what was she expecting at this point? Maybe she could ride out the same way she rode in? The idea made Ives nervous and felt like a dead-end, but hey, maybe she could find an immortal line to ride out...

Ives took a breath, opening her inner eye once again. It was easier this time, almost instantaneous. The downside was Hel's world was as devoid of threads as it was devoid of life except for the goddess herself. Ives bit back a gasp as she studied Hel. Hildr's assumption was incorrect. Hel wouldn't—no, *couldn't*—help them. The same red threads that trapped the Valkyrie were tethered to Hel, ready to tighten on her at any moment like marionette strings, forcing her to dance to the song of the apocalypse.

Identical to the Valkyrie, a damning loop of crimson thread encircled the goddess's throat. Did anyone survive Ragnarök? To her surprise, the sight made Ives angry. For a goddess, Hel didn't seem all that bad. She certainly was nothing like the imposing goddess Ives had met before. Honestly, what had Hel done to deserve such a fate other than be sired by the wrong god? From Ives's fuzzy recollection of the myth, she realized none of Loki's children survived the battle. She made a promise to read up on all of the damn myths as soon as she got out of this mess, which was going to be difficult without the Valkyrie's aid and with a goddess about to go apocalyptically postal.

Ives's thoughts ground to a halt. Wasn't this what she was supposed to do? Her *raison d'être* and all that jazz? To free people, immortals and mortals alike, from ill-begotten fate. She warily eyed the threads winding around the goddess. The pattern was denser and more intricate than anything she'd seen before, far more complex than the last prophecy she attempted and failed to undo.

Her stomach clenched at the memory. Not just failed, she'd crashed and burned spectacularly, so much so it cost her the man she'd been in love with. And that was a piddling prophecy by comparison! How could she possibly hope to free a freaking goddess from a prophecy that had had centuries to take root?

The evil red thread taunted her, seeming to pulse with defiant energy as she watched. Her palms began to sweat. Ives had to try. How could she not? If she could free Hel from the bindings of Ragnarök, there was a chance she could stop the whole shebang. But there was more to it. It might have been easy to call it pity, but when Ives looked at the goddess, she felt a flicker of the same emotion that drove her to save a random fae girl. She wished she had Jules by her side now—for moral support if nothing else.

"Hel?" Ives wondered if it was appropriate to address a goddess by name. Ah, well, it was an odd situation, to begin with.

The goddess looked up at her. The haunted expression on her face solidified Ives's decision.

"If I help you, could you get out of here?"

"How could you possibly help me? You don't even know what's coming for me. It doesn't make sense. How could he be free, now, before my brothers? Who sent you—"

"I can free you from your fate." Ives tried not to cringe at the goddess's incredulous expression. Okay, so her statement was a big, fat lie. She had no idea if she'd succeed, but it would help her confidence if Hel sort of believed she could.

"Wait," said Hel. Her single eye widened. "No way. A Fate Cipher? But, you— you're a myth, a fun, little, bedtime story they tell to young godlings," she said and took a cautious step toward Ives. She continued to shuffle forward until they were only a few feet apart and reached out with her flesh-covered hand to poke Ives in the shoulder. "And you're... *mortal*?" The goddess of death looked downright mortified by the discovery.

Ives gave her a weak grin. "UPS isn't the only thing that takes forever to deliver."

Hel worried the fleshy part of her lip. "Sorry, but what exactly can you do? You can't Google Fate Cipher."

"Uh, well, if I understand my job description correctly, I kind of, um, untangle fate?" Ives tucked her fidgeting fingers behind her back. Could she sound like a bigger idiot?

Hel looked down. She twisted her fingers together, bone against smooth skin. "Do you *really* think you could help me?"

Ives sighed. "I will try. I've never tried to unbind a goddess before. Honestly, I haven't had much luck unbinding anyone. I'm a bit new to this gig. It... It could get a bit messy."

Hel was silent for a moment. "I'll take the chance."

Ives nodded and placed her hands on the goddess's shoulders. "Here goes nothing."

She blew out a breath and slid her hands down. Her perception shifted as her now-intangible fingers sank into the tangled mass of red thread. The contact brought immediate discomfort as the goddess's fate pricked at her skin. The thread began to buzz as Ives tried to tug and tease the knots apart. Red filled her vision as she sank further and further into her task. The minutes crawled by. Nothing was happening. The knots remained as tightly fused as before.

The failure dragged on her. Who was she kidding? She couldn't do it. Once again, she couldn't perform the role her mother handed her. And was it any surprise? She'd avoided it for so long, had no skill or practice. She was doomed to fail from the start.

She began to disengage, wondering how she could break it gently to the goddess that she was a massive failure when the red threads seized her. Barbs shot into her skin, drilling down, drinking her essence with vampiric gusto. A web of pain ensnared her.

Ives began to scream.

NINE

DEATH WEARS A RAINBOW BRITE HOODIE

As a child, Ives never gave much thought to the idea of fate. She barely thought of it at all except maybe in terms of 'Happily Ever After' and soul mates. If they existed.

Ives thought those concepts were bullshit too. It would be too cruel otherwise, after watching her father pine for her absent mother throughout her childhood. She was keenly aware of how fairy tales and movies that preached the mantra of 'Happily Ever After' cut the story off when the hero and heroine reached their 'Happy for Now'. How long were her parents 'Happy for Now'? Ives learned the hard way, the day she turned eighteen, that fate was a bitch.

"You're lying. This can't be real. I'm dreaming, I'm—" Ives yanked her hands out of her mother's hold. "You can't be real."

Fate Cipher. The foreign words tumbled through her thoughts. Her mother laid it all out on the table. She told Ives what she was, why she'd disappeared from their lives, all of it. It meant nothing to Ives. It made no sense to her.

She couldn't understand how much her life had changed at that moment, how nothing would ever be the same again. She didn't understand her mother's desperate urgency to teach her and how much she failed to pass on the whole lesson.

"Please, Ikepela, don't shut me out," her mother pleaded, reaching for her again.

"Don't call me that name," Ives hissed. Tears stung at her eyes. For years, she'd imagined so many reasons for her mother's disappearance. From elaborate fantasies where her mother was a superhero who had to keep her identity a secret to save the world, or that she made some incredible sacrifice to save Ives's life. Not this, not this impossible, improbable burden she waited to shove off on her teenage daughter. Her mother, the immortal who fell in love with a mortal man.

"This isn't real. I-I can't do this. I *won't* do this," said Ives. She shot out of her chair, out of her mother's reach. There was hurt in her mother's eyes before they hardened to chips of violet ice.

"There is no choice. You will do it because there is no one else."

Ives shook her head, refusing to accept the inevitable. "So I can change everyone's fate but my own?" Her tone was angry. She wanted to throw something but there was nothing in the room but the table and seats, and the mother she couldn't stand to look at.

Her mother dropped her hands to the table, her lovely face worn and defeated. "It's not your destiny, my daughter. It's your biology. I'm not handing these powers over to you *by choice*. It's in your blood. Whether you want it or not, blood will tell."

☗☗☗

Pain spiraled through Ives. It burned like magma in her veins. The threads of Ragnarök were vile, poisonous. They leeched away her strength and ate at her essence. They shredded her thoughts and stripped down all her defenses until she floated, blank, her life ebbing away. She was an insect caught in a thunderstorm, no match for the forces powering the prophecy of Ragnarök. It pulsed through her. It tried to etch its intent into the fibers of her soul. It wanted to devour her, absorb her into the cycle of death and violence as the world went up in flames. Not just this world, but all worlds. It would continue its ravenous destruction until all of creation was ash.

The barbs sank in like teeth to chew her up. There was no one to stop the onslaught of Ragnarök, no one to stop that unquenchable thirst for destruction. There was no one else.

It was in her blood, dammit.

Ives grit her teeth as she shoved back. She refused to give in to the onslaught. This wasn't just some ridiculous prophecy flung out into the universe to be rectified with a bit of unraveling on her part. Ragnarök was a ravenous monster. It seethed hatred and chaos. There was no rhyme or reason for it. Ives seized those poisonous threads and pitched her essence through the thorny maw to wrap around its core. There were no gentle tugs this time, no soft attempts to undo the knots of fate. Ives allowed instinct to guide her, as that coiled power inside her wrapped about the scarlet knots and ripped them apart. It tore the threads of Ragnarök to nothing but shreds that slowly dispersed into oblivion. Ives slowly sank back into her skin. Her head spun, a surge of vertigo at the expenditure of so much energy in one go. She almost missed it, caught between exhaustion and the fading threads, the strange hint of another's dark influence hidden within the core of Ragnarök's thread. It slipped through her fingers as she snatched at it, but not before she got a taste for it, the truth of it. She struggled to commit that vital piece of information to memory, so she could examine it later, but her mortal limitations caught up to her. She slumped forward.

A shocked Hel caught Ives as she lost consciousness.

ᛟᛟᛟ

Fenrir rocked back. A tingle ran through the ruff of his neck as a piece of his fate came undone.

What glorious magic was this? For a brief, precious second, he had his first moment of pure clarity in centuries. He inhaled deeply and caught the scents of a new world, of strange chemicals that burned his nose. The bouquet of humanity had vastly changed over the past millennium. The mass of the reeking unwashed populace now coated itself in floral scents, sweet alcoholic rubs, and pastes. He did not know if he considered it an improvement as it made his nostrils itch. And the light, so much light. He could see the settlements from here, lit up brighter than the day, so bright it blotted out the stars overhead.

He padded through the surf after the arduous swim to the mainland. How long had he been trapped? How many years had he atrophied away, chained to a frozen rock, while the world passed him by? A surge of fury seized him, so fierce it made his legs wobble. He wanted to rend and tear it apart. He would find the All-Father and—

No!

No, this wasn't what he wanted. He could feel it, another will that twisted and warped his own. He could feel its hooks digging into his mind. He shook his head to clear his thoughts with minimal success. It was amazing he could wrest his mind at all from the choking grip of destiny. What gave him that moment of clarity?

Fenrir lifted his nose, scenting the air. He could find anything, anyone, if he desired it enough. He caught the faintest whiff of fading power and sneezed his disbelief. *It was a myth.* The Norns insisted no such creature existed, and yet...

Kill, destroy, find the one-eyed bastard, and devour him.

Fenrir launched across the land, chasing a scent as tangible as sunshine, trying to outrun fate nipping at the pads of his feet.

ᛏ ᛏ ᛏ

Something hard tip-tapped against Ives's cheek. She smelled olive oil and vanilla, a strange combination to be sure, made stranger when she cracked open her eyelids to see a cluster of metacarpals gently slapping her face.

Bemused and more than a little groggy, Ives swiveled her head around. *That woman only had half a face.* Such a shame. She was quite lovely once you got past the grinning skull bit.

"I can't decide if you're flattering or insulting, but I'm happy you're awake," said the woman.

"Oh, bother. Did I say that out loud?" Ives hiccupped and began to fall over. The skeleton lady caught her. Lady skeleton? Skellady? Ives giggled and covered her mouth. "Am I still talking?" she whispered.

The Skellady made a face, as she slung her fleshed out arm around Ives's waist. "Easy there, little lady. I don't think you're exactly a hundred percent yet."

Ives couldn't agree more, mostly because she couldn't get her head to do more than droop around like a great bag of sand attached to her neck. It was if she were floating

65

across the room as the lady helped her into a posh four-poster bed. She settled with a sigh on top of black silk sheets. Ives began to drift back to sleep when memory snapped like a rubber band.

The Strawberry Shortcake comforter slid to the floor as she folded upright. Ives panted and gripped her knees tight as she willed the world to stop spinning. Her vision finally settled on the goddess Hel, who sat cross-legged at the edge of the bed.

"Oh, good. You're awake. I was worried you'd be out for days."

"What?" Ives reached up, trying to wipe the sensation of cobwebs off her face. "You just put me in bed."

"Sweetie, that was hours ago. Though for a mortal, you recovered pretty damn quick from all that power flow." Hel whistled through her teeth. "Color me impressed."

Ives tried to summon her abilities. They fizzed and sputtered like a light bulb about to burn out, utterly depleted. "Did... Did it work?"

The goddess rewarded her with a smile. Despite the skeletal half of her face, there was such warmth and joy it transcended her appearance. Ives blinked at her in awe. How could the gods hide such a beautiful smile so deep in the earth?

Hel killed the moment with a girly squeal and made jazz hands. "It worked!" She fist-pumped the air.

Ives couldn't help the laugh that bubbled up, muffled by her hands over her mouth. She sobered up after a moment. "I thought it would kill me," she admitted.

"You and me both. When you started glowing, I thought you were going to explode on me, and let me tell you, it took me decades to collect these posters." Hel flicked her fingers at the walls. "I would be quite put out at having to clean bits of Fate Cipher off my vintage *Rocky Horror* poster."

Ives stared at her, wide-eyed. "I glowed?"

"Yeah, and there was screaming, lots of screaming. Your skin got hot, like molten hot, and there was that bit you muttered at the end."

"What bit?" Ives frowned. She *did* feel she'd forgotten something vitally important.

Hel clicked her bony fingers against her exposed teeth. "You know, I'm not sure."

Ives rubbed her temples. The information dangled frustratingly out of reach. "Why can't I remember? Gah, maybe Jules can help me." The color drained out of her face. "Oh, crap. I'm stuck here, aren't I?"

Hel stopped midway off the bed to glance at her. "Not to mince words, but a deal is a deal. I'll get you back topside. I am curious—how did you manage to get here in the first place, being disgustingly mortal and all?"

"Oh, it was that arrow, the one the damn Valkyrie shot me with. Some lifeline that turned out to be."

Hel cocked her head. "What did it look like?"

Ives patted herself down. When had she lost the very thing that shot her? "Like crystal. The string was almost invisible, like a forgery of a lifeline. When the arrow hit me, it sent me here, but about halfway down, the line snapped."

"How in the nine worlds did you survive?"

"I hitchhiked on a dying soul."

"Clever girl," said Hel, a note of admiration in her voice. "Well, it just so happens I know where the back door is. Come along, sweets."

"Really? Just like that?" Ives jumped to her feet, noticing the goddess's attire for the first time. The PJ bottoms were gone, switched out for a pair of faded jeans covered in doodles. A ratty ACDC t-shirt peeked through the gap of a large black zip-up hoodie with rainbow cuffs. Hel pulled up the hood, hiding most of her face in the recesses of cloth.

"You totes lived up to your end of the bargain. Besides," she said, squeezing Ives's shoulder with her flesh-covered hand. "You set me free. I can—I *will* help you find my father."

She spun around for the door and revealed an embroidered image of Rainbow Brite across her back. Ives grinned at the image and fell in step behind the goddess.

"You have an idea of where he might be?"

"Yeah, once I get a feel for it."

Ives paused as she processed the goddess's words. "Wait. Once you get a feel for it? From some Underworld control panel?"

Hel waved her skeletal hand over her shoulder. "*Pfft.* I'm coming with you. Haven't had a vacation in centuries."

TEN

GOOD VIBRATIONS

FENRIR WASN'T the only one who felt the fate of Hel unravel. The aftereffects rippled through gods and immortals alike. Most didn't know what it meant or what could be the cause. Most believed the Fate Cipher was a myth or a line that had died out long ago. Only those pinned beneath the wheel of fate dared to believe and kept the information quiet.

Unfortunately, not all who believed the Fate Cipher existed had good intentions. The hooded figure stopped mid-stride, sneering as the bindings of Ragnarök frayed at the edges. This was unacceptable. The Fate Cipher must be eliminated. The figure looked out over the water, standing on a lone jutting rock in a forgotten corner of the world. Ah, well, here was the opportunity to kill two birds with one stone. Two horns dangled from the figure's waist. It was not yet time to sound the other. That would come soon enough. First, a bit more disaster was required. The Jotunns were moving into place, rousting allies and eliminating foes as they went. It was time to add another player to the board.

The hooded one lifted the second horn to his lips, one carved with the Ouroboros around its mouthpiece. The sound was too low for human ears, but the being beneath the water heard the summoning that vibrated through the cold, dark, deep ocean. The water receded from the shore. It frothed and churned as a leviathan rose from the depths. The head crested first, large enough to swallow a cruise ship whole. The World Serpent drew three stories above the water and angled its massive head to peer at the cloaked figure on shore with one great sea-green eye.

There was only one reason to summon Jormungand from the bottom of the ocean, only one task he was destined for, but the hooded figure had another errand for the World Serpent.

ᛟ ᛟ ᛟ

"What do we do? What do we do?" Jules slammed her tiny fists against the wall to disguise her sniffle. "What do we do?" Ives was gone, vanished, vamoosed, and she just sat there as it happened. That was hours ago. This was the longest they'd been apart since Ives had saved her life. She didn't know what to do with herself. That oaf of a Valkyrie was no help, either.

Hildr claimed to be in contact with her 'sources,' trying to find an alternative way to extract Ives from the underworld. She'd given Jules a blank look when she asked if the cabin had Wi-Fi. Of course, it didn't. That would mean the Valkyrie was, in any way, aware of the twenty-first century. Jules paced. She was useless, while Hildr sent carrier pigeons or whatever old-school method she deemed effective. Did the Norsemen not believe in a backup plan? Jules would never have sent Ives into such a situation without more than two escape routes and a bucket-load of info. Hildr insisted her absent roomie had met with success in the underworld, claiming a thread of Ragnarök had come undone. If that was the case, then where was Ives? It was fast approaching the twenty-four-hour mark since Jules watched her best friend sink through the floor with a mystical arrow in her chest.

She debated punching the wall again just to relieve some frustration when she heard a wolf's howl. This wasn't very odd by itself, considering their location—except Jules was still indoors and the howl sounded as if it was in the same room. The odd factor ramped up as tremors shook the lodge. The Valkyrie burst into the room, sword in hand, panic etched into her face. A bad feeling settled into Jules's gut. A frightened battle maiden was not a good development.

"We have a problem," Hildr gasped, backing up against the wall beside Jules.

"Oh, goodie, another problem. We don't have enough of those," Jules snapped. Another howl rolled over them, an overwhelming, mournful sound. The support beams creaked as the shaking intensified. Jules shuffled closer to the Valkyrie and pulled a knife from her boot. The blade was only five inches long, but being armed made her feel better. "Er, I don't suppose that would be your Hound buddy checking in?"

Hildr shook her head, her face tight as she held the sword in front of her, both hands on the hilt. Grim determination emanated from her stance as the ground lurched beneath them, nearly throwing Jules off balance.

"Have I mentioned how much I hate dogs?"

"Ta-da!" Hel stepped back with the flair of a game show hostess. The rune she'd traced into the trunk of a tree rippled, and the bark melted away from a very familiar-looking set of doors.

"Hell has an elevator? That's some sort of poetic truth there." Ives followed the goddess into the cozy compartment, complete with cushioned benches for those long upward hauls. She tilted her head at the faint strains of music cranking through an ancient set of speakers attached to the wall. "Is that—"

"Sugar Hill Gang, yes," said Hel and surreptitiously prodded a rune on the wall.

The doors slid shut. Ives's stomach dropped as the elevator began its ascent. She settled on one of the benches, studying the goddess out of the corner of her eye. She wondered at Hel's motivation for coming along but hadn't questioned it. Considering Hildr and her boss had no idea where to find the key player of Ragnarök, she wasn't going to turn down any help, no matter what form it came in. Speaking of forms, though...

"Hel, what do regular people see when they look at you?" Ives didn't miss the goddess's nearly imperceptible flinch.

Her hands twisted together, flesh over bone. "I'll keep the hood up," said Hel, her voice soft, pleading. "I have a pair of gloves in my pocket. I'll stay out of sight, I just... I just want to see the world. Just a little bit."

"You can't glamour." Ives couldn't wrap her head around something so unfair. Didn't all the gods have the ability to glamour themselves? Why was Hel, the goddess of an entire realm, denied that? Wasn't Loki a shape-shifter? She pursed her lips, remembering the trickster's other monstrous children. Did any of them have the ability to change form? Why wouldn't they? In every myth she could remember, gods could change their form at will, not only to blend but so they didn't overwhelm humans. That Hel couldn't do so was troubling and didn't make sense. There had to be something Ives could do. Or, maybe not her, but Ives certainly knew someone who *could* help the goddess.

"I need to introduce you to someone," she said. She began to say more but tensed when Hel spun around and stared up at the ceiling.

"That will have to wait," murmured Hel. "We seem to have an unwelcome visitor topside." She poked another rune in the wall.

"You can see them? Do you know who it is?" Ives gripped the railing, thankful she was sitting down as the elevator increased its speed. Her ears popped from the pressure.

Hel made a face. "My brother."

☗ ☗ ☗

"Aaaaugh, aaaaugh, throw it a steak or something!" screamed Jules, leaping from the fireplace mantel as the giant wolf snapped his teeth through the space she'd recently occupied.

The creature was out of his wits, his eyes vacant. Impossible to reason with. The Valkyrie was usefully buried beneath a pile of rubble from the animal's entrance. The great bloody beast had burst through the wall like a toddler through Lincoln Logs, raining broken pieces down on them. Hildr didn't move with a fae's speed, which left Jules to distract him until the Valkyrie managed to extricate herself from the debris.

The next snap barely missed. Fangs caught on the hem of her dress. Jules screeched and spun to stab the wolf's foot. It was as effective as a rose thorn, but she managed to nip the vulnerable pad on his hind leg and sent the beast reeling against the opposite wall. There was no time to congratulate herself as he turned with a snarl and went straight for her. She attempted to go left and promptly slipped on a scrap of fur from the destroyed couch. She face-planted, stunned as she waited for teeth to close around her. There was a frantic scrabble of claws and a series of grunts.

"Get up, now, small fae idiot," said the Valkyrie in a strained tone.

Jules peeked through her fingers. Hildr had lodged her sword in the wolf's mouth, and the blade kept those terrible jaws from closing. The wolf snarled and chuffed around the weapon, pressing down on the shieldmaiden, whose muscles shook from the effort. Jules scrambled to her feet. There had to be some way to neutralize the wolf before he overwhelmed the Valkyrie. She refused to let that blonde giant die while protecting her. Hildr still had to break Ives out of the underworld.

Jules ran for the broken couch. There were advantages to being light and small. She jumped down onto the springs, launching through the air with a high-pitched war cry that startled the two figures locked in battle. Jules landed squarely on the giant wolf's nose.

The creature went cross-eyed trying to peer at the dainty girl on his snout.

She offered him a malicious grin and stabbed him between the eyes.

ELEVEN

GROUNDBREAKING

THE RIDE WAS A LONG ONE. Too much silence begged to be filled. Ives didn't know what to say, but the goddess had plenty of words, built up from long lonely years in the black marbled halls of the Dead.

"I remember things, small things, from before," Hel began, her voice hesitant, possessing a raw vulnerability. "I remember running through vast fields of tall grass, Fenrir at my side. I remember the warmth of the sun on my face. My brother loved nothing more than to run, the chase. He hunted the great stags of the wood. He hunted those who did ill to the gods. He was never malicious or cruel. He never killed without swift mercy. I remember him braiding wildflowers in my hair…"

That didn't sound like the Fenrir Ives had read about, the monstrous wolf meant to devour Odin, the All-Father. There was a beat of silence, Hel's expression lost as she sank on the plush seat beside Ives. The goddess kept an inch of space between them, as if she were afraid to touch Ives, or that Ives would reject the contact.

"I can't… I can't see the time before the prophecy in my

mind," she said softly, fiddling with a fraying patch near her bony elbow. "It's like all memories of who I was before have been scrubbed away, stolen by the weight of Ragnarök. And now that it's lifted, I feel free. But I also feel empty, like all my memories for the last thousand years are little more than shadows. Nothing is solid. I don't remember who I am, who my brothers were."

"I don't remember my mom," said Ives, oddly at ease with sharing something so personal with the Goddess of Death. "I only met her once, right when she dumped the whole Fate Cipher thing on my head and bailed. Well, not really 'bailed' so much as 'imprisoned.' I never really used those abilities or wanted to before I met you." She shook herself. Leave it to her to overshare while a goddess had a small breakdown. She gave Hel a gentle nudge. "What else do you remember of your brothers?"

Hel studied her mismatched hands. "We weren't always monsters." The goddess looked up, her gaze filled with a swirl of emotion. "I don't think our father was one either."

"I've been thinking about that myself. Something about this whole apocalypse has felt tilted from the start. I don't know what it is yet. I haven't tangled with enough prophecies to pinpoint why my spidey senses are tingling."

Hel looked stunned. "What are you saying?"

"That this whole apocalypse reeks and I need to talk to my fae roommate."

"That may have been the most puzzling statement you have made in my presence," said Hel.

Ives shrugged. "You'll like her. By the way, any idea how to stop your rampaging monstrous brother?" Really, how big a wolf could he be?

Hel clicked her teeth. "I'm sure we will think of something."

The elevator of the underworld came to a halt with a quiet *ding*. The doors slid open, revealing the same picturesque snowy landscape Hildr had brought Ives to from her Pacific home. She shivered, the cold sapping her without the Valkyrie's cape. Hel noticed and snapped her bony fingers.

"Here," she said. Reality wobbled as the goddess plucked a sweatshirt from some extra-dimensional pocket. Ives was too grateful for the extra layer of warmth to care about the *My Little Pony* print.

A crash echoed through the woods, followed by a howl that made the world vibrate around them.

Hel's entire face paled to the sickly shade of bone. "Oh, no." She whirled on Ives, clasping her shoulders so tight her fingers dug into Ives's shoulder. "Please, please help him. He didn't want this. None of us wanted this."

Ives nodded. There was no question about it, even if her grasp on her abilities was shaky at best. They took off at a run. She could see the lodge roof through the trees, the sounds of a furious battle echoing through the picturesque scenery. Hel and Ives cleared a row of evergreen and skidded to a stop on the snowy, torn-up lawn as chaos erupted through the broken front wall of the lodge.

"How the frack do we stop that?" yelled Ives.

Fenrir wasn't just a large wolf; he was *gigantic*. He had to be larger than a bull elephant, though his muscled form was lithe and agile for a creature of his size. He scuttled backward, his tail fluffed out on end, as he frantically shook his head from side to side. Ives saw the reason, and her pulse tripped.

Jules clung to the wolf's bloodied snout, stabbing him over and over in the sensitive flesh of his nose. Her knife was minuscule, little more than pinpricks against something Fenrir's size, but he must have been properly pissed by the fae's actions as he tried to fling her off his face. A strangled noise made her tear her gaze away long enough to glance at Hel, who had both hands clapped over her mouth. A burp of laughter squeaked between Hel's fingers.

Fantastic. Jules was fighting for her life against Hel's psycho brother, and the goddess thought it was hilarious.

"You going to help or stand there, giggling like an idiot?" Ives snapped. She needed to interfere before Jules got hurt or worse—killed. Where was that damn Valkyrie?

On cue, Hildr burst through the broken wall, spinning an oddly shaped hammer as she charged into the fray with a blood-curdling scream.

"Okay, time to interfere," said Hel.

Ives didn't see her move. One moment, the goddess was beside her, and the next, she was tackling the Valkyrie in the snow, leaving Ives to save Jules. She was still far too far away when the wolf jerked his head hard enough to send Jules into the trees. Ives screamed. A ball of crackling fire churned in her gut.

The ground beneath Fenrir shifted and tore open with a thunderous crack. Steam shot up, enveloped the wolf, and blinded him. The fount of steam was so strong it knocked him off his feet so he hit the ground with a tremendous thud. He lay there, dazed and panting. The fight went out of him.

Ives gaped. *How the hell had that happened?*

"Ives?"

She turned, trying to uncurl her fists. Jules poked her head through the branches. Ives's knees wobbled as the fae descended from the tree and rushed to her companion. Her small body slammed into Ives. The strength of Jules's thin arms crushed her for a moment before she shifted far enough away to assess her condition.

"I'm okay," Ives whispered. She gave Jules a similar treatment.

The fae had a few scrapes and pine needles tangled in her hair, but that was the only evidence of her tango with the giant wolf.

"I can't believe how crazy brave you are," Ives said.

"Only because you taught me how to be," said Jules.

Ives gave her another tight squeeze, letting Jules cling to her side as the two approached the fallen wolf. Fenrir was not in good shape. The fur along his ruff was crusted with blood. The pads of his feet were raw from running great distances after long disuse. The eyes were the worst. Beneath the apparent vacant sheen, there was a storm of fear and desperation.

Fenrir was a creature ridden hard by the demons of fate. Ives took a breath and reached for her abilities. They rose swiftly now at her call with only a hint of concentration. Practice made perfect. She opened her innate senses and looked at the wolf. Her heart twinged with sympathy. Ragnarök had a far more vicious hold on Fenrir than his sibling. It appeared as a coiled chain of rope around the wolf's bloody throat instead of a tangle of threads. The red threads of Ragnarök were burrowed deep in Fenrir's skin, like grounding spikes more than hooks. It was a destiny that dogged his every step. How had he ended up here? The strain of resisting it had to be incredible, and yet here he was instead of standing beside the enemy.

Who had he tracked here? The goddess?

A strangled sound drew her attention as Hel fell next to them, still wrestling the frothing Valkyrie to the ground.

"Would you tell this idiot the fight is over?" She pleaded to Ives.

"Hildr!" Ives clapped her hands to get the Valkyrie's

attention and shattered the haze of battle-lust clouding the woman's vision.

Hildr shuddered as she felt the bony arm of the goddess wrapped around her neck. She eyed Ives and Jules standing beside the fallen wolf.

"Did we win?"

TWELVE

LIFELINES

HEL WHISTLED, toeing the crack in the earth. "Didn't realize earth-shaking was among your Fate Cipher abilities." She tapped her bony index finger against her exposed teeth in thought.

The action made the Valkyrie twitch. Once she'd stopped fighting, Hildr had gotten one good look at who had her in a choke-hold, squawked, and scrambled atop the nearest large rock, twirling the hammer between her fingers as she eyed Hel with suspicion. It was apparent when she sent Ives to ask for the goddess's help, she had not expected Hel to aid them in person. But the uneasy Valkyrie was the least of their problems

Ives snorted. "I didn't do that."

Hel raised her brow at her.

Ives crossed her arms, unsettled. "I didn't?"

"Was that a question?" Hel gestured to the ground. "I certainly didn't do this. Though that would be a pretty cool hybrid-class thing," she muttered. She bit at her knuckle, puzzled by the crack before her brother whined and tried to move. The mystery was forgotten as Hel fell to her knees next to him and placed his massive head to her lap.

"Sister?"

Ives jumped. Jules yelped and tightened her grip on the back of Ives's borrowed sweatshirt. Hildr shifted from her position on the rock, gripping her strange hammer. They'd all heard the odd voice, both spoken and not. It wasn't exactly inside their heads. The voice was a faded echo in the air as if Fenrir's words traveled down a long corridor to reach them. The effect was unnerving.

"I'm here," said Hel as she tenderly stroked the wolf's bloodied snout.

Some of the frenzied light dimmed in his eyes. He closed them and leaned closer to his sister. The sight made Ives's chest tight. She pulled away from Jules to kneel beside Fenrir. The action caused a series of aches to cascade through her. Ives ignored them. The siblings were counting on her. She wasn't sure if Fenrir could last much longer without succumbing to the unending pull of his fate. Her hands shook as she reached for him.

"What are you doing?" Jules hissed. She tugged at Ives's arms. "Are you trying to kill yourself?"

"Jules, I did it. I freed Hel earlier. I can do this," said Ives.

"It's true. She was incredible," said Hel. Her lone green eye shone with faith.

Jules scowled at the goddess. "And where do you think her energy comes from?"

Hel blinked, glancing at Ives sidelong and swore profusely. "I'm an idiot."

"I thought so," grumbled Jules.

Ives threw up her hands in exasperation. "Mind sharing? Cause I gotta tell you—your bro here isn't going to hold out much longer."

Jules pursed her lips. "Do you have any idea how depleted you are, Ives? Your energy is flickering like a candle at the end of its wick. Your abilities as a Fate Cipher are fueled by your life force, or do I need to remind you how very mortal you are, my friend?" She nodded towards Hel. "I know you did something amazing down there, but if you try to repeat your efforts any time soon, you will snuff yourself out."

"How can she stop Ragnarök with such a weakness?" Hildr rested her chin on her fist. "I did not realize her powers were so meshed to her lifeline, small fae person."

Ives stared down at her hands. Jules told the truth. Her body ached all over. Wrestling Hel's fate had drained her to the point of unconsciousness. Her energy hadn't had enough time to recover from such an onslaught. *If* it recovered. Mortal energy didn't operate like immortals. Figured, she'd finally embraced her abilities, could access them with a snap of her fingers, but the reality she'd ignore was that her power came with one hell of a handicap. It was a stroke of dumb luck her success rate was nonexistent until now. Her ignorance of her limits would get her killed.

Hildr frowned at the crevice. "What about that weird energy spike she had when she defeated the great wolf?"

"I told you that wasn't me," Ives insisted. She had no idea what happened when the earth ripped open, but she was one-hundred percent certain that it didn't come from her.

"No, the ground wasn't your doing," said Jules, "but that is not the issue here." She flapped a dismissive hand at their speculative expressions. "Not sure how Ives managed to harness it when she's never managed to before, but she can't do it again."

"Yes, yes, we get it, the weak mortal can hear you." Ives hated this. The way Jules ducked down and looked guilty made her feel like crap. Ives desperately wished for a hot shower and maybe nine cups of coffee, if only to banish the exhaustion from her veins. The adrenaline long since dried up, her mind was a fuzzy mess. She couldn't think straight to see an alternative answer out of this mess. The wild lost look in Fenrir's eyes brought on a wash of guilt. She had to help him—somehow. Her efforts couldn't be so utterly quashed before she'd even begun. "There has to be something I can do, some kind of workaround."

Hel's skeletal hand slipped into hers. The play of bone over her skin should have freaked her out, but it didn't. Only Hel's obvious pain and worry for her sibling did.

"You're no good to him dead either," said Hel.

Ives looked up at her, meaning to apologize. She blinked as an epiphany struck; a physical sensation as if invisible fingers plucked a chord and cleared the brain fog away, revealing an idea with crystal clarity.

"I have an idea. It might not work. It will probably just hurt a lot."

Hel sniffed. "Sounds like most of my P.U.G. runs."

"Ives?" Jules tilted her head at her friend and companion, unable to glean her game plan.

"I think I got this, but just in case, be ready to, uh, pull me out."

The fae stamped her foot. "That does *not* fill me with confidence."

Ives didn't have much confidence in this plan either, but waiting wasn't an option, and dying was on her list of things to avoid. She turned to the wolf. Fenrir's dazed eyes were on her. A flicker of hope lurked in their brown depths. It was a lifeline of courage Ives wrapped around herself as she opened herself to the Fate Cipher power.

Ives was going to ride a lifeline again. Only this time, she'd tap an immortal one. Jules's description of her energy was generous. It was like sipping the backwash dregs at the end of a bottle of beer. Ives dug deep and laid her hand on Hel's bony shoulder. Free from the crushing chokehold of Ragnarök, Hel's immortal lifeline shone with a radiant golden glow. The plan was a sound, in theory. If Ives's mortal lifeline didn't possess the necessary energy to unbind Fenrir, why not borrow the immortal energy of his sister? The problem was Ives had no idea what to expect. Her mother never mentioned doing anything like this. Then again, their conversation on the subject of a Fate Cipher's role and abilities had been far too brief.

Jules danced anxiously beside her. Hildr was on the edge of her rock. The siblings waited for her patiently, trusting her. *This might be the stupidest thing I've ever done.* Ives made an internal shift and grasped Hel's lifeline.

She might have fared better grabbing a live wire.

Ives's scream knocked against the clouded underbelly of the sky as the goddess stiffened under her palm.

Jules grabbed for her in a panic. She pulled at Ives's locked fingers to no effect.

The goddess's energy sizzled through her blood. It washed over her skin in sheets of invisible flame. Ives dropped her head forward with a moan as she rode the pain, oblivious to what happened outside the torrent of energy coursing through her. It threatened to fill her up until she burst. The energy needed somewhere to go, a purpose. Ives seized on that idea in pure desperation and molded the energy to suit her needs. She shifted her focus to Fenrir.

The spiky coils of Ragnarök sensed Hel's energy. It bristled as Ives plunged forward. Wielding Hel's energy was akin to riding an atomic chainsaw. Instead of the fearsome wrestling match she'd encountered earlier, Ives sliced through the wolf's fate with a sword's edge. The red threads curled back like vanishing smoke.

There it was again! Vanishing with the rest was another curl of that intrusive black thread. What was it?

She'd vanquished the repulsive fate easily this time. Far too easily. Ives tried to stem the flow of the goddess's energy and detach herself from Hel's immortal lifeline. It continued its agonizing pulse up her arm and slowly ate her up. She wondered briefly if the energy would just keep flowing into her until she blew up in a splatter of flesh. Maybe then, they'd release her mother to do the job properly.

Tears tracked down her face. For being the only Fate Cipher available in the world, she was laughably ill-equipped for the job.

A noise reached her pain fogged brain. The snap of broken thread. The following silence was dreadful but carried a note of expectation. A presence covered Ives in a blanket of warmth far different than Hel's crackling energy. It felt...like home. In her mind, there was an impatient cluck of a tongue against teeth. It was distinctly feminine.

A tingling surge of heat rose from her gut and shooed the blazing energy of the goddess from where it didn't belong. Her fingers finally unlocked from Hel's shoulder as the presence retreated with a soft sigh. Ives had no time to ponder what or who came to her rescue as she collapsed face-first into the snow.

Thirteen

GLAMOUR

IVES FLOATED BACK to consciousness on a cloud of steam. The gentle warmth was intoxicating after the snow and far, far, more pleasant than the electric heat of a godly lifeline...

Oh, dear.

She jerked up with a gasp, patting herself down. To her amazement, she wasn't riddled with cracks, like a badly patched porcelain vase. She fell back with a thud. Whatever padding she slept on was thinner than she expected. Her head thumped against the hardwood floor.

"Ow," she said.

"You do need to quit it with these little mortal episodes of yours," a familiar voice teased.

Ives turned her sore head to find Hel watching her, knees drawn up to her chest.

"You gave us a bit of a scare."

Ives cautiously sat up, letting her body regain its equilibrium. Jules slammed into her a moment later. The fae was light enough that her tackle didn't take Ives to the floor again, but Ives could tell by the tremble in her friend's small frame she was shaken by what had happened.

Ives wrapped Jules in a fierce hug. "I'm sorry."

She could feel Hel's eyes on her. The goddess studied the pair of them with a mixture of curiosity and another tinge of emotion that Ives didn't recognize at first. Not until the Valkyrie strode into the room and she banished the look from her face. The goddess of the underworld was slightly jealous. Ives wondered why until she saw the flicker of discomfort on Hildr's face at addressing Hel.

"Your brother is still resting. I fear his snoring may shake down the rest of this abode before long."

Hel snorted. The sound whistled through her empty nostril cavity. "Give the guy a break. He was imprisoned on a desolate rock for centuries. He's a bit worn out."

Hildr sniffed and twiddled with the weapons hanging from her belt. "Be that as it may, we need to discuss a few things, such as why you've left your post."

The goddess tightened her arms around her legs. "I guided Ives from my realm with the understanding I would aid in the location of my father." Hel's tonal shift did a one-eighty. It wasn't like the quiet strain from before, discussing her past, but cold and aloof—the voice of the Goddess of Death.

"What's going on?" Ives shared a confused look with Jules.

"We can find the Lord of Lies without the help of his daughter," said Hildr. "She should return to her station as appointed by the All-Father."

Ives frowned at the Valkyrie. "It seemed pretty self-sufficient without her from what I saw. I think the underworld can spare her for a few days while we track down her old man."

The coolness eased as Hel considered her. A grin tugged at her stiff lips. "Hate to spoil it for you, Ivy, baby, but he looks nothing like an old man." Her single green eye winked at Ives. Or perhaps she blinked. It was difficult to tell with one eye.

"She is not going anywhere with us," snapped Hildr. "And neither is her foul brother."

"What the heck is your problem?" Ives stumbled to her feet to get between the two immortals, quite the tenuous place to be, judging by Jules's fidgeting.

Hel sighed and placed her hands on Ives's shoulders to move her aside. Hildr's expression turned incredulous. For a moment Ives didn't get it, then she realized what bug crawled up Hildr's butt—the disdain over her casual contact with Hel.

It occurred to Ives that Hel was 'gifted' a station in the underworld, far from the sight of mortals and gods alike.

Hildr threw up her hands. "She cannot venture into the general public. The children of Loki do not possess the ability to cast glamour or shapeshift. Do you wish to induce a mass panic at the sight of a giant wolf and skeletal goddess walking the streets?"

"I can keep it hidden," Hel hissed and drew farther into her hood.

"Your brother cannot, and I doubt he'll stay here."

"Then what are you suggesting? That I banish him to the underworld in my stead?"

The two women were still a couple of feet apart, but animosity sparked between. There were visible flickers of lightning coming off the Valkyrie. They were likely one or two comments from swinging fists when Jules wedged herself in front of the Valkyrie and pushed the much taller Hildr away.

"Okay there, blondie, back it up. I think I can help with this little problem."

Hildr peered down at Jules, her eyebrows creeping up to

meet her disheveled hairline. "I do not follow, small fae creature."

Ives bit down on her smile, happy her companion took the initiative without her asking. "Jules is indeed fae, and like all fae, she has a wallop of magic in her."

Hel's interest was piqued while the Valkyrie scoffed.

"This diminutive creature? She's what, a brownie? What magic do they possess besides a bit of household sprucing?" Hildr flinched at Jules's kick to her shin. "No offense meant, of course."

"First off, brownies perform tasks according to how indebted they feel to an individual. There is usually a bartering that takes place, an exchange of goods for services that makes them inclined to spruce up the place, but they're still fae. Their magic is potent," said Ives with a shrug. "Second, we're not sure what species of fae Jules is."

Hel blinked. "Wait what? How—"

"Never mind the technicalities. My magic extends beyond menial household tasks." Jules pinched her pointed chin high.

Hildr folded her arms. "Yes but I doubt you are indebted to the parties involved as you spent a good five minutes stabbing the great wolf between the eyes."

"Which I admit was rather glorious," Hel muttered.

Jules shook her head. "Okay, the wolf is not my favorite god-person, but I owe Ives everything. I will do anything I can to help her achieve her goals. I would have traveled to the underworld with her if it were possible. Creating an intrinsic glamour for Loki's children barely dips into the debt I owe her."

"A whose-a-ma-whatsit?" Hel squinted at the fae and tapped her fingertips against her kneecaps.

Hildr looked at Ives with blatant surprise. "I commend

you for inspiring such deep loyalty, but can your fae person truly glamour them?"

Ives hated the praise. She recalled the very incident which landed her with her indebted fae, a blood debt. It was another result of failure to properly use her ability, though Jules insisted their situation was better than the alternative. Ives met her roomie's determined gaze. "Time is a-wasting, my friend."

Hel raised her hand. "What exactly do you intend to do?"

"As you know, this isn't my true form," Jules gestured to herself. She snapped her fingers and vanished in a golden shimmer. In her place stood a creature barely ten inches tall. It was still Jules in her varying shades of earthen brown, from her disarray of muddy curls to skin the rich dark hue of freshly turned soil. She gave a twirl for the goddess and Valkyrie. At the end of the whirl, she shot up to her alternate height. Hel frowned and poked Jules in the arm with her bony index finger. Jules shivered at the contact but said nothing. If Ives accepted the goddess's unusual appearance, it was good enough for Jules.

"If this was a normal glamour, it would be impossible to physically interact like this without giving away your natural appearance. How are you doing this?"

"The fae have their secrets, just like the gods." Jules winked at her. "Would you like me to try?"

Hel didn't answer immediately as she cupped the skeletal half of her face. "Could you... Could you really make this go away?"

Jules worried her bottom lip. "Well, I've never glamoured a godling before."

Ives took up the mantel for her. "I'm not one-hundred-percent sure it will work, but she will do the best she can. It might not look... completely normal, but it will help you blend."

"Will it feel like solid flesh?" Hel whispered.

"Yes," said Jules.

"Then I don't care if I look like Sloth from the Goonies. Go for it."

Jules nodded. She crouched in front of the seated goddess. She placed her small hands over Hel's face. Jules drew a deep breath and slowly exhaled. She smoothed her hands up and over Hel's face. Knowing how Jules operated, Ives watched for Hildr's reaction. She knew her friend was successful when the Valkyrie's expression opened with awe.

Ives looked back to give Hel a once-over. "Wow," she said.

The perfect features of Hel's face were now complete, symmetrically perfect, inhumanly beautiful. Overlaid on one half of her face were the tattooed contours and shadows of the human skull. The tattoos continued downward, covering half her body in delicately sketched anatomical detail. The effect was lovely and haunting. On Hel, the tattoos made her striking rather than marred her divinely crafted face.

Hel's hand trembled as she reached up. When she felt the tattooed flesh, she caught her breath and brushed her fingers along her filled-in cheek. A tear fell from both green eyes. Hel rose to her feet and darted down the hall to the bathroom. She didn't emerge for several minutes.

When she finally rejoined them, she wiped at her tears, a heartbreaking smile lit her face. "Thank you, Jules."

Jules blushed to the tips of her ears. "It's nothing. The real challenge is going to be your brother. Not only is he another godling, but I haven't done animal-to-human glamours before. This could be tricky."

Hel looked thoughtful and absently ran her thumb along the side of her face. "Maybe, maybe not."

Ives raised a brow. "What are you thinking?"

"I told you we weren't always monsters." Hel's stunning green eyes shone like buds in spring. "My brothers weren't always animals."

"You remembered?"

The Valkyrie gaped. "What's this?"

Hel nodded hesitantly. "It feels like a dream, but it's there."

Jules clucked her tongue. "Like a human form that's been locked away?"

"That might be it exactly," said Ives. She remembered it now, hidden in the tangled weave of Ragnarök. There was something else at work within the prophecy, something dark and poisonous connected to the trickster god and his family. She wondered what it meant and what she would encounter when they, at last, caught up to Loki himself. Ives wished she could voice her thoughts to the group, but something held her back. It frustrated her to no end, but she didn't know how to describe what she saw to them. It was something only she could see, and anyone she could discuss it with was out of her reach.

Ives sighed. "You are going to have to dig deep to find it, but I believe Hel."

Jules nodded to her and led Hel out to the main room where Fenrir slept in the hole he'd left in the wall. Ives turned to find the Valkyrie eyeing her, a frown on her face. She appeared deeply troubled.

"Out with it," said Ives.

"The children of Loki have two forms? If this reveals itself to be true, that provokes some unsettling questions."

Ives snorted. Didn't she know it? If they had two forms all along, then the children of Loki were locked in monstrous bodies against their will. It was bad enough they were already hooked into the terrible prophecy of Ragnarök, but the thought of being locked to a half-rotted body or a wolf's form sat ill with Ives. Did the other gods, the supposed good guys, sanction this as some sort of divine punishment? The methods they used to imprison Loki made her wonder. The question was why? Maybe the mystery was tied to the previous generation of Valkyrie, the one Hildr admitted someone had silenced for unknown reasons. The more Ives considered the whole suck sandwich, the uneasier she felt.

Hel skidded into the room and slid to a stop in front of Ives with a squeal of glee. "Oh, my gods! Oh, my gods! You need to see this!"

She grabbed Ives's elbow and tugged her along into the now-drafty front room.

Jules stood near the door, her eyebrows high on her face as she stared at the unconscious figure on the floor. She met Ives's questioning gaze and shrugged her shoulders. "I didn't expect it to be that easy, but it was there, hidden right under the fur."

Ives looked down at the figure. "Oh... my."

She wasn't sure they should take the great wolf out in public after all, though for very different reasons.

FOURTEEN

THAT WOLF IS SMOKIN'

THE BLACKJACK TABLE SAT EMPTY. His game, like so many others, lay abandoned.

Loki, the great Trickster, Father of Lies, and god of fire, sat on the plush carpeting of the casino floor. He leaned back against the cool faux marble of the wall as he tried to ease the fever in his blood, rolling the glass of lukewarm scotch across his forehead. From the outside, one couldn't tell, but it took every ounce of concentration to stay right where he was. What must he look like to the passing humans? Little better than a strung-out junkie, shaking for a fix, scarred and broken, yet the female eye was irrevocably drawn to him.

The strings of his fate tugged him incessantly, their hooks driven deep. Their pull was a strange pain, though not quite as fearsome as the serpent's venom, and so he continued to resist the song of destruction. He could sense the Jotunn roaming the earth, as they sought him. Every god and goddess knew those clumsy brutes were about since they crossed territory lines with careless abandon. The Trickster was smart. He'd found the hottest place he could stand to evade them. But hundreds of miles was still not far enough away. His presence would draw them here eventually. For now, they wandered to the south, somewhere in the Pacific. The rousting of the allies had begun. No doubt Surt himself had crawled out from his hole to lead the charge.

All Loki had to do was give in. He could join them within a day and sway every divine being born of fire and chaos to his call. *Then he could tear down the gods, destroy the false one he once called a brother who'd left him to rot in the dark.*

The glass cracked in Loki's grip. Dripping liquid hissed against his burning skin. He dug his heels into the carpet, and the muscles of his neck and back strained as he fought the pull. It was only a matter of time now before he couldn't fight anymore.

🂡🂡🂡

Deeper in the casino's shadowed recesses, veiled by cigarette smoke, the hooded figure watched the god's struggle. He'd whispered the lullaby of Ragnarök in the god's ear, eaten away at his defenses as it wound coils around him, but the Trickster continued his stubborn resistance. Not long now. Then the Father of Lies would be nothing more than a puppet, a means to an end, and the grand architecture of Ragnarök would be complete.

The man beneath the hood smiled, a wink of gold in the dark.

🂡🂡🂡

Ives tapped her fingers against her cheek as she considered the formally monstrous wolf. After a solid minute of pondering his appearance, she rounded on Jules and pointed an accusing finger.

"Couldn't you give him a hook nose or something? A lazy eye?"

"That's not how this works, and you know it. I drew on what was already there." Jules fisted her hands on her hips, her gaze sliding back to her 'work.'

Hel crouched beside her brother and rubbed a lock of his hair through her fingers. "He looks so much like our mother," she said, her voice full of wonder.

Ives considered the siblings. She racked her brains for who the heck their mother was. "Cinder something or other?"

Hel's mouth puckered. "That she-bitch Sigyn? So *not* our mum."

"Then who?" Ives murmured. The comment earned her a jab in the ribs from Jules.

Jules shook her head.

"Giantess," Hildr whispered in her ear from the other side. "Bit of a sore subject."

"I can hear you," said Hel in a singsong voice. She looked up at Ives with a bittersweet expression on her face. "She got a bad rap, but she loved us."

Ives could understand that. Her own mother's reputation was a bit iffy these days.

Fenrir groaned and shifted his bulk. The light fell on his perfectly sculpted torso, dusted with dark hair, and a scattering of scars that just added to the whole rugged package. Ives fidgeted. Finally, he was waking up, and they could cover that massive slab of distraction. His eyes fluttered open, the same shocking shade of green as his sister's. The non-related females in the room sucked in a collective breath, minus one immune Hildr. Ives thought animal magnetism was a myth until this very moment. She bit down on a giggle. Jules was not so subtle. She covered her mouth with both hands as the Valkyrie rolled her eyes, exasperated with the two of them.

As a human, Fenrir would fit right in with the Hollywood set, like he dropped in from some historical epic action piece for the day. From his finely angled jaw, with the perfect amount of scruff, to his long patrician's nose and sensually formed lips, he was the definition of 'hunk.' His curling black hair had streaks of gray, a carried-over attribute from his wolf form. Add in the dazzling green eyes framed by long lashes, and he was almost too pretty to be real if not for the scars. One ran from the corner of his mouth to his chin. It gave him a roguish appeal. The fact that he wore nothing but a carefully placed towel didn't hurt, either.

Those green eyes studied the gathered group of women, full of mild confusion. His pupils dilated. He blurred to his feet, shifting to a fighter's crouch, a growl rumbling through his perfect chest. The towel fluttered to the floor. Jules squeaked.

"Don't look now. He's armed and dangerous." Ives snickered and slapped a hand over Jules's innocent eyes as the Valkyrie drew her sword, ready for battle.

"For the love of the gods, please find him some damn pants," Hildr snapped.

Ives politely averted her gaze ceilingward after she'd gotten an eyeful.

The growl tapered off in a burble of puzzlement. "Sister?" His voice was hoarse from long disuse but what a voice!

Ives shivered. Now there was a voice capable of talking a lady out of her clothes. She was *so* not taking him anywhere.

"Least he speaks normally now," said Jules as she casually attempted to pry Ives's fingers from her face.

"Yeah, Fen, mind covering up the goods there, bro?" Hel choked through barely restrained laughter.

"What?" Fenrir looked down at himself and went pale. He scrambled for the towel and cleared his throat as he held it over his genitals with both hands. "Um, I seem to be suddenly human?"

Jules waved, her eyes still firmly covered. "You're welcome."

�☠☠

Pele frowned down at the smoking remains of an unfortunate Jotunn. The perished frost giant wasn't as swift as the rest of his brethren beating a retreat to the safety of the surf. She prodded the giant's scorched leg with her toe, getting a dose of the most ungodly stink. The Jotunn reeked of burning fur, rubber, and plastic, such a gag-worthy combination due to the bits of modern debris braided into the giant's scraggly hair. There were hubcaps, tires, and what might have been a porta-potty seat melting into the river of lava now coursing over the ground.

The Hound whined from his station next to Lavi and danced away from the fiery liquid bubbling along the ground to keep from burning his paws. Lavi wasn't affected by it, though the soles of his boots were melting off. He stepped away, placing a hand on the Hound's ruff to quiet him as he solemnly studied the ruined landscape. His eyebrows rose with unspoken chastisement.

"If you weren't a whelp of my bloodline, I'd slap you," Pele muttered. Her temper once again got the better of her and literally erupted over the land, soaked it in molten rock as she drove Surt and the Jotunn back to the sea. The fire giant retreated with a plume of steam, up to his knees in seawater rather than tangle with the irate goddess.

Pele stormed through the smoldering trees. She flicked a few glowing coals from her dress as she scowled at the fresh spill of lava. She hadn't meant to take it so far, but Surt got on her last divine nerve.

"That primeval upstart thinks I'll just bow to his whim? That I want the world to be nothing but a barren wasteland? Fool." She snarled over her shoulder. "Not all beings of fire are alike, dolt." She glanced back to Lavi and the Hound, marooned on an island of untouched earth. She snorted and stomped the lava down until it was cooled black rock. Flowers petulantly burst through the nutrient-rich ash as soon as she lifted her foot.

"I know, sister. I know," she yelled at the new growth. The plants didn't seem to be listening, they burst upward at an extraordinary pace. A vine rose above the rest. It grew fat and thick as it coiled in on itself until it looked like a snake. A tremor of shock passed over Pele's face. It echoed through the ground under her feet. "Fair warned, Haumea."

Lavi's head snapped up. "I know that look. That look means nothing good. What is it?"

"One of your other aunties gave us a heads-up," said Pele, her tone brisk and authoritative. "We need to get to higher ground, my boy, and—"

The goddess stilled. Through her the connection of their blood, she felt Ives burning alive as she rode a storm of divine energy that ate up her mortal body from the inside. That foolish chit! A continent away, Pele's reach was severely hindered. If not for their familial connection, there would be nothing she could do, but blood trumped distance. Pele's present physical form vibrated, slightly out of focus. She sighed as she held out her hands to the empty air, her inner focus thousands of miles away. By some work of divine luck, she managed to pull the girl back before her body disintegrated.

"That child needs to learn control," said Pele. She turned to Lavi with narrowed eyes. "Move it, boy, before we are caught out in the open."

Lavi looked near to bursting with questions. "Child? What child? My Ike? What's happened? What's coming?"

Pele squeezed his shoulder. "Your daughter is fine. Though I do hope that odious trio of females are watching so they can see the folly of their punishment." They had to be watching. If Pele didn't know better, she could almost feel their touch on Ives's essence, even now…

Lavi's jaw clenched at the reminder of the worst day of his life. "Likely not in my lifetime."

The goddess didn't answer at first as she glanced out at the boiling sea. Surt and his forces were regrouping. If Pele would not join them, they'd make sure she couldn't aid the other side. Soon they would have an ally Pele couldn't beat. Godling or not, few could stand against *that one*. The wheels of the Norse doomsday were spinning faster. Pele didn't look at her mortal nephew. She thought of that woven prison. Gods rarely admitted mistakes, and the Fates were the worst for it, but they royally screwed up. So had Pele, for allowing them to dictate the situation. It sat all the more ill with the goddess because, by mating to her nephew, the insufferable woman was family, and Pele protected her family above all else.

"They may not see their folly in anyone's lifetime."

FIFTEEN

DEATH RIDES A TRIPOD HORSE

IVES WASN'T QUITE sure how they rolled in Valhalla, but she doubted a war council consisted of a group of women, and one former wolf, huddled around a plate of freshly baked cookies courtesy of one anxious fae with domestic tendencies.

Fenrir sat next to Hel, double-fisting cookies and leaving tantalizing smears of chocolate at the corners of his mouth. "These are the best things I've ever tasted," he said in a disgustingly attractive spray of crumbs.

Jules fanned herself.

"Yes, she is fantastic," Ives sniped, feeling a bit put-off. She'd forgotten how the perfection of immortals could make even the most confident person feel after prolonged exposure. If she was honest with herself, it was one of the many reasons she and her ex would have never worked out, though her heart liked to lie. "Can we please get back to the problem at hand? We need to find Loki, like, yesterday. Do either of you have any idea where your father might be holed up?"

"Depends on what state of mind he's in," said Hel. She pulled at the ends of her hair. "This is a damn good cookie."

Ives took a breath for patience. "What do you mean by state of mind?"

Hel swallowed and glanced at her oblivious brother for support. She rolled her eyes as he continued to stuff his face. "Well, you saw how my brother fared under the reins of Ragnarök."

The word made Fenrir crush the food he held and growl down at the table. Ives raised an eyebrow at his teeth, far too wolfy to pass for human. He stilled at his sister's touch on his arm.

"My brother's role was larger and more demanding than mine. I could have resisted its call until the very end, but Fenny was far more tangled up in it. It would have forced him to massacre all who stood in his way until he devoured the All-Father himself." Hel leaned over and rested her head against his shoulder. Her eyes teared up. "The grip it has on our father is ten-fold worse."

Ives stared down at her hands. She suddenly felt very small. She refused to worry the others and allowed herself to scream herself silly in the confines of her head. Breaking Fenrir's bonds took the added power of a goddess, power Ives woefully did not have. The effort had almost killed her twice, and she wasn't quite sure what saved her the second time. She doubted she'd have that kind of luck a third time. It struck her as fair strange she *was* this lucky. Was there another unseen influence at play, like the black threads she couldn't be certain she saw or imagined? Or was the universe laughing as it strung her along for a glorious blowout? With all the gods and immortals in play, it was hard to keep track of who and what could be manipulating *her* strings. She had suspicions though no solid theory to back it up. Still, divine influence aside, her likelihood of surviving Ragnarök was rather dim.

"If he's resisting it, where would he go?"

Hel's fingers rapped the tabletop. "Somewhere hot and dry. It wouldn't stop the fire giants from seeking him out, but it would keep most of the Jotunn at bay for a while. He'd probably want somewhere densely populated, somewhere he can hide among humans."

"Well, that narrows it down to half the world," grumbled Hildr.

Ives spared the Valkyrie a glare and turned her attention back to the siblings. "What would he do to hide? If he's anything like your brother over there, he is probably a bit of a standout."

"He likes games, revelry, places where people are desperate and willing to make deals."

"The more desperate, the better," said Fenrir. He stared mournfully at his crumbled cookies. He shoved his palm against his face to lap up the crumbs.

"Isn't chocolate bad for dogs?"

The others all turned to look at Hildr, who didn't even have the grace to look embarrassed.

Fenrir licked a bit of chocolate from the corner of his mouth. "Do you have something sweeter for me, Valkyrie?"

Hildr sneered and stormed from the room.

Hel punched her brother's arm. "Stop flirting with the Valkyrie."

He gave her a 'what gives' expression. "Want me to go apologize?"

"If you value your new manly bits, you will not leave this room," said Hel. She wagged a finger in his face.

Jules giggled. "Aw, come on. The man's been a wolf for hundreds of years." Ives bit back her retort, certain Jules wanted to see the Valkyrie mete out some punishment to an idiot male.

"See, the tiny fae girl gets it. Who knows? She might be

receptive. What happens in the lodge stays in the lodge," said Fenrir, absolutely oblivious.

His words made the hair on Ives's arms stand on end. It was so similar to another well-used turn of phrase, one she had used repeatedly after her somewhat recent catastrophe there.

Hel made a face. "Maybe you've been a wolf too long. That Valkyrie is more likely to wear your guts as a garter—"

Ives slammed her hands on the table. "Son of a bitch!"

"Hey!" said Fenrir.

"Jules, remember my birthday last year?"

"When you maxed out your credit cards and lost your MINI Coop at poker?"

Ives gave Jules's hair a yank. "Yes, Miss Blabbermouth, where did we go?"

A light of understanding winked in Jules's gaze. "Vegas."

"And where is Vegas?"

"In the middle of the desert," Jules grinned. "Your dad never stopped wondering what happened to that car."

"What happens in Vegas stays in Vegas," said Ives.

"I don't understand, is Vegas some sort of resort?" Hildr inquired from the door, drawn back to the conversation.

"Better," said Hel as she caught on. "It's a casino."

"A regular den of iniquity," said Ives.

"Oh, good, we should go there then," said Fenrir. He stood to stretch in Hildr's too-small sweatpants. They rode high up on his calves. "Especially before our brother makes landfall."

The table fell silent.

"Jormungand?" Hildr's voice was a hoarse whisper.

Hel shot a worried look at Ives.

"Our brother should still be slumbering, Fen. His role has not yet come due," Hel said.

Fenrir cocked his head to the side. His expression turned distant as he listened to something only he could hear. "No, our brother is most definitely on the move, though his path is a strange one. He should've made landfall by now, but he's circled back. He's headed for a grouping of islands off the North American continent."

Ives fell off her chair.

"What?!" Jules yelped and jumped onto the table.

Hel looked mystified. "Why is that important?"

A crow landed on the table.

The siblings scrambled away from the bird until they hit the wall.

Hildr detached from the doorway, her face growing pale and pinched as the crow cawed at her. "It is where the fire giant Surt and his army have made landfall. They are attempting to roust the local deities."

The crow gave Hel and Fenrir a meaningful look before launching off the table to exit through the broken front wall. Once the bird was out of sight, the two visibly relaxed into mutual puzzlement.

"Okay, Surt consigning more gods is not good, but if Father isn't there, then we might make it to him first," said Hel. "If we're lucky, those local deities will stall Surt and crew long enough to find—"

"We're going," said Ives. She headed for the front door. "Hildr, summon your magical sled or whatever it is."

Hildr cringed. "Ives, you know our priorities."

"Screw your priorities!" Ives stopped. Her hands curled into fists. "My father is there," she whispered.

Hel went wide-eyed, shoving her brother to the side as she half-tackled the Fate Cipher. "Your father lives on these islands?" She shared a worried look with her sibling over the mortal's head.

"If our brother joins the fray, they'll be slaughtered," said Fenrir.

Ives sniffed. "Then we stop him from doing so. If all three of you are untethered from Ragnarök, it might give me a better chance of helping *your* father."

"Uh, Ives, I'm not sure that is such a good plan," said Hel.

"I feel fine, completely energized," insisted Ives. She lied through her teeth. On the surface, her energy appeared stable, thanks to her divine top-off: Goddess of Death energy fuel, the gift that kept on giving. The high buzz almost let her ignore the bone-deep ache that sapped at her limps every time she moved or the alarming brown spots that continued to dot her vision. But her dad was all she had, and the only defense he had was some random Hound and an accurate throwing arm.

Hildr made a defeated sound. "I might agree with your reasoning, Fate Cipher. Jormungand's fate is a grim one. He will be as difficult to unbind as his brother."

Hel shrugged. "No biggie. She can use me for some godly intervention if need be."

Ives couldn't quite hide her flinch. "Yeah, I'm sure it will be fine."

Hel narrowed her eyes. "Something you aren't telling me, woman?"

"Ladies, if we are going to do something about Jormungand, I suggest we do so soon. He's about to make landfall," said Fenrir. He scratched at his ear.

Ives turned to Jules and clasped her hands. "Please," she said.

"You know I can't refuse you unless it endangers your life," said Jules, her tone careful.

"If one of you doesn't take me right this second," Ives said, "I swear—"

"I got this," said Hel. She lifted her fingers to her lips for an ear-splitting whistle.

Hildr pointed at her. "You didn't," she hissed.

Hel snorted. "Don't get your thong in a twist, Battle Barbie. He is completely neutered since the days of yore."

The back wall exploded inward in a shower of splinters. A sad-looking excuse for a horse plodded into the room, somehow maintaining its balance despite the use of only three legs.

"All right, I admit he's still incredibly stupid," said Hel.

Ives blinked, unsure how to proceed.

"What the heck is that?" said Jules.

"Our ride. Trust me. He's completely safe and family-friendly," said Hel. She swung up into a moldy looking saddle. She tapped it twice, which caused the saddle and the horse to casually lengthen to accommodate more passengers. The sight was beyond unnerving, complete by the chewing motion of the horse's jaw. What it was chewing on was a mystery that none of the present company wanted to solve.

Despite her misgivings, Ives was desperate enough to let Hel heave her up into the saddle behind her. Jules immediately followed and kept a firm on Ives's waist.

Fenrir eyed the beast dubiously. "I'm not getting on that plagued horse," he said.

"Helhest has had his shots. Quit whining," Hel said.

Fenrir took a step forward. The horse's flea-bitten ears flattened against its skull. He sighed. "Right."

"Ride with me, idiot," said Hildr. A flash of distaste creased her brow. She hooked her arm around his neck, none too gently, and dragged him away.

Fenrir flashed them a stupid grin.

Hel shook her head. "Poor lad. She'll murder him. All right, ladies, hang tight."

Helhest lurched forward. The world blurred and left their stomachs behind. Ives would have thrown up if it weren't for the fact she was ninety-percent sure it would fly back in her face. She dug her knees into the horse's bony sides and prayed for the ride to end. Her wish came true with an abrupt jolt. They hovered high over the water. Ives caught the brief sight of the churning ocean far below, the coastline of her home still miles off. Smoke choked the air in great plumes. Heat lightning crackled in the black clouds, the warm air threatened a storm. The height proved to be too much as Ives tipped sideways and promptly tossed her cookies. Even though Jules baked them all the time, it still felt like a waste. Jules slid forward and held Ives's hair away from her face as Hel kept them in the saddle.

"Sorry about the rough ride," said Hel with a sheepish grin and gave her ragged horse an affectionate pat along his neck. Ives was about to respond with a few chosen expletives, but the ocean heaved below them, a sinuous form beneath its surface.

Her eyes widened.

It was massive, so large her mind couldn't comprehend what she was seeing. Its body had to be wider than the length of a great white shark, maybe two of them nose-to-fin.

"Oh, dear, we have less time than I thought," said Hel, strain evident in her voice.

"That's your brother?" Ives felt her stomach roll as the shape continued to scroll along, longer and longer beneath them.

"They call him the World Snake for a reason, Ives," Hel said.

The air twisted beside them as Hildr and Fenrir joined

them in the sled. He had his arm around her waist, which she casually removed with an audible crack, murder in her eyes.

Her icy expression shifted as she looked at the sea below them. "What course of action do you propose, Fate Cipher?"

"How am I supposed to unbind that thing?!" Ives screamed. "That's not a snake. It's a damn sea monster."

Hel released her and turned in the saddle to gesture to the creature in the water. "Come on, Ives. We didn't look much better," she pleaded. "I'll be with you every step of the way."

"Tail!" Jules clamped her arms around Ives's waist.

Hel cursed. She heaved on the horse's mane to jerk them to the side as a tail the size of a redwood whiffed through the air where they'd just been. Hildr wasn't so lucky. The tail caught the back end of her sled and sent it careening toward the far shore. She would've been thrown free if not for Fenrir's hold. Not that the Valkyrie would be happy with him when they landed.

"Aim for land," Hel shouted after them and turned to the others.

But she was alone in the saddle.

Sixteen

FINISH HIM

FALLING to her death was becoming a hobby.

Jules was doing her best to slow their descent under their combined weight, but physical strength was not among her many fine attributes. They were falling too fast for Jules to displace them. Ives could feel the strain and drag as Jules fought to slow their plummet to a survivable pace—with little luck.

"Let go," she said, her eyes tearing up from the wind. In a few seconds, they would crash into the water.

"No," Jules screamed.

Ives thought about pushing Jules off her to save both of them from going *splat* against the ocean's surface when the leviathan broke the water's surface. Both she and Jules screamed as the tail reappeared to snap them up in mid-air. Their fall came to an end with an abrupt jolt against a wet expanse of sleek, scaled flesh, speckled white like dirty snow. Ives struggled to suck in a breath, the air pushed from her lungs. All Ives could see and feel all around her was the constricting wall of reptilian skin, squeezing them together as they shot higher and higher, so fast her stomach gave another mutinous roll. If she hadn't already emptied it, Jormungand would be wearing those cookies.

The wall of flesh squeezed them upward until Ives and Jules were crushed up to their waists. They stared into the face of the World Snake.

"I think I'm gonna pee," Jules whimpered.

"Try to hold it in, dear," Ives wheezed, though she was also tempted to void her bladder as those slit pupils focused on her.

The snake's eyes were the same shade of green as his siblings and would've been almost lovely if they hadn't been full of madness and violence. Jormungand held them at eye level, far too high off the ground and far too near to his gigantic mouth for comfort.

"What now?" Jules shivered against her.

Ives would have grabbed her hand if she could reach it. "We stall?" She glanced around for Hel, but the sky seemed empty. To her shock, they were nearly on the beach of Kauai, the great snake chilling in the shallows off the shore. Ives wracked her brains for something to say to a big monster snake. Her constricted airflow doubled the spots in her vision. She hoped the world snake shared the same urge to resist as his brother and sister did when a hissing voice filled her head and pushed out every other thought.

Kill... Kill the Fate Cipher.

"Jules! Time to act," said Ives. Panic flooded her veins as the snake squeezed them again.

"What do I do? What do I do?" Jules shrieked and thrashed against Ives's back.

"Can you glamour an unaware monster?" Ives's pushed the words out, gasping on air she didn't have.

"I've— It's never worked on anything so big before," said Jules. She sounded breathless.

Ives prayed Jules's delicate bones wouldn't crack under

the pressure. That worry was forgotten as the snake opened his mouth. Broken bones, eaten alive—neither was something she wanted to experience.

"Now, Jules! Try it right now!"

There was nothing left to lose. If her companion failed, the end wouldn't be pleasant either way. Jules's voice rang out in a chiming language Ives never heard her speak before. The air hummed and smelled of violets. The snake stopped moving. Ives swore she saw an expression of astonishment in that giant scaly visage before he disappeared completely. Ives and Jules hung in the air a moment before the inevitable pull of gravity caught up to them.

"Oh, bother," said Ives.

They plummeted to the surface below.

***

Hildr didn't know how she survived. One moment, she was barreling at an unstoppable pace toward the ground, prepared to meet her fellow battle maidens in the sweet embrace of the afterlife. The next, she was floating at a swift but much slower pace to the earth. She blinked in an attempt to get her bearings. The knock she took when Jormungand hit them had nearly sent her unconscious. Her head was still spinning. She glanced straight down to find a male backside clad in her far-too-small sweatpants. Oh, right, there was her former canine now sexually starved ingrate of a traveling companion.

Fenrir the man had her slung over one bare shoulder and controlled their descent to the ground by launching them from the sled. He held her firmly in place with one arm across the back of her thighs, his hand spanned over her right butt cheek. Hildr resisted the urge to stab him in the kidney, still too woozy to land properly on her own.

"Good sir, do remove your hand from my posterior before I remove it from your arm."

The god-son had the nerve to chuckle at her as he slid his hand down to a more appropriate position. "Can't blame a man for trying."

"Yes. Yes, I can," said Hildr.

The ground came up fast. Fenrir crouched into the fall and left a small crater with their impact. He did no more than grunt and set the Valkyrie on the ground with care. Hildr patted herself down, ensuring all her clothing was to rights. She turned to the wolf, punched him squarely across the jaw, and knocked him down to the dirt.

"Thank you," said Hildr.

He rubbed his chin with a happy sigh.

ᛏᛏᛏ

This was how Ives was going to bite it. Not going out in a blaze of glory as she wrestled the nasty piece of work that was Ragnarök. Not helping her ex, Mordred, with his now seemingly piddling problems. Not even a proper human death like a car accident or a heart attack. No, Ives was going to die by face-planting on shallow surf. It would be akin to hitting cement. The fall was just horribly long enough to realize this lovely little fact. She closed her eyes, unwilling to watch her death come up to meet her.

Ives plunged into seawater, a swell so high she ran out of momentum before she touched the sandy ocean bottom. *What the hell?* She kicked upward and gasped for breath as her head broke the surface. Jules was a few yards away from her, just as bewildered they'd survived a fall into the thigh-high water.

"Did you see the wave?" Jules pushed the hair out of

her eyes and spat seawater. The water nearly came up to her shoulders.

"No I— Look out!"

Ives's scream came a moment too late as a pair of arms shot out of the surf and seized Jules. The man tossed her like a rag doll onto the sand. Ives fought against the undertow and made for the beach, where a small giant crouched over a shrieking Jules.

He had her by the throat as he hissed at her. A pair of dripping fangs descended from his open mouth. He paused over her; the fangs receded. "A woman?" he croaked.

Ives burst from the water and tackled him with a guttural scream. They fell back into the surf, choking and coughing on seawater until he rolled her under him and slammed her against the wet sand. He easily pinned her wrists with one hand as he stared down at her without comprehension. Ives gaped up at him. She wouldn't have recognized him without the green eyes, the pupils contracted into slits. His features bore a striking resemblance to his brother's, though his human form was much larger and his coloring was different. He was also quite naked. Ives tried to use that to her advantage and kneed him between the legs. He sat on her and leaned in close to peer into her face. The surf dragged saltwater around her.

"Who are you, female?"

Ives froze, not certain how to answer. He wanted to kill her a moment ago. Did he not recognize her now? Had Jules's glamour disoriented him?

"Where is the other one?" Jormungand lifted his face, searching for the fae.

Jules landed on his back and wrapped her thighs up over his shoulders as she yanked his head back by his hair. She pressed her knife to his throat. Her fierce brown eyes blazed down at his bemused face.

"Let her up," Jules snapped.

Jormungand's tongue flicked out and tasted the air. "A fae? So far from home?"

"Let her go," Jules yelled in his face. She dug her tiny blade into his skin until a trickle of blood ran down his neck.

"Jules," said Ives. Jormungand tensed over her.

"I think not," he said. He only held Ives down with one hand; the other twisted around to grab at the girl on his back.

"Free hand, Jules. Free hand!" Ives yelped.

Jules barely jumped clear in time. She landed on the beach and spun in the sand with her knife up and ready.

"Such a fierce creature," Jormungand murmured. He stared down at Ives. His brow creased. "I know you... Something important..." His eyes went wide and blank. "*Kill the Fate Cipher.*" There was another voice threaded through Jormungand's, a voice of shadows and secrets.

A part of Ives recognized that voice, though she'd never heard it before. She shivered.

His other hand circled her neck. Ives renewed her struggles. Jules released another piercing shriek and charged. Hel got there first. She appeared at the corner of Ives's fraying vision and swung her clasped fists against her brother's temple. Jormungand went down and crashed beside Ives.

Hel stood there, chest heaving. She was soaking wet and covered in seaweed. "Holy shit, my finishing combo worked."

SEVENTEEN

THE THREADS BENEATH

HILDR KICKED the remains of her sled and swore under her breath. So far, she was doing a bang-up job on the All-Father's mission. Seek out the Fate Cipher, guide her through the unwinding of Ragnarök, stop the apocalypse. They were simple, noble tasks though she expected the Fate Cipher to be somewhat trained on how to use her abilities. Ives's delicate mortality was an unforeseen complication. Not to mention the strangely loyal fae in her company. The jury was out on whether Jules was a boon or a hindrance. She'd never seen a fae so attached to a human. The children of Loki were another blasted mess, a rather distracting one, as they also raised questions, questions that would rock the halls of Valhalla.

Fenrir hovered by her side, wearing the same smug grin that made her want to clock him one. She remembered Jules's face when she finished her glamour, how shocked she was by the man's appearance. What if she'd merely pulled the human beneath the wolf to the foreground? What if Loki's children were truly cursed to be monsters? Who would do such a horrid thing to a child?

Fenrir growled. Hildr frowned and turned to her

companion. If Fenrir still had fur, his hackles would be rising. She drew her sword, searching for the threat. She didn't see it coming until the shadow loomed over them. Fenrir rushed her. He moved so fast she couldn't track him until he scooped her up with one arm and jumped. He seemed rather fond of this gesture. A Jotunn crashed down in the space they'd been.

"Sweet Freya!" Hildr gasped.

The frost giant was on fire. The local deities must be putting up one hell of a fight. The giant groaned and thrashed. He knocked down a few trees as he attempted to right himself. A man burst out of the woods with a mighty bellow as he brought a sledgehammer down between the giant's eyes. The Jotunn stilled, down for good. Hildr gaped at the newcomer and nearly dropped her sword.

"He smells familiar," said Fenrir.

Lavi Ives stood, brushing a few stray cinders off his charred jeans. He raised a brow at Hildr and her half-naked companion in too-small pants. Chester the Hound trotted into the clearing, wagged his tail at Hildr, and sat on Lavi's feet. The man casually scratched his ears, his large sledge-hammer in one hand.

"Where is my daughter, Valkyrie?"

☗ ☗ ☗

Ives watched as Hel stripped off her hoodie and draped it over Jormungand's manly bits while Jules checked Ives's neck.

"Your psycho brother could have killed her," Jules snarled, clearly shaken. The fae appeared mindless to her own bruises on her upper arms and shoulders.

"Sorry. I would have stopped him sooner had my damn

horse not bucked me into the ocean," said Hel, who looked equally peeved and apologetic.

Ives sighed and winced at the pain in her ribs. She didn't want to think what her body looked like after nearly being crushed to death by a giant snake. She peered at the snake—the man—in question. Part of her wanted to hate and fear him for what he'd done, except that blank look on his face gave her pause. And there was that echo of another voice riding within his own. Someone was after her, who wanted to stop her from unraveling Ragnarök, and they sent Jormungand to do their dirty work. His large body shuddered and twitched.

Ives took a breath and called on her abilities. The effort was like flipping a switch, to her great relief. The power came to her instantly; her mother would be proud of her. She looked at the World Snake.

"It wasn't his fault," she said. Jormungand was trapped in a similar web to his brother, the hooks of Ragnarök buried deep. She could see the other thread now, black shot through with gold, that dangled from his closed mouth. She had to free him of that compulsion first, or he would keep trying to kill her. Ives reached for it, tugged it.

Jormungand convulsed. Hel tried to hold him down until his fist slammed into her chest. Hel went flying and tumbled end-over-end across the beach. Jormungand grabbed Ives by the shoulders. He gagged. His fingers dug into her skin. She grunted, gritted her teeth, and kept pulling. Jules yanked at his hands, trying to dislodge his hold.

"Jules, get ready to catch him," Ives said and pulled with everything she had.

Jormungand coughed violently, as a withered knot of black thread emerged from his throat. He collapsed into

Jules's arms. She staggered under his weight and landed in a heap beneath him.

Hel crawled over. She gaped at the dissolving mass of thread in Ives's hands. "What is that?"

"You can see it?" Disgusted, Ives wanted to fling the slimy mass of thread away from her, but Hel could see it. That was a new development. Had her mother mentioned other beings seeing the threads? "It's the compulsion someone placed on your brother to make him kill me. What does it look like to you?"

"Gross," said Hel.

The thread dribbled away into nothing and left an oily film on Ives's hands. She scrubbed them clean in the sand. Her knees wobbled, exhaustion tolling through her veins as if that small task sapped all the energy she'd borrowed from Hel. She shook her head and pushed the feeling down. She couldn't afford to be exhausted yet. "Could you see the bindings of Ragnarök when I freed Fenrir?"

Hel looked thoughtful. "No, though I did see you light up like the frickin' sun when you started channeling me."

Ives walked on her knees over to Jormungand, his head in Jules's lap. Jules absently ran her fingers through the man's black-flecked white hair. It was the exact opposite of his brother's and looked finer than silk.

Jules's expression flickered with anger and pity. "Someone put that poison in him?"

Ives found Jules's reaction interesting. If Hel could see the compulsion, could she make them see the prophecy? It was a small experiment.

Ives placed her hand on Jormungand's bare chest. His skin was chill to the touch. Hel gasped and clapped a hand over her mouth. Jules's eyes widened. Oh, yeah, they could see it now.

"That's what Ragnarök looks like," said Ives. She

reached down, carefully parted the layers of barbed red lines until she found what she was looking for. She pinched the thread and separated it to examine it—black, sparked with gold. Immortal gold.

"But why can we see it now?" Hel knelt next to her and slipped her hand in her brother's.

"This is new," said Jules, "and kinda scary."

"I wish I knew," said Ives, her voice laced with frustration. Making the threads of fate visible wasn't the only difference. Ives could see *more* now. She could see the very fibers that bound fate together. She could read the words, feel the rhythm, and hear the cadence of the prophecy. "Who makes your prophecies, Hel?"

Hel raised a brow. "The Norns, three women, nasty lot. Got a constant stick up their collective arse."

"No men?"

Hel's brow rose higher. "No. Why? I mean, we already knew the Norns decreed Ragnarök centuries ago."

"I can hear it, the prophecy," said Ives. She listened hard to the faint song vibrating through her fingertips. "It's woven into the thread, and I swear there's a male voice mixed in."

Jules and Hel shared a look.

Hel gently poked her arm. "Ivy, dear, you're glowing again."

"Yes," said Ives. Jules said something, but her voice was far away, too far for Ives to hear. There was another voice, no *voices*, speaking to her now, whispering instruction. She canted her head, listening. They explained it perfectly. It was so simple now. She could see all weak points along the thread, the frayed spaces where it connected the siblings. She gripped a worn point, where Fenrir's and Hel's fates bled into Jormungand's and tore it free.

Hel shielded her eyes. "Holy—"

Jormungand gave a hoarse bellow and grabbed fistfuls of sand. His chest heaved. He opened his eyes. Slit pupils widened and contracted as he focused on them.

"Oh, good. It worked," said Ives. There was an internal sound of snapping thread, loud as a gunshot inside her head. Her eyes rolled up as she fell backward.

☗☗☗

Hel caught her. "She needs to stop doing that." She lowered the unconscious Fate Cipher to the sand. A worried frown creased her brow as a trickle of blood leaked from Ives's nose. "She's going to kill herself like this."

"Indeed she will," said a new voice, a woman's voice that resonated with a beautiful song of destruction.

Hel looked up at her approach. There was no question in her mind the woman was a goddess. She truly looked like one, whereas Hel looked like a tattooed skater punk. A wild collection of curls fell to the woman's waist, the tips lit like embers that gave off wisps of smoke. A gauzy dress the color of the setting sun licked the luscious curves of her bronzed skin like an affectionate flame. Hel could feel the heat coming off her as she left footprints of melted sand in her wake. The woman dropped to her knees beside them and brushed a stray strand of hair from Ives's face.

"Pele," said Jules, her voice full of awe and fear.

The goddess's gaze snapped up, her eyes burning coals in her face, as she gazed at all of them with a fierce expression that made even Hel, a child of Loki, shrink in her skin. "Ikepela cannot free your father. It will kill her."

"You don't know that," sputtered Hel. She cowed under the chaotic power of Pele's gaze.

"But I do," Pele said. "Had she not been on home soil, bolstered by the bloodline of her ancestors, she would have

122

perished just now freeing the Great Snake. Even then, it's a marvel she survived."

Jormungand's eyes widened with awareness as he sat up. He moved an arm to shield Jules behind him.

"Peace, child of the fire god, you are no longer a threat to us," said Pele.

"What ancestors?" said Hel. "And *why* is she mortal? I thought her mother was an immortal fate cipher."

"But her father is a child of my mortal sister's bloodline," said Pele.

"That explains so much," muttered Jules. She poked her head out from behind Jormungand's back. "Lavi isn't just some random human her ma fell in love with. He's practically a demi-god. Why would they punish her mother for that?"

"Okay, they lost me," said Hel. She looked at her brother, who shrugged.

A bitter smile played on Pele's lips. "That decision was out of my hands. This one, however, isn't. Ives cannot undo the bindings on Loki. This is too much for her. But in freeing his children, she has given you a fighting chance to stop this prophecy."

"What... What are you saying?" Hel felt sick, certain she knew what Pele implied, but unwilling to put it into words.

"You three are capable of stopping him."

Jules darted out from behind Jormungand and put herself right up in Pele's face. "You can't ask them to kill their father," she snarled.

Jormungand plucked Jules off the ground and calmly placed her behind him. "I don't think you realize how powerful our father is," he said. "The only reason the world isn't aflame at this very moment is his continued resistance to Ragnarök's pull."

"The world will still burn. Stopping him might cost you

your lives, but you might survive. Ikepela will not." Pele looked away. "Not as she is now."

"I think you underestimate her," said Hel. "I think she has abilities you aren't aware of."

"Like the power to channel a goddess?" Pele glared at Hel. "If I had not broken your bond, she would have burned up from your power. She has no control."

Jules popped up over Jormungand's shoulder. "And whose fault is that?"

"It is not a matter of fault, fae. I want Ikepela to survive long enough for the Fates to learn from their mistakes," said Pele. "If she continues this way, she will not last the week."

"I think she might surprise you." Ives sat up and wiped her nose. Her eyes were shards of flint as she met Pele's gaze. "This is my path, my choice, not yours, and certainly not *theirs*."

Pele's expression hardened, smooth, and dark as volcanic glass. "What would your father—"

Ives ground her fist into the sand. "You do not get to bring him into this. Not now, not ever."

"Bit late for that Ike."

Ives's father led an interesting party up the beach, complete with one Valkyrie, one Hound, and one son of Loki. He was streaked from head to toe with soot, holes were burned in his clothing, and a nasty cut marred the side of his face. A sledgehammer was lazily perched on his shoulder, the metal misshapen from striking surfaces it was never meant for.

Ives teared up at the sight of him. "Dad? What are you—"

"About that," he sighed, letting the sledgehammer slide to the sand. He leaned on it, weariness emanating from his frame. "We need to have a long-overdue talk."

EIGHTEEN

THE SHINING GOD

The hooded figure watched the gathered group of gods and mortals through the Veil, tucked safely In-Between, keeping well out of their sight and Sight as he studied the situation. Things were not going his way. The Fate Cipher was still alive despite numerous opportunities and brushes with death. Instead, she seemed to have *befriended* Death. He sneered at the tattooed Hel. He wished he could rip the glamour from her, show the monster she was to the world. What they all were—abominations, children of a wicked god, and nothing but the vile creatures they were cursed to be. They were *supposed to* set the grand plan in motion, to force the others to fall into their roles. Instead, they doted on that mortal bitch like she was their savior. It would not do, not at all. After centuries of waiting, after so many setbacks and risks, Ragnarök was finally set to come to fruition, and he refused to let a slip of a girl halt his plans.

He listened to the goddess of fire and chaos admonish the others for risking the Fate Cipher's life. Pathetic, the lot of them. It was a relief to his growing sense of incredulity when the mortal father appeared and led the group away.

The hooded figure sighed through his nose. He thought

he'd pulled the rug out from under the Fate Cipher years ago when he used an ill-gotten technicality to bring the wrath of the Fates down on that horrid woman. Her daughter was supposed to perish before Ragnarök was even a whisper, but Ikepela Ives proved surprisingly resilient. Or lucky. There was no such thing as simple luck in a world of divine powers. The girl had someone's attention. He could almost admire the minutiae of these power plays if not for the fact he needed her dead. He turned the fire goddess's words over and over, tasting them for good measure.

Attempting to free Loki would kill her. It was a risky maneuver bringing the two of them together, especially with his children now released from the bindings of prophecy, but if the hooded figure killed the Fate Cipher himself, the Fates would turn on him. There had to be a balance, even if it was an unfair one. The Fate Cipher was the counterbalance of the Fates, but if she perished in the line of duty, her mother would be released from her punishment to take her place—drained, bitter, and far too late to stop the progress of Ragnarök. For his plan to work, he needed it to look like a true sacrifice.

He needed her to *want* to save Loki. To die for him. It wouldn't take much of a push. The Fate Cipher already felt sympathy for the god's children. If she were to fall in her duty, not only would the gods and his children rally against Loki, but the Fate Cipher's divine brethren would add fuel to the fire. Such a glorious fire. He would show the Trickster what true wrath was, comeuppance for what was stripped of him by the so-called 'God of Fire.'

He waited until Ikepela Ives separated herself from the others to move the pieces into play.

☗ ☗ ☗

Ives needed air. There was too much damn drama in the house, and the revelation of her father's family filled her with quiet anger she couldn't give voice to. All these years he could have told her. All these years he could have warned her what to expect. Only for 'Auntie Pele' to force him into some deal that kept her in the dark about both sides of her family. Like hell was she calling that jerkoff of a goddess 'Auntie.'

She still couldn't believe it, though the strange occurrences made sense now. Was Pele responsible for the cracking earth beneath Fenrir? Her godly relatives the ones who coaxed the ocean wave that caught her and Jules as they fell? She guessed her Divine Island family lent her a hand where they could. Pele herself kept Ives from taking too much of Hel's power. It was a shame that they couldn't deign to tell her of their connection when they ripped her mother from her, that her father couldn't tell her how it was all connected. She wanted to scream into a pillow for about a year.

Ives made for the backyard. She wanted nothing more than to breathe in the warm, salted air and get her bearings. Truthfully, she wished to swim in the ocean as a good dip in the surf always cleared her head, but there were still too many giants roaming and the beach was on fire.

She needed to get away from the crowded house of immortals and gods and just be Ives, alone in her skin.

She tiptoed out through the workshop, the forge cold for the first time in her memory, and snuck out the back door. 'Yard' described the area loosely. Her family home sat at the edge of a lush tropical forest, a generous word for the small spate of growth that provided semi-isolation from the rest of the island. The air was always drenched by the sea breeze, perfumed by fragrant wildflowers, and filled with bird song. Tonight, it was eerily quiet, and a smoky haze hung in the sky. She sighed, hugging her elbows. The whole world would be silent and burning if she failed to stop Ragnarök.

What had Pele said to the others before she came to? Hel and her brothers were rather aloof during the evening conversation, huddled together around the kitchen table. Jules made them coffee, which they held without drinking until the liquid went cold. She meant to ask what was wrong before her father went and ambushed her with his godly origins.

A slight movement made her turn. She wasn't alone out here. Hel stood among the trees, her face lifted to the smoky sky. The island breeze teased her midnight hair so inky strands fluttered over her cheeks. The skeletal tattoos lent her a haunting beauty, otherworldly beneath the moonlight. She had her eyes closed, appearing to simply enjoy the feel of fresh air on her skin. A tear tracked down her cheek and slid off her chin.

Ives could feel her pain now. It buzzed against her senses. It didn't matter what Pele said to the siblings. It was enough to see she'd hurt them. Ives slipped beside the goddess and slid an arm around her shoulders. Hel stiffened for a moment before turning to Ives for a hug. She buried her face in the crook of Ives's neck.

Ives ran her fingers through Hel's hair, like cool silk, until her shoulders stopped shaking.

"You're the first person besides my father and brothers whose ever touched me," whispered Hel.

The confession hurt. She didn't want to let go of Hel.

"What did she say to you?" Ives pulled away to look at her, but Hel wouldn't meet her eyes.

"It doesn't matter, Ives. How did it go with your father?"

Ives snorted and gave Hel's nose a tweak. "Doesn't matter. There are other important issues to deal with."

Hel blew the hair out of her face. "We should probably head back inside and discuss what happens next."

"Go on ahead. I'll be there in a minute. Just need to clear my head."

Hel nodded and clapped a hand on Ives's shoulder as she passed. Ives copied the goddess's pose of reflection, lifting her face to the heavens. She wished she could read her friends' sorrows in them.

"The island goddess wishes for the children to slay their father rather than risk one of her own."

The voice slithered over her skin. The hair on her arms stood on end. Ives peered through the dark as a man emerged from the trees. She caught her breath. Not a man. This was another god, a beautiful one. The square angles of his face and a dusting of hair along his jaw kept his appearance masculine. He shone in hues of silvered gold beneath the moon—pale hair, pale eyes, and skin so white it glowed.

Her reaction to his appearance folded beneath the weight of his words. She dug her fingernails into her skin. "She did *what*?"

The god paused at her tone, bemusement in his eyes.

Ives checked herself, certain it would be a royally bad idea to piss off any other deities. "My apologies."

He nodded. "I merely wished to answer the question the stars cannot tell you."

Ives frowned at him. "How do you know what Pele said to them? You weren't on the beach." *How did he know what she asked the stars?* The idea of a mind-reading god made her uneasy at a fundamental level.

A small smile played on his lips. "Forgive me, Fate Cipher, for not introducing myself. I am Heimdallr, the Foreseer."

"The who and the what now?"

A flicker of annoyance passed over the god's face, though the smile didn't move. "Norse god, the Watcher, the Herald of Ragnarök?"

Ives quickly wiped the blank look from her face to avoid irritating him further and kept her lack of knowledge private. "Okay, back up. Pele asked them to kill their father? Screw that. There has to be another way."

Heimdallr gave her a pitying look. "She asked them to save your life. You have performed admirably Fate Cipher, and you have given us a chance to win against the Father of Lies. We will have the might of his children on our side when the time comes."

Ives's lips parted. Didn't the god see the horror of his statement? As angry as she was with her father, she could never imagine a situation where she could strike him down. Except the fate of the world didn't hinge on Lavi Ives. It rested on the actions of one individual, the 'evil' father of lies. If Loki was truly evil, perhaps he *should* be put down. The thought struck a chord of wrongness the moment she had it. After meeting his kids, Ives didn't believe the hype. Not when his children fought their fates so hard, not when the world itself was still turning. Loki was out there somewhere. He resisted the pull of Ragnarök instead of rushing to join team evil. Someone like that deserved to be free from their fate. They deserved a chance.

"I can't let this happen," said Ives. "I just can't. It's not right, even if I have to risk my life."

"The goddess of these lands is certain the effort will end you," said Heimdallr quietly.

She looked away, listening to the muffled crash of the surf as her thoughts churned in time with the ocean waves.

"It doesn't matter." Ives met his silvered gaze. Determination burned within her. "If there is even a fraction of a chance I can help unbind him from his fate, I can't sit here and do nothing."

"The others will never let you go," the god remarked.

Blast it, she knew he was right. For 'her own good,' even Jules would flat-out refuse to help her pursue this. Hel's refusal to inform Ives of what Pele asked of them made her certain his children would stubbornly attempt to keep her safe as well. This path she would have to forge alone.

"Heimdallr, could I ask a boon of you?"

He blinked at her. "What may I do for you Fate Cipher?"

She inhaled a deep breath for strength. "Can you take me somewhere?"

Jules would kill her when she found out. None of them would be happy with her for this, but the sight of Hel's tear-stained face committed her to her course of action. She *liked* the goddess of Death as a person, and in their short time together, she felt a connection to Hel, similar to what she shared with Jules. The two women were similar in many wonderful, endearing ways. She wanted to help Hel, protect her, as a friend.

Heimdallr smiled. His teeth were a startingly metallic gold, glinting in the filtered moonlight. "Of course." His smile faded. "Though the others will worry fiercely about your absence."

Ives nibbled her lip. She tried to think of something that would distract the lot of them from tracking down. "If you can port me there, at least I'll have a head start."

The god chuckled. "Perhaps I can suggest a course of action for them? Loki's wife has surfaced once again. Cracking her secrets could stall them for some time before they came after you."

Ives bowed her head to the errant god. "I would be indebted to you."

"Now," he said, "where shall I bring you, my good lady?"

"Vegas."

NINETEEN

SPLITSVILLE

HEL COULD FEEL the world twist in on itself. She stood up abruptly and ignored the calls and complaints of her brothers as she tried to pinpoint the source. Absently running her fingers along the walls as she wandered through the house, she felt the pulse of the land. There were many stories about Hel in the old world, cruel stories of the monstrous goddess, she who must be feared and respected in equal measure as the Lady of Death. The job title did have its perks, but it was also a misnomer. Death was not the only thing she could sense.

There was also life. The two walked hand-in-hand together, eternally entwined. Everything had a pulse, even so-called inanimate objects, many created from pieces of once-living creatures and plants that still echoed with the pulse of their life. Pulses were important. They could tell you numerous bits and pieces of information if you listened hard enough. Hel could hear the pulses of the island, of the wood in the walls beneath her fingertips, of the foundation rock, of the metal supports. The pulses beat with alarm. Her hackles rose.

Hel moved faster toward the workshop. "Ives, what have you done?"

She'd been out there far too long. Something was amiss. Lady Death emerged from the house just in time to catch a glimpse that filled her with dread. The shining god swept Ives up into his arms. One silvery eye winked at Hel before the pair of them vanished. She could feel reality settle in their wake. It prickled at her skin. He'd taken her through the between ways, instantaneous travel and nearly impossible to track.

Well, impossible to track by her brothers, who relied on their powerful physical senses. Not for her. She relied on other abilities. The between ways were known to her, likely more than to that tosser who'd abducted their fragile Fate Cipher. She paused to glance back at the house. Unfortunately, the trail would go cold if she spent too much time arguing and dilly-dallying with explanations. There was nothing for it.

"I'm going to strangle that girl," she grumbled and stomped her heel into the ground. A few precious moments passed before an elevator box rose from the ground. Hel entered, humming along to 'Rapper's Delight' as the box followed a trail as tangible as smoke and dust.

🎃🎃🎃

Ives moved through corporeal shadows in the marble embrace of a god. The shadows stroked her skin, cool and silky, full of regrets and promises, joys, and tears. Emerging from the strange passage was not a delicate experience, as Heimdallr dumped her onto the Vegas sidewalk like a sack of potatoes.

The shining god took a look at their surroundings, an unreadable gleam in his eye. Ives winced as she picked herself up off the sidewalk. She managed to skin both elbows and one thigh on her short tumble to the ground.

"Thanks," she muttered. She debated the wisdom of giving Heimdallr a piece of her mind when she noticed she was alone. Scraped up, in her shorts and t-shirt, still damp from her impromptu tussle in the sea, with no shoes. She'd conveniently left them on the welcome mat thousands of miles away. Unease slid down her spine in drops of sweat as the acrid desert heat pressed on her. Why would he vanish now? Hadn't the god offered to help her? Or was he the dine-and-dash type? Ives considered her bare feet. She did not relish the idea of maneuvering over the sticky sidewalk, still hot from the day and littered with patches of gum, cigarette butts, and who knew what else. She hoped her tetanus shot was up to date.

A caw made her jump.

Ives looked for the source. Finally, she craned her neck to stare at the power lines over her head. A large crow sat on the juncture of wires tethered to what appeared to be a gentlemen's club, where it pecked at the knotted laces on a pair of dangling sneakers. A few taps of its beak brought the shoes down, which landed with a *plop* at her feet. They were a bit ragged and weatherworn, but a cursory glance told her they would fit.

Beggars couldn't be choosers. She made a face of disgust as she slid them on, prayed they didn't give her athlete's foot and glanced back up at the crow. It had cocked its head to peer down at her with one bright black eye. It emitted another abrasive caw and took off, flapping its wings against the heated air. A single feather floated down. Ives caught it and put it in her pocket. She wasn't one-hundred-percent sure, but she suspected the bird was the same one who visited the Valkyrie before. Ives was open to any little favors, including token feathers, even if she didn't know what they were for. Yet.

The shoes squelched as she walked. She tried to ignore the unpleasant sound as she eyed the flashing casino signs. She was looking for one that screamed, 'Here Gambles the Father of Lies.' It would be awesome if a giant flashing arrow would just materialize over the right one. She sighed and ducked through the doors of Echelon Place. Maybe she'd get lucky.

Like her first time in Vegas.

👻👻👻

Jules froze when Jormungand sat up and peered toward the back of the house. His tongue darted out, a flash of pink so fast she would have missed it if she hadn't been looking. She turned away and continued to furiously scrub down the floorboards. Lavi's house miraculously survived the battle for the island despite his proximity to the action, but ash and soot were everywhere. It coated the walls, floor, even the ceiling. Jules occupied herself with tidying and tried to ignore the greatly oversized males keeping them company. The Valkyrie was no help, unfazed by either of them, and deflated by her failed efforts to stop Ragnarök through the Fate Cipher's intervention. Pele had declared Ives unfit to stop the apocalypse and had sunk back into the Earth, which left Jules to console her human.

If Jules was honest with herself, she was also disappointed. Not only because the siblings would now have to face down their father, but Ives had come so far with her abilities in the last couple of days. She suspected her friend was on the verge of finally mastering her powers, but her mortal limitations were too worrisome to ignore. No matter how much she pitied Hel and the others for the turn in their fortunes, she was secretly relieved Pele pulled Ives out of the game. The sight of Ives, her bludfend, unconscious and bleeding from her nose, had shaken her to her core. She couldn't lose her, not after everything they had done for each other.

"You've been scrubbing the same spot for several minutes, faeling," said a silky voice.

Jules squeaked and fell over.

Two large hands steadied her. They spanned the entirety of her waist.

"You're too quiet," she snapped. She peered over her shoulder at Jormungand.

He crouched beside her, studying her actions with intent curiosity.

"Shall I stomp up behind you next time?" Jormungand asked with a tilt of his head. His untidy hair fell in his eyes.

Jules bit down on the urge to straighten it, perhaps a quick trim. "Yes," she said, bristling.

He was too big, *too big*. The memory of their encounter on the beach was too fresh in her mind. The cut on his throat had already healed, but her bruises were a sickly yellowish-green, fading, and still painful to touch. He was staring at them now, his expression blank. His fingers flexed.

A tremor rocked the ground. Jormungand snatched her up before she could react. He tucked her between him and the wall as he searched for the threat. Jules couldn't process why she was pressed up against the scantily clad giant of a man, so she focused on sounds and finally relaxed when she heard the squeal of the Jeep's brakes.

"Chill," she said. She gave Jormungand an awkward pat on the back. "It's just Lavi. Remember? He went to grab you and your too-large brother some clothes?"

Jormungand gave her a bemused look as he tasted the air again. "There's something else."

Lavi burst through the door. He dropped a blue plastic bag on the floor, his swarthy face pale. "The Jotunn are gone."

The room grew smaller as Hildr and Fenrir joined them.

Fenrir wore a thunderous expression as he nodded to his brother. "They aren't the only ones," he said.

"Our sister?" Jormungand licked the air, his eyes narrowed. "And the Fate Cipher."

Jules dropped her cleaning rag and slumped against the wall. "No. How?"

"I left her with you for five minutes!" Lavi shouted.

"She was here but a moment ago," Hildr said, her face dark with shame. "She claimed the need for air after your disagreement and retreated to the rear yard." She glanced at the others. "She couldn't have been out there more than a few minutes."

Lavi rounded on the brothers. "What has your sister done?"

"Not what you are accusing her of," Fenrir growled and shifted his feet.

His lean face took on sharper, meaner angles as she watched, shadowed by a promise of violence. Jules didn't know what to think. Would Hel abscond with Ives when both knew the risks? She didn't know. She didn't share a bond with the goddess as she did with Ives, but she *did* know her human. She set her teeth, determined to ream out Ives later. In the here and now, she had to keep a group of anxious mortals and immortals from tearing each other apart. She darted under Jormungand's arm, got between the three angry men to push her small hands against Lavi and Fenrir's chests.

"Enough! Why are you arguing when Ives is out there

somewhere? We need to find her before she gets herself killed."

"And their sister?" Lavi gripped the hammer tucked in his belt.

Jules smacked him in the arm. "Does it matter why she left or who helped her? I know I'd rather spend my energy on tracking her down than on tossing accusations."

"The small fae person is right," Hildr said. She used her size to shove the men further apart.

Jormungand put an end to the conflict by hauling his brother up by the waist and physically tossing him into a chair. "Our energy would be better served searching for her than challenging one another. The Jotunn might be setting an ambush—"

Jules's senses crackled with alarm.

"That is incorrect." A god stood in the corner of the room. Had he just appeared? Had he been standing there the whole time? It had to be the former since he was impossible to ignore as if he'd been wrought from marble and gold.

She had a moment to register the immense power wafting off him like a pungent cologne when Jormungand appeared in front of her again to place his massive body between her and the new threat. *What was he playing at?*

"Heimdallr," he said, bowing his head in respect, maintaining formality despite wearing little more than a bedsheet. The gesture was all show as his hands curled behind his back.

Jules could read the tension in the big guy's shoulders. Jormungand was not happy to see the newcomer. The Valkyrie fell to one knee while Fenrir backed up against the wall, his teeth bared in a forced grin.

Lavi raised a brow, beautifully unimpressed. "Who's

this guy? Does he know where those sneaky Jotunn slunk off to?"

Heimdallr's smile might have been indulgent, but it was off-kilter, laced with too much annoyance. "I am the Watcher of Ragnarök, here to uphold my duty to the gods as an informant of our enemy's movements. Surt and his army march on the mainland. They will make landfall on the Californian coastline in less than a day. They may continue to seek allies. There are quite a few native gods to roust in those lands. However, they've set a punishing pace, as if they have a destination in mind."

Jules sucked in a breath through her teeth. Surt and his army would be just a state away from possibly reuniting with their apocalyptic boss in Vegas. "What happens when the giants find Loki?"

Heimdallr turned his silvery eyes on her and pierced her with his crystalline gaze.

She shivered.

"I will sound the horn and the All-Father shall lead the Aesir into the final battle."

Jules's jaw tightened at his tone—flat, emotionless, and all the more horrifying for it. If her human had gone after Loki, she would either get herself killed trying to undo Ragnarök or she would be caught between the Trickster and an army of irate giants. "We have to find Ives."

"That could be quite difficult. She has traversed through the hidden ways."

Jormungand went so tense over that nugget of information that Jules was certain he would snap in half. "Pray, do you have a suggestion as to how we could locate the Fate Cipher?" he said.

Jules saw the emotion that passed through the shining god's eyes, a momentarily flash, but she curled her fingers around Jormungand's arm and palmed her dagger.

"If the Fate Cipher has gone to find the Trickster, then you must find him as well," said Heimdallr. He smoothed his immaculate hands down the front of his robes.

"We have a possible lead," said Jules as she studied the god's every reaction. There wasn't even a slight pause at her words.

"If you want to truly pinpoint his whereabouts, you should seek out his wife."

A hiss escaped through Jormungand's clenched teeth, echoed by Fenrir's growl.

The Valkyrie lifted her head, puzzled by the god's decree. "But, Heimdallr, the small fae is right, our lead is a good one—"

"Vegas, Valkyrie?" Heimdallr sneered. "Do you have any comprehension of how many gambling pits are on the North American continent? The world? What made the Fate Cipher so sure of her choice? No, to search there would be a futile endeavor. This order comes from the All-Father himself."

"But—"

"Your disregard of the All-Father's orders places you in a precarious position, Valkyrie," Heimdallr said. His cold gaze shifted to the sons of Loki. "Your present company is already questionable. Who gave these monsters a human shell?"

Jules was ready to stab the god in the leg when Jormungand's hand moved to clasp hers. She caught the imperceptible nod he gave her and kept her mouth shut.

Lavi, however, was not so silent. "You're a bit of a dick, mate," he said as he casually twirled one of his hammers between his hands. "Spit out your order already and trot on your merry way, yeah?"

Jules forced down on a grin. She recognized that tone since she had accompanied both father and daughter to many drinking establishments over the years. It was the voice Lavi adopted moments before he sent some poor idiot to the floor.

Heimdallr blinked at the man. His puzzlement turned to uncertainty the longer he stared, obviously puzzled Lavi wasn't ardently worshipping him like some mortals. He shook himself. "Sigyn vanished at the same time as her husband. Unlike the Trickster, we were able to capture a few sightings of her flight. She was last spotted on the North American continent, in upstate New York. Find her, extract your information, and turn her over to the All-Father."

Heimdallr disappeared with zero fanfare, poofed away as if he was never there.

Hildr stood up, stress etched in her features. "None of this makes sense. Why didn't Odin contact me directly? Why traverse the whole continent to track down Sigyn? She won't tell us anything."

The brothers shared a look while Lavi opened the door and let the Hound in. The dog's ears flattened to his skull at the lingering scent of the god. Jules could sympathize.

Lavi scratched the Hound's ears. "What are you lot going to do now?"

"I think we should split our efforts," Fenrir said. "Two of us shall go after Sigyn. The rest shall pursue our original course and head to the land of Vegas."

Lavi was quiet for a moment. "I'm afraid I cannot join your efforts. I am bound to the land by the same forces that bind our gods. It is the price of my bloodline, and it is a fate my beautiful daughter cannot undo." He looked to each of them. It clearly cost him, to place his trust in this divine and immortal jumble of beings to save his daughter. "Do what you have to, but find my girl, and bring her home."

Fenrir and Jormungand sobered at his request.

"We will," said Jules. "That Lite-Brite idiot did have one valid point. Vegas is a big place. Which one of you is the better tracker?"

Fenrir shrugged. "I work better in the country."

"I shall accompany you, Jules," said Jormungand.

She glanced up at him and realized they still held hands. "Um, what about travel arrangements?" She looked away, anywhere else but up.

"Oh, Jorm can get you there in a jiff. Don't you worry. Us on the other hand, hm?" Fenrir scratched his head.

The light bulb appeared to finally click in Hildr's head at his words. "You're traveling with me? Oh, joy of joys."

"We could always borrow my sister's horse." Fenrir's smile promised mischief.

Hildr blanched. "You must be joking."

TWENTY

LOKI AT LAST

THIS WAS the sixth casino Ives had searched. Her hair reeked of stale smoke. A constant stream of sweat trickled down the dip of her spine. The sneakers squelched and left a swampy muddy feeling between her toes. She leaned against the cool faux-marble arch and caught her breath while trying not to cough on the casino smog. She'd searched the worst pits of the gambling halls, the shadowy dank corners where people wagered their fortunes to the click of dice and shuffling cards.

This one had to be the worst of them. Ives could feel the desperation here, a pungent presence that left an oily taste on the tongue. Despite the late hour, the room was fully occupied, a perfect place for a trickster to hide. Unfortunately, there was another hiccup. In all her dealings with Loki's children, she never got a description of what their dad looked like. She doubted he'd turn up wearing a horned gold-and-green suit like his comic-book equivalent. Or anything simple like a shirt that read, "I started the apocalypse and all I got was this lousy t-shirt."

She searched male faces for hints of Fenrir and Jormungand, looked for the same chiseled features and height. She'd bet money they shared those gorgeous green eyes. She'd used some of their all-too-brief downtime scanning a mythology primer at her dad's house, but her attention had been split between the siblings before her father came in and ruined her concentration.

There was one detail that stuck in her mind. The myths were not kind to Loki. Though he seemed to help as much as he hindered, the punishments were so cruel, so violent. Yet he was referred to as Odin's brother, not in blood but name. How could he go from such a position of honor to the most hated god among them? What changed? None of it made sense to her.

Ives sighed as she peered through the dim. More than one person was slumped over the table while they cradled a drink. A woman in a stained fur stole, despite the outside heat, laughed loudly and revealed lipstick-smeared teeth. A middle-aged gentleman ran his hands through his greasy black hair, his tuxedo was rumpled and sweat-stained. A man with violently red hair, so long it obscured his face, was slumped against the wall to her left.

This casino seemed to be a bust. The only thing left to do was double-check the atmosphere with her other senses. She held her breath and opened them.

The redhead stilled, his lips parted with a sharp exhalation.

Ives looked at him through the Fate Cipher's filter. Her vision blazed with the crimson snarl of Ragnarok. The man with red hair loomed over her between one blink and the next. He clapped a hand over her mouth. She met his gaze, stunned by his lovely green eyes, cracked with madness.

Ives shrieked into his palm.

"Shhh, easy now," said Loki. He broke eye contact to scan the room. His skin against her lips scalded her and made the hot air seem like a breezy spring day in comparison. Seeing him, Ives finally understood Pele's warning. She was so far over her head that the surface was invisible. Any moment, she would drown beneath the overbearing pressure of Ragnarök spilling from the Trickster, and it would strip her mental defenses to swallow her up. Her limbs started to tremble from its weight.

A tear fell from the corner of her eye, over Loki's fingers. He stared at the droplet as it slid down his knuckles. A shadow passed through his eyes. He closed them and took a bracing breath. She could feel the pressure lessen. Those poisonous coils sank beneath his skin. He turned a shade paler and rocked on his feet. His hand slipped from her mouth as he began to tip backward. Ives caught him and hauled him up with all her strength. She had a few years of practice hauling a drunken Lavi home after a game night at the bar, but her father had nothing on the weight of a god. She feared her knees would buckle and send both of them to the floor. A tattooed arm slid into view, shored up the sagging god, and grabbed Ives's hand with a gentle squeeze.

"You're an idiot," Hel hissed as she tucked her father against her shoulder.

"Yes," Ives conceded and pulled Loki's other arm across her shoulders. "But you can yell at me later. We need to get him somewhere private."

Hel grunted and snagged a passing waiter. She gave him a sweet smile, completely oblivious to the look of beguiled panic in the man's eyes. Ives doubted he got cornered by goddesses all that often.

"Pardon, could we snag a room for my fath—friend here? He had a bit too much, you know." She held her hand to her mouth to make the universal drinking gesture. The man stared at her lips, mesmerized until she frowned at him and waved her hand in front of his face. "I think I broke him."

"Yo!" Ives snapped her fingers in front of his face to knock the mortal loose.

He jumped to attention. "Right this way, ladies. We have a complimentary room for our high rollers."

"High rollers?"

Ives looked at Hel, who answered with an exaggerated eye roll and mouthed, 'Trickster'.

They managed to drag the semi-conscious god between them away from the foggy den, to a hallway of plush royal-red carpeting that eased Ives's sore feet. The man led them into an elevator and pushed a button for one of the upper floors as Ives and Hel propped their charge on the holding bar. In the gold plating on the walls, Loki's red hair looked like a flame and obscured his face. She couldn't tell if he was awake or not, though his weight seemed to shift off her when the elevator started moving. The doors slid open with a quiet *ding*, their guide skipped out and paused at a door down the hall for them to catch up. He graciously held the door open for them, even lifted the god up by his boots as they shuffled his body onto the hotel bed. Hel looked ready to ream her a new one until they realized the man stood waiting.

"Go tip him," said Ives. She gave the goddess a wink.

Hel looked like she barely stifled her urge to clock Ives as she turned to the man with a forced, bright smile to she lead him out.

Now that she wasn't hauling his weight around or on the verge of screaming her head off, Ives got her first good look at the god behind all of this chaos. Loki shared the height of his sons, his long legs dangling off the bed, but his frame was leaner, a lithe build of wiry muscle. His hair spilled down to his shoulders in fiery tangled curls, like a fox given human form. His face was shockingly young, an odd juxtaposition next to his full-grown children, though the strain of bearing Ragnarök was clear in the shadows surrounding his closed eyes and the lines framing his scarred mouth. Her hand was outstretched to touch him before she stopped herself, shocked by the action. She puzzled over the urge, the way her heart thumped painfully in her chest at the sight of him.

He was attractive, certainly, though not her type, and she couldn't forget the absolute insanity he'd shown her the brief moment their eyes met. Sure there was a magnetic quality to his presence that tugged on her subconscious, a dangerous charisma that made her whole body fidget but it was no more potent than any other god or immortal she'd met. The effect was broken at his pained intake of breath. His perfect features crumpled as the prophecy's suffocating energy throbbed. In that spare second, Ives saw him, really saw him, and realized the source of the pull. His need to be free of the prophecy called to the core of her gifts, the depth of his suffering so intense she couldn't look away. She brushed a hank of hair away from his lean face. She had to free and survive. She had to.

Resolved, she bit her lip and wrapped a length of the god's hair around her fingers. The contact grounded her as she took another look at the coiled serpent of Ragnarök squatting inside him. It bared its fangs at her, attempted to sink its teeth into her skin. She batted them aside, determined to see if her suspicions were correct. Loki was the source of it all, the lynchpin, and if she *was* correct, she would find something other than Ragnarök in those woven threads.

Loki twitched, still unconscious. Ives smoothed her fingers over his forehead as he cried out silently. Shadowed threads flickered into view. They covered his mouth.

She focused harder, forced the faint, gold-tinted black threads lacing his mouth shut to manifest—an additional compulsion that bound him to the violent intent of the prophecy. She could see them now, strung throughout his body, taut and unyielding, as they wore down his willpower and tore away his resistance piece by piece. Ives couldn't imagine the strength of will Loki possessed to keep such a nasty spell at bay.

"Um, awkward," said Hel.

Her voice broke Ives's concentration. She jolted and realized in the course of studying the threads binding the god, she'd clambered on top of him and straddled him so her bare knees pinned his arms in place.

"Oh, um, sorry, yeah, awkward," Ives sputtered. She started to roll off him. A pair of hands clamped on her thighs and made her yelp. She glanced down to find Loki watching her. His maddened gaze met hers for a second. The bottom dropped out of her stomach as a deep primal fear swamped her, the urge to flee so strong her muscles tightened to spring.

The moment broke as he looked away to focus on a point just over her shoulder.

Ives shuddered and gasped for air, more than a little terrified. Was that Ragnarök or his unchecked divine potency? Her momentary mortal terror faded as his hands kneaded her thighs.

"What the—"

"It's been a while since I've had a lovely, scantily clad lady on top me," he purred. His words slid over her skin like warm silk. *Oh no, no, no.*

Hel's brothers had nothing on their old man. If she wasn't so freaked out by him already, she might have melted under the lusty influence in that voice. *Ugh, he's worse than Mordred.* The thought of her ex was enough to sober her up.

She glared at him. "Great. You're a horndog, too," she said. She slapped her hands on top of his and dug her nails between his knuckles.

Rather than release her, he grinned, and a flicker of interest lit up his face. Ives prepared to unleash the potency of her swamp feet on the god when Hel's mortified voice doused his ardent attentions.

"For the love of Valhalla, Dad!"

Loki's hands froze. He sat up so fast Ives slid off his lap and half off the bed, still anchored by his hold on her thighs.

"*Hel?*"

"You can let me go now," Ives wheezed.

Loki abruptly released her. She crumpled into a heap on his feet. Hel hauled her up by her armpits and helped her stand. The moment Ives was clear, Hel tackled Loki in a fierce hug. He returned the affection, stroking her hair as he held her close. The gesture was so tender Ives felt a pang, she wished she could have shared a reunion like this with her mother, not one of fire, anger, and fear. She pushed the selfish thought aside, she refused to begrudge Hel such a reunion. When he pulled back to smooth a hand along the side of her face in wonder, Ives decided it might be a good idea to take a walk and leave them alone.

"What made this possible?" he asked.

Hel smiled. "A very helpful small fae person."

Loki's brows drew together. "I didn't know they were capable of such magic."

She shrugged. "Not sure she was, either, but she had a pretty powerful motivator." Hel winked at Ives before her expression shifted to worry at how close she was to the door.

Loki's attention shifted to Ives again. A range of emotions flashed over his face before settling on a strange sort of irritation that frayed her nerves. "Sorry for the grab hands, love. Did you need payment? How much for your services—"

Hel slapped a hand over his mouth before he got any further with that line, but Ives felt a small stab at her self esteem. She risked a glance down at her burned and torn outfit, complete with unpleasantly damp sneakers. Did he think her a hooker in this getup? Honestly, what kind of standards did he have?

"She's not a prostitute," Hel hissed, mortified as she turned to Ives. "Um, could you give us, like, five minutes for me to get him up to speed?"

"I think I'll take advantage of your complimentary shower," Ives mumbled as she plodded into the bathroom. She locked the door, stripped out of her abysmal outfit, and snapped on the hot water. The stream did wonders, eased the stress and tension from her shoulders. After a few moments, she hugged herself, and a hysterical sob escaped her lips. Mistaken for a hooker by a god was a scarp book worthy memory.

❦ ❦ ❦

Hel was torn between the desire to embrace her father and strangle him. Ives had found him—*she'd found him*—and Hel found herself splintering inside. Her relief at locating Ives before something had happened to her was palpable and far more intense than she'd expected. Seeing her father first grope then embarrass and dismiss Ives irritated her. And then there was the shard of dread at seeing her father here, in the flesh. Pele's words still rang in her ears. They tainted the joy of the moment and left a sour taste in her mouth as she watched her father.

Loki stared at the bathroom door in pure bafflement. "That was the Fate Cipher?"

Hel curled her fingers in frustration. "Yes, yes, and you just insulted her. How could you not recognize her? You accosted her in the hall before I got to you. What were you trying to do to her?" She eyed him nervously. What if he was under the same compulsion as Jorm?

"I did?" Loki's vacant expression lifted as he strained to focus on the moment. He gasped and clutched his face as an internal battle raged she couldn't begin to fathom. "I—I can't..."

A battle he was losing.

Hel swallowed hard, the unfamiliar prick of tears in her eyes. This whole shitstorm was so bloody unfair. "Hey, it's okay. It's okay. It'll work out."

Loki gave her a sad smile and tugged a strand of her hair. The gesture was painfully familiar, one she remembered from long ago when he was simply her father, free and unburdened.

"You're worried, little one," he said, his eyes drawn back to that closed bathroom door. "She can't undo this, can she?" His tone was void of hope.

Hel couldn't bear this. She squeezed his hands and tried not to think of the inevitable.

"The goddess of her home island said it would kill her," she admitted quietly. "Ives came here anyway. Alone, if I hadn't followed her."

Loki somehow picked up on the hint of admiration and exasperation in her voice.

"You care for her," he said.

Hel stilled. "She freed me and my brothers. She risked

her life for us. She…" Her mother once warned her of mortal attachments, how their fickle natures and brief life spans would leave her full of bitter sorrows. Her father never eschewed mortal company and believed their changeable nature and passion were good for immortals. Then the gods locked her away in the Underworld with only the dead and her monstrous self for company. Before the advent of the internet, Hel's existence had been a tightening noose of loneliness and madness. Even the community she found online wasn't enough, not until Ives stumbled into her world and touched her without disgust, without fear. "She's my friend." A simple word, that wasn't nearly adequate.

Loki went silent next to her. There was so much unsaid between them, but her father sighed and took her hand. "I am grateful she's helped you three. I am at peace with dying if my children can live."

Hel crumpled and heaved a great big sob. Her father knew what would be asked of his children if they were free from the prophecy. His immediate resignation infuriated her as much as it broke her. "No, you don't understand. They asked us—"

He silenced her by pressing his lips to her forehead. "I know," he said against her hair. "My family would be the only ones strong enough to bring me down when Ragnarök took hold." He let her cry against him. The inevitability of their situation finally sank in. "I wish I could have seen my sons again."

Hel sobbed harder. She wished she could throat punch the Norns for chaining them to this horrible fate.

"Daughter, I must ask a favor."

She shot out of his arms so fast she left him reeling. "No. No! We will find another way. I will petition the fates myself. Ives said someone tampered with the prophecy. If the Norns find out someone mucked up their gig, maybe we can convince them to stop this insanity."

"By the time you manage to gain an audience, I will have long succumbed. Please, you can stop me now, while I am still myself." He reached for her and placed her hand on his chest, centered over his heart. "You have the strength to do this, Hel. Your brothers would fight me to the end."

"Because they love you," she sobbed and curled her fingers away. She wanted to smack him, to rail against him, but he held her hand in place. "I can't do this." She loved him, too, in a way her brothers couldn't fathom, which was why the plea on his face undid her.

He smiled, tears clogged in his fine red-gold lashes. He gripped her chin and forced her to meet his gaze. "Please."

She inhaled sharply at the panic and fear in his eyes, the bottomless well of pain. Her father was holding on by a thread, a hair's breadth from snapping and giving in. Her hope shriveled under the sobering weight of his gaze, and the cost of her burden settled on her, a crushing weight that threatened to drag her back into the bowels of the Earth.

"Okay," she said. She wondered how she would explain it to her brothers. They would never forgive her. She didn't want them to. Her tattooed hand rested on his chest, the power of death whispering beneath the skin. The fae might have recovered Hel's human form, but she'd never felt more like a monster. Her words were choked as she spoke. "I love you, father."

Loki braced himself as her tattooed hand blurred, the glamour of flesh lifting to reveal the ivory bones beneath. He held her hand tight, as if afraid she'd pull away, even now, but she was committed, and there no more options.

Hel sucked in a pained sob as she plunged her skeletal hand into his chest.

TWENTY-ONE

PINNED AND SEARED

HELHEST SET DOWN with a clumsy stumble, his three hooves crunching the late autumn leaves. Hildr promptly slid off the wretched beast and dry-heaved. Feeble sparks of electricity spat from the ends of her hair. Fenrir was far less affected by their method of travel. He fiddled with the mobile phone the small fae person gave to him on their departure. He was simply fascinated by the device—by any technology they encountered— cooed over it with such obvious delight she wanted to shove him off the horse.

She'd spent most of the ride with her face plastered against Helhest's foul-smelling flank. She cursed the All-Father for giving her this impossible assignment, cursed the horse for his deplorable lack of hygiene, and cursed the wolf for his obnoxiously cheerful nature. The same wolf slid easily from the saddle and leaned against a tree as she recovered. Helhest ignored them both to graze on a patch of dead grass.

Hildr sneered at the beast as she wiped her mouth before glaring at Fenrir. "Shouldn't you be looking around rather than playing *Angry Birds*?"

"My nose is on task," said Fenrir, "Ha, take that, arrogant green pig monster!"

Hildr frowned at their surroundings. The leaf-strewn lane lacked the layer of crushed rock humans used for their roadways and was little more than well-traveled dirt. Trees lined the avenue, branches bare in preparation for winter's embrace, their smooth trunks bleached by the moonlight. The air held just a hint of the coming season, cool against her skin and a welcome change from the Fate Cipher's sweltering tropical home. What in the nine realms would bring Sigyn here?

Fenrir inhaled deeply. "We're definitely in the right place. Sigyn is close."

Hildr retrieved her sword. "Your nose is accurate."

'Close' was an understatement. Helhest had brought them directly to the goddess. Even Hildr could register the stink in the chill air.

Fenrir blanched and dropped the phone amid the fallen leaves as he caught sight of the figure beneath the tree, a massive specimen, an oak ancient when the rest of the reaching trees were mere saplings. It had seen war and peace, feast and famine. A few shriveled leaves still clung to its weathered branches like warning rattles in the wind. At the base of the thick trunk, curled among the jutting bones of its roots, was Sigyn.

Her pale face was serene beneath the night sky, ivory cast in starlight. A soiled white silk dress spilled around her, the dirty cream a puddle on the leaves. Hair fine as corn silk clung carelessly to the oak's bark and gave her the appearance of a pinned moth, fragile and gossamer. This comparison was emphasized by the sword protruding from her chest that pierced her and the ancient tree.

Sigyn was quite dead.

"How could this be?" Even Fenrir looked horrified and

bewildered. It was no secret Sigyn never got on with her divine stepchildren. Hildr herself never knew the goddess of fidelity well, but she'd lived up to her namesake by entombing herself in the mountain with Loki and giving what relief she could to his misery. Hildr admired such selfless sacrifice. To find Sigyn like this enraged her. Such a foul act demanded justice.

She approached the slain goddess. "We shall have our answers," she said, her voice filled with dark promise.

Fenrir turned to her with confusion. "Little late for answers now, Valkyrie."

Hildr ignored him, her gaze fixed on the sword piercing the goddess's heart, on the pale bloodied hands gripping the blade. She swung her dark gaze on him, like a caress of ice.

"Prepare yourself."

ᛏᛏᛏ

Jules patiently listened to Jormungand's explanation of how he'd get them to Vegas. "You know what? Let's not."

He had the nerve to look puzzled. "Why not?"

"For one, I don't think I could ever pull off a glamour of that size again. For another, I don't think the people of California would appreciate a giant snake emerging from the sea like Godzilla on vacay."

Jormungand's baffled expression was somewhat endearing.

She placed a hand on his arm. "What I'm saying, big guy, is I got this." She hoped. Ives was one thing. The human was at least normal-sized for a person. A son of Loki was another matter. She never attempted to displace a godling before, never mind anyone approaching seven feet. Of course, before this little adventure, she'd never managed such strong glamours— and on the children of gods, no less. She considered it a freaking miracle to find a condensed human form for the World Snake, even if he was totally over large.

One of those ridiculously large hands landed on the top of her head, gently craning her face to look him in the eye. "You got this? Pray, please explain."

The intensity of his stare made her shiver. She felt very much like the mouse in the cobra's sights, but she turned on her smile. Ives called it her razzler-dazzler. It seemed to work by the dazed look on his face. He shook himself and raised a brow.

"I can displace us there," she chirped. She ignored the disarming smile on his lips.

"Forgive me. I am not familiar with that form of fae magic."

Jules narrowed her eyes and wondered if he was making fun of her. "That's my terminology for it," she said. "Watch and learn, bucko."

She made to hug him and froze, eye-to-eye with his navel and far too close to his belt buckle. This was a rather unfortunate development. Thankfully, her complexion mostly hid her blush.

She cleared her throat. "Um, do you think you could, uh, give me an arm up?"

To his credit, he turned his reaction into a polite cough as he wrapped his hands around her waist. He lifted her until they were truly at eye level. She hadn't been this up and personal with his face since she'd held a knife to his throat. This close, she could see the wound hadn't vanished completely as she thought but had healed to a fine white line nearly invisible against his pale skin. She reached out without thinking and brushed the scar with her fingers.

"I'm sorry for that," she said. She felt his grip tense ever so slightly.

His jeweled green eyes darted to the fading bruises on her arms. "I'm sorry for what pain I caused you," he said, a husky note in his voice that did funny things to her stomach.

This was burgeoning into awkward territory, so Jules placed her hands on his shoulders. She closed her eyes, twining herself deep in the power that allowed her to slip through space. The air began to blur and immediately locked back into place. She frowned and attempted it once more with the same results. Sweat beaded along the base of her spine and the dip between her breasts. *Why wasn't it working?*

Frustrated she opened her eyes to find Jormungand tracking a bead of sweat on its path down her chest. The look on his face made her mouth dry. Could he be that much of a distraction? All the other instances of moving with Ives were a cakewalk. All it took was a firm hug, and whammo!

Jules could have slapped herself for such an obvious mistake. Her power worked best under proximity. She shifted in his grip to wrap her arms around his neck. Jules ignored his surprised huff against her cheek as she reached for her power once more. The world shifted. The heavy heat of the island evaporated under the dry heat of the desert. Lights and sounds filtered in, the sharp horns of traffic and the blazing signs of the strip. Jules concentrated on setting the world to rights before she dared to pull away.

Jormungand's expression was filled with curiosity and a bit of awe. "I didn't realize fae could move through the In-Between spaces," he said. He knelt to set her on her feet.

She frowned at him. "What do you mean? All I did was

move us from point A to point B." She moved her hands in tandem to her words.

Jormungand caught her hands. "Jules, you said you called it displacing. What do your sister fae call it?"

The sting was so fresh that the years between vanished in the face of such an innocent question. A blood debt—owed to the human who saved her, who offered her home and hearth when Jules wandered lost, broken, her immortal fate wiped clean and sheared away. Ives had only seen her fate line once, had seen that it appeared as if someone had ripped the fate from her, and with it her memories, her life.

"I have no sisters," said Jules, her voice small. "I have no one to call my own but Ives."

"We'll get her back," said Jormungand.

She looked up at him, touched by the promise in his words.

The moment was ruined by the smell of burning asphalt.

Jules spun around. The streets of Vegas were lit by more than the flashing neon signs. A giant wreathed in flame made his way down the center of the road. Cars veered away from him; horns blared as human minds tried to comprehend a mythological creature stomping down the Vegas freeway. The ground gave a roll beneath their feet.

"The giants are here."

🂠🂠🂠

A wet towel smacked into Hel's face. She jerked back, both hands up and clear from Loki's chest. He bowed over and coughed. Ives exhaled in a gush of relief she'd caught her in time. Hel wrestled with the sodden cloth while Loki turned on Ives with a frustrated expression. Ives stood at the bathroom door in a pair of damp shorts and a tee shirt. Water dripped down her bare arms and legs.

Ives was mid-shower when the threads of Loki's fate twanged through her soul. She'd heard it, that black oily voice that throbbed in her head and squeezed the air from her lungs, and she knew if she didn't get out there ASAP, the Trickster would be dead. She flipped her soaked hair out of her eyes.

"Oops, sorry," she said, far too chipper for the situation. "Hey, Hel, sweetie, would you run and get me some ice? I took a fall outside when I got here, and I have this nasty bruise down my back." She winced and rubbed at the base of her spine.

Hel yanked the towel free. Her bewildered expression shifted to teary-eyed gratitude as she snagged the ice bucket off the desk. "Be right back," she rasped and gripped the door handle so tight it creaked in protest. "Don't do anything stupid."

That made Ives smile. "I won't," she said, not that she could necessarily keep that promise. The moment the door clicked shut, she rounded on the Trickster.

He had both hands over his chest, his eyes cast to the floor, sightless. Ives inhaled for strength and tiptoed closer. She could see it from here. It swirled around him like a woolly storm cloud. The black threads were winding tighter. They moved outside of Ragnarök's sphere of influence to end him one way or another. At that moment, Ives realized the Norse apocalypse was more personal than prophetic. Anger seared her anew. A Fate Cipher existed to balance the harshness of Fate, to wipe the slate clean. Fate was messy, it could be cruel, but it always came with a loophole, a cinch point the Fate Cipher could tug on until the whole game came toppling down. Ragnarök possessed no loopholes. It was multi-layered and cunning in a way a prophecy should never be. Someone buried their influence deep into its core and twisted it to their means. The prophecy itself might have been manipulated from the start, created from the beginning as nothing more than a tool of diversion for the culprit behind it.

Pele's warning dogged her conscience. Ragnarök would kill her if she tackled it head-on, but there had to be something—anything—she could do with the power she was finally beginning to understand. The power her mother entrusted to her. Did her mother realize the toll it would take on her or was that another little detail no one realized when they shoved the Fate Cipher's power into her mortal body?

Ives bit her lip, as she examined Loki with that other sense. He was ready to give up. He had begged his daughter to end him. The pain in that plea echoed between her ears. She'd heard it since she'd shut off the water by then. No, she couldn't take it all, not in one go, but what if she sliced off pieces at a time, as much as her mortal stamina could handle?

Aware she didn't have much time before Hel came back, she placed her hands on Loki's and gently moved them aside. Her abilities hummed just beneath the surface of her skin now. She let them rise and bloom inside of her. Loki's gaze shot up to meet hers. Ives caught her breath. It wasn't madness that clouded his eyes. The black threads were there, too. They served to blind him. They sealed his mouth, clogged his sight. It amazed her he managed to resist at all when he was assaulted so thoroughly. She lifted her hands and traced them against the corners of his eyes until she caught a frayed edge of the darkness.

"This might hurt," she whispered.

This time, she shoved her power through those dark lines like a battering ram until her light shone through and burned them to ash. Loki hissed, gripping her wrists. She flinched at the strength of his grip but kept going until the shadows in his eyes cleared. His hold on her wrists loosened as he stared at her. Her vision wavered for a moment before she steadied herself. She could do this for him, for Hel and her brothers. Ives could destroy that disgusting black thread's hold on him. It wasn't a true thread of fate, only a hateful shadow that needed to be burned out.

Loki's eyes widened as Ives dropped her hand to his chest again and flooded him with light. It seeped into his skin, tore at the darkness within him. A golden glow flickered over her skin. She was mindless of it, of the sparks that ran through her damp hair and crackled in her irises.

"Dazzling," Loki whispered.

She did react, locked in to the power that swept through him. It didn't burn away the hunkered down entity that was Ragnarök, but it attacked what it could until the black thread crumbled away. Next, she focused the power on his lips as she dragged her fingers through the binding threads there. The god blinked at her, wide-eyed, his breath hot against her hand. She hooked her fingers there and yanked hard. Loki gasped. The scars around his mouth vanished to reveal pale, smooth skin, dusted with a coppery five o'clock shadow. With the absence of those marks, the Trickster had the same staggering beauty as his children.

"There you are," whispered Ives as she slowly leashed the power. She felt hollow inside. Her heartbeat thundered in her ears. Too fast. It stuttered. At last, the power slowed to a trickle as she pulled her hands free. The world started to spin. That was her only warning before she pitched forward and blackness ate at the edges of her vision. Loki caught her and smoothed her hair off her now sweat-soaked forehead. He stared down at her with something uncomfortably verging on reverence.

"I think I overdid it," she tried to say, but her tongue was too thick in her mouth.

Loki's expression shuttered as he carefully set her on the bed. "Please, don't expire on me, Ives. My daughter will be most upset with me," he said.

Ives wanted to protest that she was fine, except she was so very tired. She closed her eyes, for just a moment.

On the fringes of her hearing, she thought she heard Hel's scream.

TWENTY-TWO

MORTAL MATTERS

THE ICE BUCKET fell from Hel's hands. She bolted for the room, as a high-pitched warning jangled through her divine senses, a pluck of threads pulled too tight, then the snap and silence.

"Ives!" In her haste, Hel phased through the door and skidded across the carpeted floor on her knees as she slammed her skeletal hand down on Ives's chest. The force jolted her struggling heart back into full gear, but Ives's energy guttered, her breath so shallow her lips turned blue.

"No, no, no you don't," hissed Hel. She concentrated on Ives's fading lifeline and willed it to stay.

"Hel." Loki placed a hand on her shoulder.

"Shut up!" she snapped, afraid if she looked away for even a second, Ives would fade. She studied the lifeline she held, a terrible truth forming. "Oh, gods, no."

"What is it? Hel, is there anything I can do?"

Hel spared her worried father a glance, shocked by the change in him. "What the hell did she do?"

"Sh-she destroyed a part of it," said Loki as he absently traced his mouth. Even the scars lining his mouth were gone. He frowned down at Ives's limp form. "Her body wasn't made to accommodate that power."

"No shit, Sherlock," said Hel. Her hands shook from the effort to be delicate, oh so delicate, as she waited for the idiot Fate Cipher to stabilize.

Loki reached between her hands.

She realized what he intended a moment too late. "Wait. No!"

A jolt of his fiery energy shot into Ives's chest. Hel froze, certain the mortal's little heart would explode, but to her shock, Loki's power lit Ives's lifeline like a burst of oxygen over smoldering coals. Ives drew a ragged breath as her lifeline thrummed and settled, still dangerously low but stable. Hel released a breath and carefully extricated herself from Ives's unconscious body as she settled her back on the bed.

"How did you know to do that?"

Loki shook his head, his expression dazed. "I just—I just knew it would work."

She didn't like the sound of that one bit. There were only so many beings that could manipulate gods and mortals with such a subtle hand. Ives was alive. For now. Hel turned away and pressed her hands to her face. *Stupid, stupid girl!* How could she be so bloody reckless? But then, Ives didn't understand. Heck, Hel wondered if even Pele understood how thoroughly screwed the current Fate Cipher was.

Her father sat beside her, full of worry and nervous energy. So distracted by Ives's brush with her side of the business, Hel missed the other notable changes in Loki. The madness was gone from his eyes. The strain she'd seen in him before she left the room was greatly reduced. Even his shoulders were straighter. Gods, how much power had Ives exhausted?

He caught her looking and reached for her tattooed hand.

Hel froze. A memory teased free from the deep fog of her past.

The smile on his face as he reached for her. Her hands rose to meet his, tiny hands, human hands. There was such joy between them. It surrounded them. She'd forgotten such a precious memory? Her father lifted her high into the air, so high she was certain she could see all of Asgard. He spun with her, her laughter clear as silver bells ringing over the land. Among the trees, the hooded figure watched them. The setting sun sparkled on something metallic within that oval of darkness, and it shone in her eyes.

"Hel?" Loki squeezed her hand as he cupped the tattooed half of her face in his attempt to snap her from the vision.

Tears slid thick and fast down her cheeks, icy cold to the touch, and full of ancient grief. She wrapped her hand around his and held it to her face.

"I remembered..." Hel looked down at the shivering figure on the bed.

Ives had said there was a male voice, tangled in with the Norns. Was that who she saw in her memory? Was the hooded figure the one responsible for this whole mess? Who was this brazen bastard to risk messing with the Norns? Or worse, what if the Norns knew about it? Hel bit her lip. Her free hand felt Ives's pulse, now steady and strong.

Loki's power, somehow, granted Ives a reprieve. It shouldn't have worked, but it did. Whatever power was manipulating events to keep the Fate Cipher alive, Hel knew the same tricks wouldn't work twice, not when her power was so intrinsically tied to her lifeline. Something the Norns also had to know. It always came back to the Norns.

"Those bitches," Hel snarled.

Loki blinked. "Who's bitches? What's wrong?"

"Her power, it doesn't just draw on her life force, her energy," said Hel.

"It shortens her life span," finished Loki. Anger sparked in his eyes. "But the Fate Cipher is an *immortal* position. Why does this woman have these powers? How did this come to pass?"

"They locked her mother away," she said.

He reared back in shock. "She's Keawe's daughter?"

Hel arched a brow. "Do I want to even know how you know her mother?" Ives had told her briefly of her situation on the long elevator ride up from the Underworld, but she'd never mentioned her mother by name. Hel pursed her lips as she tried to puzzle out Ives's power.

The Fate Cipher was meant to be a counterbalance to the immortal fates, but she couldn't use her abilities without literally killing herself in increments. She'd narrowly escaped death several times now, or she would have if she'd approached her power straight on. Ives should have burned up before she finished freeing the siblings. Except, when Ives channeled another immortal, she managed to bypass her mortal energy, though it also overloaded her system. Tricks and loopholes aside, this power was a catch-22 for Ives, and Hel thought it bloody unfair. No, it was downright unjust. Having spent centuries as the Goddess of the Norse Dead, shunned by her fellow gods for her father's supposed trespasses and her unwitting appearance, she had a pretty good grasp of the concept of fairness. The only true hope her father had, the world had, was an *immortal* Fate Cipher, but Ives likely didn't know where her mother *was*.

"I can feel the pull of Ragnarök but it's…weaker. I can fight its call for now." Loki glanced out the window at the dazzling glow of the Vegas night. "Why would they allow this? This isn't right. This doesn't heed the balance."

"I don't understand it, either," said Hel. She studied Ives's flickering lifeline. "When she unbound me from Ragnarök, she blazed like a falling star. I thought I'd killed her then."

"Didn't she draw on your energy?" Loki made a face. "She didn't draw on mine, either, for that little performance."

"Not that first time, no. She used herself up like a matchstick. When she freed Fen, she tapped me, but she didn't know how to stop. The goddess of the island had to cut her loose before she went up like a puddle of gasoline."

Hel clicked her teeth. "She freed Jorm on her home soil. I think that buffered her. Probably the only reason she's not dead is there's something else at play." There was a bitter snap to her words. She wanted to punch the wall. She was pissed—pissed at the Valkyrie for dragging Ives into this, pissed at the gods for this whole mess, pissed at whoever or whatever kept pulling Ives through every divine loophole imaginable, but mostly pissed at herself for not noticing so glaring a weakness sooner.

"Why didn't I see it?" Hel pinched the bridge of her nose. She suddenly felt exhaustion built up over eons. "Balls."

Her father snorted. "This is far from your fault, my dear."

"Bloody Pele, Hildr, the whole freaking lot of them should have known better," Hel snarled. "They gave her no guide, no teacher. She had no real practice with her abilities until now."

"A completely untrained Fate Cipher," said Loki, his

expression one of sympathy. "It's like they wanted her to die."

Hel nibbled her lip. "They might have. Dad, we need to wake her up. I have to have a bit of girl talk with her."

"I'm not sure that's wise," he said.

Hel rolled her eyes as he pouted. "Oh, please, go eavesdrop from the bathroom like you were planning to do anyway." She shooed him off as she cradled Ives's head in her lap.

Her father gave Ives one last glance before disappearing out of sight, one of longing and hope as if Ives was still the answer to his grand dilemma. Hel sighed. He might try to convince her to help him again. One miniature disaster at a time. She placed her forefingers on Ives's temples and listened to the hum of power in her veins. She could sense the echoes of her brother's power, her own faint shade, a taste of the island gods, and the more formidable flux of her father's energy, possibly what sustained the girl now. There wasn't a trace of any other divine power, though it had to be there. Hel was still curious how easily Ives's body soaked up her father's power or was it her life force that diminished?

Hel prayed Ives was still somewhat receptive to her energy as she gave her a trickle, like a desperately needed drink of water through parched lips. It was the wrong kind, but it was enough.

Ives groaned. Her dark eyes fluttered open. "Is he okay?" she croaked. Her words gave way to a dry cough.

Hel couldn't help the relieved smile at the sound of her voice. "You go and nearly do yourself in again, and you're worried about that tosser?" She bent over and touched her lips to Ives's forehead. "He's better. Don't you dare scare me like that." A hot tear splashed over Hel's hand.

Ives stemmed the flow from her eyes by pressing her

forearm over the bridge of her nose. "I'm sorry. I can't help him anymore." She sounded so forlorn like she'd failed them.

It pinched at Hel's heart. "Ives, do you know what happened to your mother?"

For a moment, silence reigned. Ives kept her arm in place to hide her eyes from Hel. The goddess could only imagine the struggle going through her head. The subject was a sore one—to both Lavi and his daughter. Hel remembered the single picture on Lavi's nightstand she spotted while wandering his home, a testament to his love for the absent woman.

"They sealed her away, deep in their realm," said Ives. Her voice wobbled from the pain of her memory. "They said she had to be punished for her dalliance, for me, that I was a mistake left alive by their goodwill."

Something cracked in the other room. Ives jumped. Hel made a face at the semi-closed door. She hoped her father didn't break anything important. As a man who'd fathered plenty of dalliances, he was mighty sore on the subject.

"Who are they, sweetie? The island gods?" Hel asked. If it was Pele and her crew, she'd ram her size-nine combat boots right up that goddess's fiery arse. She wiped the tears off Ives's face.

Ives puffed out her lips in a shuddering sigh. "No." She swallowed. "The Fates. They took her away, and I don't know how to find her. They said she would be imprisoned until my life came to an end. It was my duty to uphold the tasks of the Fate Cipher in her stead."

Hel could picture it now, those tawdry bitches. They certainly got their kicks off of making people miserable. Pleasant prophecies were rare for a reason. But to punish a little girl just for being born? To shove such a dangerous and lethal power into her and then leave her defenseless, unguided? Even for the fates, that level of careless cruelty baffled Hel.

"We should go break her out," said Loki, perched cross-legged on the end of the bed.

Hel and Ives both startled.

"Rude," Hel snapped.

"How does he move so quietly? Dude's over six feet tall," said Ives. She peered bleary-eyed over her arm at the god. "What do you mean break her out? I don't even know where she is."

Loki shrugged. "She's in the realm of the Fates. Simple enough to breach."

Ives sat up, a mixture of hope and exasperation on her wan face. "Where? How? Do you know how to get there?" The very prospect of seeing her mother again seemed to banish her fatigue.

Loki raised a brow. "You've been there before. Its essence still clings to you and my daughter."

Hel gasped and clapped her hands over her mouth so her shrill exclamation was muffled. She took her hands away to punch her father in the shin. "You mean they've been there the whole bloody time?"

Ives looked ready to throttle them both. "Where the f—"

"The In-Between," said Hel. "They lurk in the same realm the gods use to travel across time and space."

An explosion rocked the room. A burning tire crashed through the window and showered the bed with shards of glass. Loki had Ives and Hel in his arms and across the room in a flash to shield them from more debris. They could hear the screams from outside, the shouts of dismay from other rooms down the hallway. The roar of fire and the screech of twisting metal rent the air.

Through the hotel window, the city of Las Vegas was on fire.

Jules knew they were in real trouble the moment Jormungand threw her over his shoulder and sprinted away from the approaching giants. For a moment, she thought they'd make it inside unseen until one ugly pisser popped up from the back end of a parked eighteen-wheeler. The asphalt melted beneath his boots. The stench of it stung her nose. Jormungand's muscles bunched beneath her at the sight of the giant. Though honestly, he was a bit on the short side in Jules's opinion, barely topped Jormungand's human form by a few inches.

The giant's skin wasn't simply dark, but black as pitch and cracked like charred wood. His eyes were similar to Pele's, like smoldering coals, but burned with chaotic violence that promised pure senseless destruction. He looked at Jormungand in confusion until incredulous recognition flared. A choking laugh burbled up from the giant's throat to emerge in puffs of oily smoke.

"The great World Snake?" he grated, a voice of tumbling rocks and crackling flames. His glowing gaze noted Jules's presence with a flicker of surprise. "Interesting company you keep, Lokison."

"Better than some," Jormungand remarked coolly.

"Yeah, step off, Shorty," said Jules. She waved her knife at the fire giant.

If possible, Jormungand stiffened further. She was afraid the man would topple over like a plank of wood.

The fire giant gaped at her before bursting into laughter. Flames spilled over his lips and dropped to the sidewalk in sizzling puddles. "I like her," he said. "She can die first."

Jormungand yanked her behind him so fast she thought she'd get whiplash. He planted his feet and released a chilling hiss that made her skin crawl. The giant struck first and rammed a fiery fist in the center of Jormungand's chest. Jormungand took the impact with a grunt and skidded back a couple of inches before he retaliated with a backhand that sent the giant flying. The maneuver surprised Jules before it dawned on her—all the strength of the World Snake must be contained in his human form. He spun on her. A fist-sized hole smoked through his shirt.

"Run to that hotel," he pointed. "My father's and sister's scents lead there. Your Fate Cipher must be with them." He gave her a shove as another contender approached up the street. Unlike the small charred giant, this one didn't skimp on his Wheaties. He towered close to twenty feet tall.

Jules paled at the sight of him.

"Go!" Jormungand yelled at her.

She darted forward and wrapped him in a fierce hug before she yanked on reality. Like hell was she leaving him to get beaten down in the street. The world stilled into darkness. For a moment, Jules wondered if she'd taken them horribly off-course until the familiar smell of cleaning chemicals hit her. Her seeking hand brushed a couple of mop handles and a rack of supplies before her fingers found a light switch. They'd landed in a janitorial closet, hopefully, within the hotel he'd pointed out to her. She was a wee bit disoriented at displacing them again so soon.

"Come on. Let's see if we at least landed in the right casino," she said. She slipped her hand into his to tug him along.

She kept her eyes forward as she looked for trouble in the form of giants and casino security, secretly thrilled as he laced their fingers together.

♆ ♆ ♆

It was Hel who got them moving.

"If they catch up to him, all is lost," she said, her voice was an electric wire that prodded Ives between the shoulder blades.

Loki was in a daze, likely from the proximity of the giants, his movements stiff, like a puppet tangled in its strings. They managed to pull him out into the hallway and lose themselves in the general chaos of people fleeing the casino. The crowd's fear was thick as smoke, and the air tasted rotten, like a hint of spoiled milk on the tongue. Another tremor rained dust and plaster from the ceiling.

"We have to get out of here," said Ives. She shared a frightened look with Hel. "Can you take us to the In-Between?"

"If I do, the giants will follow. You think we're in trouble here? At least we can hide among the humans." Hel dragged them in the same direction as the fleeing people.

Flames sparked and ignited along Loki's skin.

Ives yelped and leaped back. "I don't think we can hide him for long." Odd, she could feel the heat of the flames, but they didn't burn her.

Hel cursed so profoundly Ives was astonished her ears didn't bleed.

"It's the bloody giants," Hel said. "They're pushing Ragnarök to the surface."

A helpless expression took hold of her. It filled Ives with dread. She thought freeing Loki from the compulsion would buy them more time, but Ragnarök was too strong. She stepped up to the God of Fire, risking a burn as she slapped him hard across the face.

"Snap out of it," she cried. His skin blazed against her palm. Hot, but tolerable. She clenched her teeth and gave him another quick slap that drove the blank look from his face.

Loki shook off the lull of the prophecy. Ives was surprised his fire hadn't done more damage.

He took in the chaos as anger and annoyance warred for dominance in his expression. "How did they find me? It should have taken them more time to track me down."

"Probably a tip-off from the same asshole who's been pulling our strings all along," said Ives. She spotted the familiar figures of her best friend and the World Snake in the crowd a second before they spotted her. "Oh, crap."

"Jorm!" Hel yelled and waved frantically for her brother.

The shock on their father's face was almost worth the fist to Ives's ribs as Jules caught up to her.

"You stupid human!" Jules practically screamed at her and punched her twice before hugging her so tight she couldn't breathe. "You just left!"

"She was upset," said Jormungand. He turned to face his stunned father. "Hello, Dad."

Loki looked damn near teary-eyed, taking a moment amid the chaos to gently pinch his son's chin.

Ives shuffled in place. She felt awkward despite Jules's death grip. "As touching as this moment deserves to be, we have a problem."

Jormungand looked at her. His pupils contracted to mere slits. "Oh, yes. I may have thrown Surt into traffic."

Jules gasped. "That pipsqueak of a giant was Surt?"

A smile pulled at Loki's lips. Hel covered her face with one hand.

Jormungand laid a hand on Jules's head. "Yes, but don't say that to his face."

Ives tugged at the fae's curls. "As happy as I am to see you, small fry, we need to play keep-away with daddy Trickster or it's game over. We need to make a fast exit."

"Not all of us," said Hel. She looked grim. "Some of us

need to stay behind and distract the giants, or they will follow you to the In-Between."

Jules went wide-eyed. "What? Why there?"

"It's where the Fates are," said Ives. She didn't like the idea of leaving any of them behind against an army of giants, even if Jormungand could toss them with ease. She hadn't gotten to know him like Hel, but without the madness of Ragnarök twisting him up, he seemed like a decent fellow. No, he was *good*. She felt that in her gut. She'd known the moment she met Hel that she was good, too. None of them, Loki included, wanted to be a part of this insanity.

Jormungand's hand clapped on her shoulder. "Jules will take you to the In-Between. My sister and I shall distract the giants."

"No," said Jules, "I can take all of us. We shouldn't have to split again—"

"The giants will not follow you into that realm," said Jormungand, his voice firm.

"They can't stay here either," said Ives. "There are too many innocent people."

"Hence why we shall lead them into the desert," said Hel as she nudged Ives with her shoulder. "We can handle these idiots. Go, find your mum, help my dad. Save the freaking world."

She said it so confidently. Ives looped an arm around her neck and tried to ignore the terrified tremor in her limbs. "Don't get yourself murdered."

Hel stiffened for only a beat and enveloped Ives in a fierce hug before peeling away to join her brother.

Loki watched them both with his arms crossed, his expression one of parental frustration. "Listen to your sister," he said.

Jormungand gave him the finger and looked down at

Jules, his expression regretful. "I may have to destroy your glamour," he said.

Jules swallowed and looked at her feet. "I'll find a way to do it again."

He slipped a finger under her chin to lift her face. "Do keep yourself alive as well," he said and knelt to place a brief kiss on her cheek.

Jules turned a rich shade of cedar brown, blushing up through her ears. "Hang on tight," she muttered as she grabbed Ives and Loki in an odd group hug. The world shifted. The trio blurred and vanished, leaving the siblings behind.

Twenty-Three

THE IN-BETWEEN

WHENEVER JULES TRAVELED with Ives like this before, it was as if the world blurred out of focus, spun so fast it made her stomach heave. She didn't recognize the shadowy realm until Jules brought them to a halt. It was the same realm Heimdallr carried her through earlier, filled with rushing shadows. Ives simply never saw it before because they zipped through it so damn fast. She sank to her knees as she tried to keep from yarking the spare contents of her stomach on the coarse stone ground.

Jules apologized as she fluttered around her. Ives waved her off and rose on her unsteady feet. The writhing shadows did little to settle her dizziness, but she forced herself to keep moving. Loki waited for them at what looked like an archway, so obscured in shadow it was difficult to identify its form.

"This is our way in," he said. He reached out and pinched the shadows between his fingers.

The effect was akin to pulling back a curtain. The gloom lifted and Ives's mouth went slack. Like Hel's realm, the air was filled with glowing strands. Not the opalescent pale threads of mortal lives, but the diverse colors of fate—the deep crimson of violent ends, morning glory blues for sorrowful tales, and more—laced the sky over their heads, humming with magic.

"Huh," said Jules "I feel like I should have noticed this before now."

"Why would you?" said Ives. She looked at the mass of swirling gray surrounding the archway like a dismal portal. "This whole place was designed not to be noticed."

"Come on," said Loki. He set a foot inside the arch, which caused the colorful threads to pulse. The colors grew brighter as if they could sense the presence of Ragnarök hiding within him.

Ives followed. The threads didn't seem to react to her presence and let her pass unnoticed. It was Jules's presence that provoked the strongest reaction. The threads recoiled from her while a burnt-ozone smell permeated the air. Jules shrank against Ives's side. They stopped as the threads parted to reveal a dark-skinned man, dressed in an outfit Ives only saw during historical island ceremonies. A kahuna, a scion to the fates of her ancestors, approached them. He glared at the trickster god, clearly displeased by his presence, but his steps came to a stumbling halt as he saw Ives and her companion.

An unpleasant sneer twisted his mouth, his dark eyes cold as he addressed them. "Fate Cipher, your visit is unexpected. I am afraid I cannot permit you to go further into our realm with your present company."

Loki appeared beside Ives in the blink of an eye. His piercing eyes stared down the haughty islander. "We have come here with a vital task. We require access to the Fate Cipher in your keeping," said Loki, his tone businesslike, belying the stance he'd shifted into, ready to spring.

The kahuna seemed unperturbed by the god's request. He brushed a bit of invisible lint from his clothes. "While unseemly, you are permitted within our borders, God of Fire. It's that one," he spat as he pointed to Jules, "we refuse to admit. An unbound fae is too dangerous."

Ives stepped in front of Jules to hide her from the kahuna's venomous gaze. "She is bound to me. Does that count for nothing?"

The man sniffed, unimpressed by her decree. "Physical bonds, nothing more. Her fate has been stripped from her, her purpose. There is nothing here for trash."

Ives was ready to kick him in the shins. "Why, you sodding son of a—"

"Ives," Jules snapped and stepped out from behind her to give the kahuna the evil eye. "If I stay outside the arch, can they move forward?"

"No, wait—" Ives began to protest.

"That will be acceptable," said the kahuna.

Jules nodded her head in acknowledgment and grabbed Ives's wrist. "There isn't time to debate. They're fighting for us up there." She jerked her head upward. "You need to find your mother and fix this." She eyed the kahuna over Ives's shoulder. "They sent *an islander* to meet you. Straight from your father's side. I think you make them nervous."

Ives absorbed her words as she watched the kahuna from the corner of her eye. It wasn't her whom his gaze kept lighting on. No, it was the trickster who kept his interest. "*I* don't make them nervous," she said.

Jules caught her drift. *Be careful*, she mouthed, backing away through the arch. The shadows flowed around her, sealing the way.

Ives felt a pang as her friend vanished from sight and left her alone with an enigmatic god. Well, she was alone with Loki and the snobby kahuna.

That statement also proved false as the kahuna bowed

his head and started to fade back into the myriad of threads.

"Wait," said Ives. She rushed forward. "Aren't you going to show us the way?"

That dark gaze snapped up at her, soaked in old anger. "We do not guide the unravelers," he said. His gaze darted once more to Loki and flickered briefly with fear as he faded into the threads.

"That was troubling," Loki said.

Ives didn't respond, burned through and through by the kahuna's words. No kidding they didn't help Fate Ciphers. It was why she was here in the first place.

🎲🎲🎲

Odin would probably frown on a second technicality, but Hildr figured it was for a worthy cause. She knelt beside the fallen goddess, the air thick with the metallic taint of blood. The blade had obliterated Sigyn's heart and shorn the divine soul from her body. Immortals, as a rule, were diffi- cult to kill, gods even more so. Which begged the questions of what and who ended the wife of Loki? Hildr cupped Sigyn's icy chin, lifted her face to the bright moonlight, and winced. Someone had plucked her eyes from her head.

"Interesting," remarked Fenrir as he shuffled behind her.

He was right. The removal of the goddess's eyes was an old trick, one that protected against a certain kind of divine magic. Her killer had ensured no one would witness her demise through her last sight. Out of sight, out of mind. The act also stole the memory of her death. When Hildr raised her, Sigyn would not be able to identify her killer.

"Thorough," she said as she stood. She placed the flat of

her blade on the goddess's shoulder and gripped the handle of the sword that killed Sigyn with her free hand.

"What are doing?" Fenrir sounded a bit frightened. "She won't remember anything."

"Of her death, no, but she might be able to tell us who set Loki free." Hildr called on the power within her, the gift of the All-Father to raise the fallen who died in battle. "Sigyn, wife of Loki Laufison, hear the call of Odin and rise." In one swift motion, she pulled the sword free of the woman's heart and tapped her blade on Sigyn's shoulder. Power flared and fizzed, passing from the Valkyrie to the dead goddess in a brilliant flash and the lingering scent of electricity.

Fenrir's footsteps crackled through the leaves as he backed away from them. His actions amused her. The big bad wolf was tilted by a little necromancy?

"Hildr, I don't think that was a good idea. Sigyn was—"

The goddess woke up screaming. Her empty eye sockets gaped open, swirling with darkness. Hildr made a noise, a soft gasp at the product of her handiwork. The awakened Sigyn seized on the sound. She flew at the Valkyrie, taking them both to the dirt.

⚰⚰⚰

Ives and Loki traversed the forest of threads side by side. It was a singular surreal moment in a week of them, to be walking through the realms the Fates with one of the most heavily bound creatures she'd ever met. The ex, Mordred, was nowhere in the same league. To think, earlier this week, she was trying to drink away her feelings of rejection. Just a few days ago she possessed a tenuous grip on her powers and no desire to use them.

Now, after she'd finally embraced her power and desired to use her abilities for good, she couldn't do so without killing herself. Maybe she had some epically bad karma from a previous life slaying puppies or something equally awful. What had she done to deserve this? Now she had to seek out the woman who'd thrust all this on her.

In the blood, indeed.

'What's the deal with you and your mum?"

Ives tripped, ready to kiss the stone floor until Loki grabbed the back of her shirt and hauled her upright.

"I don't see how it matters or why it's any of your business," Ives sputtered as she straightened herself.

Loki looked thoughtful. "I got pieces from Hel, and from what you said, about how they took her from you, but I don't understand the anger."

"Excuse me?" Ives squinted at him.

"You—you're furious with her. Do you blame her for what happened?"

"What? No, I know it wasn't her fault."

"It was the Fates who imprisoned her, wasn't it? If you should blame anyone, I'd put my money on them."

"Look, this really is none of your business," Ives protested.

"So, if you don't blame her for being imprisoned, what do you blame her for? There's something, something that's filled you with hurt and rage. That will make it harder for you to listen when we find her."

"I'll be fine," she snapped, fed up with the conversation.

"Do you even want her to be free? Or do you think she deserves to be locked away? To be kept from her loved ones?"

"Back off," said Ives. She walked ahead of him, but Loki pressed harder.

"Perhaps you do want her to stay locked away. What

could a mother have done to deserve such coldness from her daughter?"

Ives spun around and slammed her hands against his chest. "Shut up," she yelled. "You don't know anything. You don't get to talk about her."

She shoved at him again, pounded her fists against his unyielding chest until he clapped his hands over hers and held them in place over his heart. His pulse was steady and calm, completely at odds with the fierce pounding of her own heart.

"Perhaps, but you need to talk about her, Ikepela," he said.

His gaze held her in place, searching for the chinks in her armor.

"Who told you that name?"

Hel, damn her. Overwhelmed, she wanted to look away. She could hear the hypnotic undertone of his voice. It lulled her, eased past her guard. The Trickster was working on her, but for what?

"Not a day passed, not a moment, of my imprisonment that I didn't think of my children, of the ones trapped in the same poisonous fate as I am or the ones..." His voice grew ragged as the words ripped his throat raw. "The ones I lost." He paused and reclaimed his composure. "A parent's absence does not equate to an absence of love, Ikepela." Ah, his great trick was brutal honesty.

She struggled to tug her hand free, seized with the urge to slap him again. Perhaps she could snap him out of his righteous philosophical bullshit. Shame washed through her. How dare she even think that? He'd just confessed what must be a private pain, and she couldn't stop wallowing in her grievances to empathize with him. She released her anger in a long, slow breath and swallowed the painful lump in her throat. Brutal honesty was a tactic that worked with her after all.

"I'm sorry," she said. She looked down at their hands. Loki wasn't at all hesitant to touch her like Hel. The stray thought made her wonder how the goddess and her sibling fared elsewhere. "What was done to you and your family was truly awful." She peered up at him. "How do you continue to resist it? After what the gods did to you, your wrath would almost be justified."

Loki made a face. "Yes, I would be completely justified razing the world for a personal grievance. It would *so* balance the scales for me to get my revenge on the gods by ripping every family on earth to shreds."

"You're sarcastic for a trickster."

The smile on his face wasn't a nice one. "If I survive this, freed from Ragnarök, I may very well take up my grievances with the gods for their part in this. But I wouldn't make the entire world pay for their mistakes. That is something *they* would do."

There was a very real threat in his words, not that she could blame him, though she wondered why he referred to the other gods as *they*, as if he saw himself as separate from them by more than the divides of prophecy. She looked away and curled her fingers beneath his hand. He had her number, that she enjoyed admitting it.

"You're right. I'm angry at her," Ives said. "Not for being locked away by the Fates or even for dumping the whole Fate Cipher business on my head before she vanished again. I'm angry for the eighteen years before that moment. I'm angry at the woman my father let me believe was dead rather than simply not there." Her sight blurred as tears stung at her eyes. "No reason, no explanation, not even a hint where she was. Just gone."

Loki nodded. "I think I understand the anger now, Ikepela."

"Stop calling me that," she grumbled. It was the name her mother gave her, the only thing she left her daughter before vanishing without a trace and never speaking a word to Ives until she had to.

"Do you ever wonder if perhaps she couldn't contact you? If she had to stay away to keep you safe?"

Ives sighed as she pulled away from him. "If that's the reason she never said a word about it." Part of her almost hoped it wasn't true. If only so she could feel as justified in her anger as Loki did.

She was distracted from her uncomfortable train of thought by the threads overhead. She'd been looking at them absently from time to time as they walked but hadn't realized the threads all held a direction, slanting downward from the sky to the left or right, intertwining overhead in a glowing corridor. Ives followed the slanting threads down, down, down to their destination.

She gasped.

The tapestries hung suspended in the air, supported only by the constant feed of threads weaving into place to form a picture. Drawn to it, she broke off from the path they followed. It was a work of art, wrought with astonishing detail down to the finest threads used to create the expressions of the tapestry's subjects. It told a story as clearly as a moving picture, a grim one, of a boy cast out by a king's fear, of the trials he overcame to return, the death of the king, the boy who took the queen for his own.

Ives felt sick as she looked on. She recognized this story, one she'd read in high school ages ago. She thought it a work of fiction, but most of the ancient stories were steeped deep in truth, in forgotten histories. This one she always thought rather disturbing, but to see it unfold in such vivid detail was a visceral experience.

"*Oedipus Rex*," she murmured. Her fingers itched. She could see where the threads were weakest, where one good pull could unravel the entire depraved work. A flash of color made her turn her head. The tapestry was one of thousands. A parade of destinies hung for miles, woven to the minutest detail. Ives walked on, mesmerized and horrified by them in turn. Some she recognized; others she couldn't even fathom a guess, set in worlds other than earth. She passed one tapestry of a realm caught in eternal spring that brimmed with fae creatures locked in a graceful dance. It was the only one she'd seen so far that wasn't perfect. The central figure was burned out, a charred mass that marred the beautiful picture. Ives stared at the broken image, confused by the sorrow in her heart. A ring of women with familiar brown curls and joyful faces danced around the charred figure.

"Oh," said Ives. She reached out to touch it when Loki's sharp intake of breath stilled her hand.

He stood before another tapestry further down from the burnt one, his gaze locked on it, filled with fury. Ives knew before she reached his side what she would see, but it didn't prepare her for the impact of the piece. Before them was the sprawling tapestry of Ragnarök in all its glory, down to the bitter ash of the end. It was longer than most of the other pieces, stretching twice as tall as the Trickster. Ives let her eyes wander over it, and her stomach turned at the details.

She was halfway down when she caught a glimpse of him. She frowned and stepped back, trying to see the bigger picture. There he was again, at the binding of Fenrir, in the group that banished Hel to the Underworld. Even in the group that slaughtered Loki's other sons, using their innards to bind him. She took one more step and stared.

"Loki," she whispered and gestured for him to join her.

He followed her, eyes wide as the picture became clear.

Throughout the tapestry, a hooded figure appeared, over and over, a presence at every tragic and grisly event of Loki's fate. This far back, they could see it all come together, the tapestry hemmed with the same black thread spiked with gold, woven through the entire background.

TWENTY-FOUR

THEY MIGHT BE GIANTS

HERDING an army of giants away from the bustle of Vegas was much easier than Hel thought it would be.

"You know," remarked Hel as she eyed her brother, "our father could have managed a little trip to the In-Between with the human in tow."

Jormungand headed for the entrance of the casino. "I wanted Jules safe."

She decided to let that line pass without comment. They had a dangerous task to do and little time to do it in. It helped immensely that the unbearable heat and the flashing lights along the strip drove the frost giants bonkers. While the fire giants probably wouldn't mind a good brawl through the city streets, their snow-bound brethren were not so inclined. When Hel appeared, waving their hotel room bedsheet like a matador baiting the bulls, they gave chase. She barely had time for a "Come and get it, boys," before she had to haul her butt into high gear.

Jormungand was far ahead of her, not so much a sprinter as a marathon runner. His long legs ate up the distance well enough, but she soon overtook him.

"Pick up the pace or they're gonna mow you over," she panted as she pumped her arms in focused rhythm.

"You forget, sister, we want them to follow, not eat our dust," he said, his voice even and unhurried. The jerk wasn't short of breath in the slightest.

Hel attempted to squint at him before a pothole sent her sprawling across the road. She groaned, thankful for divine healing as she peeled herself up. A chunk of asphalt the size of a Buick slammed down beside her. She yelped and rolled away as another projectile landed with the crunch of crushed metal. It might have been an actual Buick. Jormungand hauled her up and tossed her off the road onto the sand as another piece of the highway flew at them. He turned into it and smashed it with his fist into a cloud of pebbles and tar.

"Dude! That's an anime power move!"

He made a face at her. "Ani-what?"

Hel didn't have time to call him on his lack of culture as a giant came hurtling through the debris. The giant slammed into her brother, both of them tumbling off-road into the desert. A frost giant, judging by the blue tint of his skin, well over twice the size of Jormungand's human form. Thick, veiny arms— a sickeningly pale shade of robin's egg — squeezed her brother's human body until Hel heard the creak of bone.

"Jorm!" She yelled, itching to help, but the thunderous vibration of hundreds of giants, frost, and fire, poured across the Nevada sands. Hel peeked through the sweat-soaked curtain of her hair as Surt strode between them, puffed up and preening as he swaggered through the ranks of his army. The stunted jackass wore a victorious smirk on his face, considering the battle already won. Much as she wanted to smack the look off his face, the gods themselves had difficulty against the giants, and the two godlings were so very outnumbered. Hel wondered if Odin and the fam were watching them, witnessing their supposed enemies fighting to save the world.

A lone crow flew overhead. Its distant caw reached her ears. She tracked it out of the corner of her vision, unwilling to look away from the gloating fire giant. *Of course*, they were being watched. Unwilling to help, the gods were probably watching to see who would emerge the winner.

"So much for the cavalry," Hel muttered.

Surt stopped a few yards away, well out of melee range, the coward. "You could still join us, Sister Death, Brother Serpent." He grinned at Jormungand pinned in the Jotunn's hold. "The war *is* coming. Our side will emerge the victor, whether you are a part of it or not."

He sounded so certain as if their fates truly were chiseled in stone. Hel glanced at her brother. Why hadn't he shed his human form? Was he stuck? If there was ever a time to let out his scaly side, it was now. Jorm was looking straight at her, his pupils mere slits.

He was waiting for her signal. Hel swallowed, realized *she* was the one stalling. She wasn't certain they would live through this battle. After centuries of existing alone in the Underworld, she hadn't had much of a shot at living. For a moment, her resolve faltered. What had the gods ever done to deserve her loyalty? Why should she throw her lot in with either side? She should let the idiots fight it out while she enjoyed what pleasures she could find topside for as long as possible.

Hel pulled up short at the memory of a touch. Ives's touch, her arms wrapped around her, a freely given embrace *before* Hel had a glamour. Hel looked at her hands, one normal one shaded by the contours of a skeletal tattoo. She liked the human, truly liked her. Ives might be the first being Hel would call a friend.

It was a bond worth fighting for.

The crow cawed overhead. A single black feather floated down between her outstretched hands. She snatched it out of the air without a thought.

Remember who you are.

Hel twirled the feather between her fingers. She was the daughter of Loki. Goddess of the Underworld. Queen of the dead. The glossy black feather appeared to drink in the light around it, emanating the familiar chill of the Underworld. Hel smiled.

She looked up at Surt, and the surrounding fire giants slowed their advance, clearly unsettled.

"I am afraid we must respectfully decline," she said.

Her glamour cracked, peeled, and fell away in curling flakes. Her empty eye socket lit up from within, a glowing pearl white flame, the same shade as mortal lifelines. The giants took a unified step backward as the ground beneath her feet lost color and bleached to a dreary gray. The gray spread and seeped into the sands. Jormungand seized on the moment and shed his human form, crushing the Jotunn beneath his bulk as his body grew and grew until he surrounded them in the scaled embrace of the World Snake.

The giants' scent began to shift, the stink of fear tainting the air. They'd seen nothing yet.

"*Come,*" whispered Hel. Her voice echoed through the empty marble halls, answered by a thousand mortals shades eager for violence.

The sands writhed as the first skeletal hand tore through the crust of the earth.

⚱ ⚱ ⚱

Hildr rolled over damp leaves and branches as she attempted to shove the dead goddess away. Growling and spitting in her face, Sigyn clawed at her and left deep gouges in Hildr's golden skin. Hardly becoming behavior for a divine being, deceased or not.

Sigyn was plucked off her within a few seconds. Fenrir carted her away by the waist as she continued to rant and rave. Silence fell as Hildr placed the bloodied sword tip at her throat.

Sigyn attempted to blink, a strange sight with her empty eye sockets. "My eyes! Where are my eyes?" Her voice echoed, her soul still clung to the halls of the afterlife.

Hildr's grip tightened on the hilt. "Who freed Loki from his bonds?"

Sigyn paused before she descended into wails once again and tossed her head to the side. "My eyes! Where are my eyes?"

"Answer the question," Fenrir growled in her ear.

Sigyn froze, her mouth slack in her shock. "Fenrir?"

Static sparked along Hildr's skin. Sigyn was not surprised by Fenrir's human form. What other secrets had the wife of Loki kept? How many could Hildr pry out of her before the reanimation wore out? Only one mattered.

"Who freed Loki?"

Sigyn paused again. Her mouth worked without sound as Hildr pushed her will on the dead goddess.

Her blonde head shook back and forth in a frantic motion, panic in the rapid twitch of her fingers. "I can't. I can't. He'll kill me. He'll kill me," she moaned.

"Sigyn," Hildr said, "you are already dead."

Sigyn appeared to consider her words but still, the goddess hesitated, the fear evident in her shaking form. The reaction spooked Hildr. Few things scared the dead.

"He's here," Sigyn said.

Fenrir snarled. He threw Sigyn aside as he dove over Hildr, his body a shield to the crystal arrow aimed at the

Valkyrie's back. He fell with a cry of pain. The shaft protruded between his ribs.

"Damn fool wolf," Hildr muttered. She eased him off her gently as she could. The arrow was high, and the angle was bad. She sucked air through her teeth as she hovered over her fallen companion, her sword raised and ready to defend.

A hooded figure stepped from the shadows. The folds of his cloak shifted to reveal the two horns that hung at his waist. She recognized one. It was unmistakable. The Gjallarhorn. Her blood turned to sludge in her veins.

The betrayal of it shook her to her core. Her vision swam as rage and sadness hummed through her. The strength left her arm, dragging her blade down to the dirt.

"The All-Father trusted you," she said. A tear fell down her face.

The hooded figure leveled a crossbow at her face, another crystal arrowhead primed and aimed at her heart. Was this how the first generation of Valkyries met their end? She understood now why none of them saw death's approach, wearing the face of the All- Father's right-hand man.

The crossbow fired.

☗ ☗ ☗

Jules wandered through the shadowy corridor of the In-Between. Urgency tugged her footsteps forward. She could sense the conflict unfolding, but her thoughts continued to tumble over her brief interaction in the realm of the Fates.

An unbound fae is not welcome here.

The words puzzled Ives. Despite the bond between them, there were pieces of knowledge Jules had never divulged to her friend. She was too ashamed.

An unbound fae, her fate stripped away, her face and name scraped from the memory of her people, including her own. She'd wandered, aimless, nameless, lost in the fog of the Well and truly forgotten, unable to recall who and what she truly was. She should have faded. That was what happened to the banished fae, but Ives had found her instead. It was such a simple thing. Jules doubted the untried Fate Cipher realized what she was doing as she grasped the severed thread of a lone fae to reel her in. The action wove their essence together, grounding the fae to Ives's plane of existence. 'Jules' was another gift, the name of Ives's favorite mortal author.

Ives never knew the truth about the state she found Jules in. She operated under the assumption something terrible had been done to the fae. In her heart of hearts, Jules knew the opposite was true. A Fae was unbound only for unforgivable crimes.

If they managed to make it out of this mess alive, she would have to tell Ives the truth. If the children of Loki lured the giants out of the city, though, she would be walking back into a hairy situation. The thought of Jormungand in danger made the muscles in her chest go tight. She focused on the siblings and blurred through reality to their location.

Chaos greeted her. Flames and ice ripped through the air. The giants were engaged in a heated battle, batting at a relentless army of—

Jules's jaw dropped. Her stomach rolled in protest at the sight of so many corpses in various states of decay. Did she leave Ragnarök to come back to the zombie apocalypse? She scanned the battlefield and caught sight of Hel in full deathly glory. *Sweet giblets, the goddess was terrifying.* Hel appeared to float above the ground. Her clothes had morphed into a ghostly shroud that clung to her half-formed figure. She wielded a wicked-looking scythe. Wherever she swung it, a giant took a dirt nap. Where was Jorm?

The ground rumbled beneath Jules's feet. She looked up, and up; her breath left in a gasp. Jormungand had shed his human skin, and his massive form was coiled around the whole of the battlefield, acting as a natural barrier that contained the giants and the dead. Giants swarmed him. Burns and gashes marred the length of his scales. For the most part, the siblings were holding their own, but that wasn't what Jules noticed. Her eyes zeroed in on the vertically challenged Surt, who tossed flaming spheres of fire into Jormungand's face with the aim to blind him.

Her lungs seized. *Like, hell.* Jules raced across the field, her blade clenched between her teeth as she dodged and vaulted her way through the battle. There were advantages to being small. In the space of a few minutes, she'd crossed to Jormungand's flank where her deft fingers found the chinks in his scales to pull herself up. She raced along his back when it happened.

Surt got in a perfect hit, a molten globe of rock and fire straight in Jorm's eye. Jules nearly lost her footing and knife as he writhed, his body crushed giant and risen dead alike. She held on for dear life. Tears pricked at her eyes as he roared in pain. She was going to murder that squat fire giant.

Jorm was falling. Her heart froze at the sight of him swaying before his upper body crashed into the sands and knocked half the field off their feet.

Please don't be dead, please don't be dead, she chanted in her head as she jumped into a sprint. Her feet blurred; she charged the blissfully unaware Surt as he conjured another sizzling ball of rock and fire. He remained unaware of her presence until the very moment she landed on his head and plunged her dagger in his eye.

TWENTY-FIVE

FAMILY REUNION

"WHO IS THIS?" Ives stepped closer to the tapestry of Ragnarök. She reached to touch the figure when instinct veered her fingers away. Her gut twisted. Something about the figure was familiar, like trying to place someone she'd seen once in a crowd. She turned to Loki. "Do you know who—"

She stopped and stared. The god was steaming. Literal smoke curled off him as his eyes glowed in his skull. His rage was breathtaking. Ives would never want to be on the receiving end of such wrath.

"I never saw it before," Loki said with silken menace, "but I wasn't meant to."

Ives looked at the tapestry again, following the path of the figure's appearance as it wove through the whole picture in a serpentine fashion. She was so focused on the hooded cloak that she stumbled on the reveal, the cowl pulled back from off his white shining face. His woven smile conveyed a vile undertone, but it was the gold thread of his teeth that made the hair rise on the back of her neck.

"I know him," she said. "He brought me to Vegas,

helped me escape the others…" She trailed off as the Trickster's wrathful gaze swung toward her.

"Helped you?" Loki's eyes narrowed. "Why would he risk you undoing his creation?"

Ives swallowed, her throat tight as she realized exactly why the gilded god had sent her on her merry way. She remembered Jormungand's intent to kill her, the dark threads driving him to destroy the Fate Cipher. The puppet failed, so the puppeteer tried a more direct tactic, the very same Pele warned her about.

"He didn't expect me to survive the attempt," said Ives.

She didn't look at Loki, though she felt the wave of heat that simmered off him. The god had a temper. She remembered what Hildr told her, the reason Loki was punished. Killing the Beloved One. So far, Ives judged the god through his children, but she was acutely aware of how very little she knew of his mythological history. She forgot he was the Norse god of fire until she saw him burst into flames in the casino.

What if he *had* killed the Beloved? Who was the Beloved? If that was the event that precipitated Loki's punishment, it was an important detail. Her eyes read the tapestry from the beginning, where the gods gathered 'round a great table laden with food. Everyone appeared joyous, their faces woven with expressions of laughter and ease. At the center was a god whose beauty, all golden hair and Adonis features, outshone all others. Loki offered him a flowering plant. In the next scene, it was chaos, the expressions frozen in shock. The beautiful god lay dead, an arrow stuck in his chest and the innocuous flower tied to its shaft.

"How did it start?" Ives's voice was soft as she pointed to the slain god. "What happened to him?"

"The Beloved, Baldr."

The heat at her back vanished. She turned to find Loki on his knees, his eyes full of regret.

"It wasn't supposed to happen. It wasn't supposed to go so wrong," he rasped. He stared at the scene, his expression distant, caught in an ancient memory. "I don't remember why I offered the mistletoe. I thought it would give him a scratch, a small annoyance. He was supposed to be invulnerable. The arrow flew straight and true, a perfect shot by Hodur, his brother. Too perfect for a blind god." Loki looked up at her. "I didn't mean to—I didn't *want* to kill him."

Ives stared at the tapestry once more. She focused on the arrow in Baldr's chest and the black thread that trailed from it.

"I don't think you did." She pointed to the thread. "His influence is here too, guiding the arrow. This whole prophecy is like one big frame job."

"What are you saying," said Loki. He gazed at the tapestry for several minutes, studying the tale as the revelation flashed through his features. "That bastard. He will pay for this." The promise of violence in his tone made her shiver.

"I'm sure he will, big guy, but now that we know he's behind this whole mess, why don't we just tell the other gods? Topple this whole scheme before it comes to fruition. It can't happen if they know the truth," she said.

She looked at Loki and jumped. There was someone behind him. Three someones to be exact—more hooded figures.

"Foolish girl," said the first in an ancient voice, her words filled with venom.

"A fate so tightly woven cannot be easily undone," one spoke in a huskier voice. Her slender hands landed on Loki's shoulders.

His face went slack as the third figure stepped around him to approach Ives.

"The architect took many precautions. The *sight* of the gods is as tangled as the Trickster's was," said the last, youthful voice.

The young one stopped before Ives and grasped her face between calloused palms. "The gods will not believe you," she said.

"*Cannot* believe you," corrected the middle one.

The eldest sniffed. "Tricky bastard."

"Who are you?" Ives breathed. She could feel their power as it twisted and writhed around her. It buzzed against her teeth.

The one who cupped her cheeks tilted her hooded face. "You already know, don't you?"

Ives knew by their power, the way it pushed and pulled against her own, two magnets of opposing forces. "Yes," she whispered, "but which version?"

The three ladies chuckled.

"The Norns," said the young one.

"The Fates," said the middle one.

"The Three Witches," said the eldest. "Crone."

"Mother," said the middle one.

"And Maiden," said the youth. "All one, all the same. We are the Weavers." She released Ives and swept her fingers down the tapestry of Ragnarök. "The Trickster is *not* the Father of Lies."

"You were correct, Ikepela Ives," said the Mother. She twined her fingers through Loki's red hair.

He looked up at her, his movements lethargic, eyes glazed over.

"What will you do about it?" The Crone looked at Ives, withered hands on her hips.

Ives blinked at them. "How could you let this happen?

This is a clear interference in fate. None of this should have been allowed to unfold."

The Crone snorted. "Are you so certain it was not meant to be this way?"

The Mother had the decency to look away. "He slithered his way in with promises and sweet words."

"The gods do not like us for what we are, though our job is as important as yours," said the Maiden. "And for what we are, we are not like the gods."

It was Ives's turn to snort. "What does that even mean? Can't any of you give a straight answer? Or a simple one?"

"That upstart mucked up our work, and we cannot fix it because of our own rules," the Crone snarled. "By the gods, Ikepela Ives, why do you think we let a creature like you into our realm?"

Ives folded her arms across her chest and raised a brow at the eldest Fate. "Wow, you know how to ask a girl for help, don't you? Would a 'please' kill you? Since it *will* kill me." She finished on a mutter.

"She's not a 'creature,'" said Loki, his voice distant. It was the first time he'd spoken.

Ives realized the Mother must have had him under some sort of hypnosis, as she looked surprised by his words. Her hooded visage lifted, gaze unseen gaze as she studied Ives. The Maiden stepped in to smooth over the Crone's blunt wording.

"We do need your help, Fate Cipher," said the Maiden, her hands clasped before her "You must understand. This situation is difficult for us."

"Unheard of," said the Mother.

"We made a mistake," said the Crone.

"We cannot undo what has been done," said the Maiden, her voice solemn.

Ives knew her words were true. The reason the Fate Cipher existed was due to cosmic B.S.

"But we can offer advice," the Maiden said.

"Guidance," said the Mother.

"We know what brings you here," said the Crone. Her voice rang with disapproval.

Ives peered hard into the shadowed hollow of her hood. "Why did you imprison her?"

"She erred," said the Maiden and looked away.

"We are not allowed to sire mortal children with immortal power," said the Mother. Her voice brimmed with hidden sorrow.

Ives wondered if the Mother committed a similar 'crime' when the Crone's sharp voice slapped her in the face.

"Her dalliance upset the balance," she sneered.

The Maiden took Ives's hand, her fingers so icy they made her shudder. Her chill touch traced along the lifeline running across Ives's palm. "There is only one Fate Cipher. There has only ever been one. Until now."

"Immortal power forced into a mortal body," said the Mother.

"A body that cannot sustain such essence," sighed the Crone.

"An essence siphoned from its immortal host," the Maiden finished, her finger paused in the middle of Ives's palm.

Ives tensed. Her lifeline ended there—abruptly. Their words confirmed what she already knew, but for the first time, she felt the true inevitability of her death creeping up on her. But what did it mean for her mother? "Where is she?"

"The only place that could sustain her," whispered the Maiden, she pointed beyond Ives's shoulder.

"We know what we ask of you, Ikepela Ives. In exchange for your aid, we will grant you a boon," said the Mother, her soft voice calming. "You will take her from our realm."

Ives turned with a start. Her gaze fell on a dark tapestry, the only source of color a small keyhole in the center. A woven prison. Her feet itched to run toward it, but the Crone's warning squelched her eagerness.

"We imprisoned her, Ikepela Ives, but what you find in that dungeon was not our doing. That mystery is her own."

Ives looked between the three women. "What do you mean?"

The Mother slipped her hands over Loki's ears, her voice barely a whisper. "We see what was and what will be, but we do not see all that is. If we possessed more insight than foresight, we would not be in such a mess."

The omission, oddly enough, dispersed some of Ives's anger. She looked at Loki, his eyes vacant beneath the Mother's influence. His ears were still covered.

Ives cleared her throat. "I'll fix your mess, and I'll take my mom home because she never should have been imprisoned here in the first place," she said. She stared at the Crone in particular. "But I'll do this because you ladies royally screwed up his fate and his families'. If you owe anyone from this mess, you owe a boon to the Trickster." For a second she thought Loki's eyes flickered in her direction.

The three Fates fell silent.

Then the Maiden spoke. "What sort of boon?"

"You could fix his kids, for starters," said Ives. "Were they truly born monsters?"

The Crone snickered.

The Mother spoke with hesitation. "Your theory is

correct. The children of Loki have long been cursed, but this has already been broken by another."

Ives blinked in surprise. "But who—"

"We will bear witness," said the Crone. "When the Shining God's plot is laid bare, we will speak on behalf of Loki Laufison."

Ives rolled her eyes. Shoddy as it was, this was the best offer she was going to get from the divine trio. "Fine."

"Ikepela, a final piece of advice," said the Mother. The other two looked at her like she'd spoken out of turn, but she pressed on. "You are a Fate Cipher through your mother, but it is not the only bloodline you possess." Her hands moved off Loki's ears. "You are also a child of Pele." Ives stared at the Mother, wondering if she deliberately allowed the Trickster to hear those last words.

The three women winked out as if they'd never been there at all. She hated how gods did that. Loki shook himself as he climbed to his feet. His expression was far too thoughtful for someone who'd supposedly spent the conversation checked out.

Ives sighed. "How much did you hear? How did you even hear through their whammy?"

Loki raised an eyebrow at her. "A Trickster has his ways." He didn't even acknowledge her other question.

Ives made a sound of disgust, ready to get the hell out of this place and as far away from the Fates as physically possible. She approached the dark tapestry and dubiously eyed the keyhole. "How am I supposed to get in there?"

"Do I honestly need to point out who you are, Fate Cipher?"

Ives hunched her shoulders. "Right." She reached for her power, burying her shock before the perceptive god noticed. Granted, not much time had passed since she'd used her gift on Loki, but it flickered and waned, little better than fumes. It wasn't replenishing. It wouldn't replenish, just continue to use her lifeline until she burned it up.

She couldn't worry about that now, though. She had to free her mother, and they had an apocalypse to stop. She shoved a wisp of energy into the keyhole and heard a physical click as the tumblers unlocked. She stepped back at the grinding sound, wide-eyed as the darkness seeped away to reveal a room.

An empty one.

"Where is she?"

"Why don't we step inside and find out?" said Loki. Before Ives could scoff at the idea he stepped forward and entered the tapestry. He turned to her. "Coming?"

She scrambled after him and met no resistance as she walked into a world made of thread. Or was it? She tentatively ran her fingers down the wall. It *felt* like stone. Ives decided she didn't need to understand how as she looked for her mom. There was a door in the wall she'd touched. She opened it to a sunlit hallway. The air was balmy with a familiar hint of brine in the air.

"I smell the ocean," she said. She rushed forward. There were no windows or doors in the hall, but the sunlight persisted nonetheless. Her steps echoed. She stopped as the hall opened into a large barren room with a single bay window.

Loki followed, silent beside her.

The glass provided a view of her island home, unmarred by battles with giants and the children of gods. A woman leaned against the wall as she looked out at the view, her face hidden by the play of light and shadow.

"Mom?" Ives's voice wavered.

The woman turned with a start, her expression one of

shock. "Ikepela?" Her mother ran to her. The light revealed her face as she enveloped Ives in a fierce hug.

Ives stood frozen, equally shocked by the sight of her. The streaks of gray in her hair, the lines at the corner of her eyes. Keawe had aged dramatically compared to the flawless youthful complexion Ives had seen only three years ago.

Her mother was *mortal.*

TWENTY-SIX

THE 11TH HOUR

HILDR REFUSED to avert her gaze as the crystal arrowhead sped toward her. If she was going to meet her death, she would stare it in the face like a true Valkyrie. She'd failed in her mission. She'd failed the Fate Cipher. Ives... Her throat tightened when she realized all her new friends would fall, Ives would fail and die in doing so. All their efforts would fail because none of them had suspected such a foe. Not one Odin trusted so much.

The arrow flew straight and true as it winnowed for her heart.

Sigyn leaped in front of her with a wail. The dead goddess absorbed the arrow and dissolved into a brilliant blinding light.

Run.

The goddess's final whisper spurred Hildr to action. She slung the wounded son of Loki over her shoulder as she bolted. Adrenaline lent her strength. The hooded one cursed behind her. The leaves crackled as he pursued them. Hildr's sharpened hearing caught the whine of a crossbow drawing tight. Another bolt would strike her in the back. She could not flee him unscathed. She braced herself at the twang of the bowstring. Fenrir hissed and bucked, toppling them both as a second bolt slammed down in front of her.

Hildr rolled. They couldn't run. They couldn't win. She lifted her sword and bared her teeth, facing off against the hooded one. "What have you done?" She screamed the question, her hilt bit into the palm of her hand as her enemy approached her, another bolt loaded and aimed for her chest. Was she fast enough to block the arrow of a god? "What other little atrocities have you committed in the shadows, Bright One?"

She sought to distract him, but he was unrelenting. As he approached, the realization dawned on her. To kill Sigyn, to wield the horn—it meant events had been unfolding long, long before Ragnarök. For a moment she felt the whisper of threaded rope around her neck, an unseen noose that tightened. No matter how many knots the Fate Cipher unraveled, Ragnarök would claim them all.

A snarl ripped the air as a massive wolf sailed over her, a shadow that blotted out the moon. The hooded god fired. Hildr stood, stunned as the bolk skimmed along Fenrir's long jaw and sank into his neck. The son of Loki ignored his wounds, intent on his prey. He clamped his jaws on the hooded god's shoulder. The two tumbled in a blur of motion, so fast her sight couldn't follow what happened. She only knew the victor when the wolf broke away with a high yelp of pain. Blood splashed on the leaves as Fenrir stumbled away. Two arrows protruded from his flank, but it was the slash across his throat, in a grisly smile, that disabled him. The hooded god crouched over him, dagger raised to strike again, to kill the feral son of Loki. The godling's animal form melted away as she watched, revealing his unconscious human form. The *innocent* son of Loki. The injustice of it fueled the rage in her veins, broke through her inaction as thunder rumbled high overhead. Static sparked and crackled along her skin.

Hildr shrieked and stabbed her sword at the cloudless sky. The scent of ozone filled the air a moment before a bolt of lightning shot down. She flung it at the hooded god as she charged forward. It was a final desperate play, her last move before the end. The lightning hit him square in the chest. The total sum of her efforts caused the hooded god to shuffle back a few feet. He remained standing.

She continued forward, undaunted. "For Asgard!"

Neither of them saw the horse.

That damn tripod of a stallion appeared in a gust of smoke and fog. It reared up and slammed a hoof down on the god's wounded shoulder. Where lightning did nothing, the horse's kick knocked him on his ass. Helhest kept up the attack, hooves landing with solid *thunks*. Not enough to kill him, they weren't that lucky, but enough to keep him down.

Hildr didn't pause to thank the gods. She was too pissed at them as it was. She hauled Fenrir's too-still form onto Helhest's back. The beast barely waited for her to mount behind him before he launched them into the sky.

Hildr could have kissed the foul-smelling creature. "Take us to your mistress," she gasped. She prayed the godling's divine healing would save him. She nervously watched the uneven rise and fall of his chest as Helhest sped them along.

※ ※ ※

The hooded god grunted as he came to.

Damn that beast of Hel.

His quarry managed to flee from him, no doubt to take word to the Fate Cipher. He clenched his fists as he rose and ripped the hood free. The glow off his skin and hair lit the clearing. It was all beginning to unravel, his millennia-long revenge. He'd come too far to fail. It was time to take matters in hand. If he had to bring the halls of Asgard down to a smoking ruin himself, he would see it through to the end.

☗☗☗

Stabbing a fire giant in the eye was not one of Jules's better life choices. Or it was one of her best. It was a matter of perspective.

Jules gave Surt plenty of perspective as she rocked back and pulled the giant with her by the handle of her blade. His inhuman screech of agony was a physical caress of heat and ash against her skin. The stink of sulfur stung her nose. Surt lost his grip on the molten sphere. Jules rolled free as it splattered him in the face and left her knife embedded in his eye socket. The fire giant tumbled off Jormungand's back and out of sight. She heard him land like a sack of wet cement on the battle-torn ground.

Jules was already up and moving. She dashed for Jorm's injured face. *Oh, gods, the blood bubbling on his skin.* Why was it bubbling?

"Sweet Avalon," she swore.

A glowing red sphere was embedded in Jormungand's skull, lodged in his eye socket, still burning.

The sizzling sound terrified her. She could *see* the orb eating away at the godling's flesh. She flashed between spaces, unwilling to waste further time as she reached for the molten rock with her bare hands. No hesitation for the pain to come. The son of Loki was dying.

"We aren't finished, you and I," said Jules.

No, this was supposed to be a beginning. She'd lost too

211

much—her sense of self, her purpose, her fate. The fragile bond blossoming between herself and Jormungand was something new and unknown, and she refused to let it turn to ash.

She didn't feel the pain at first, the orb so hot her hands went numb. She felt *cold*. This was worse than the heat. The pain rode in a moment later, where her seared nerves came alive, exposed, and raw. The breath in her lungs burned as she tipped her head to the sky and screamed.

A raven's caw answered. Jules peered up at the circling bird through blurred eyes as tears spilled across her temples. The sounds of battle fell away beneath the agony and the heavy sound of her breathing. The sensation in her hands fell away, gone.

The raven coughed another sharp caw. Jules could feel her body falling as the sphere came free with a wet crackle of charred flesh.

Let go. Let go.

She didn't know if she managed to get her hands free or if they burned away. The sphere landed beside her, still flickering a dull bitter orange. It rolled up by her head, where it emanated enough heat to dry the tears on her face. She turned away and stared at the circling raven. She'd pushed her body beyond its unknown limits. Not that she believed she could handle that ball of fire unscathed. She knew it would hurt, but it was worth the risk.

Was he still dying?

Jules wanted to go to him, to see if he survived, but her limbs refused to obey. Was that Hel shouting her name? She blinked, slowly, for it took so much effort to lift her eyelids. An abyss grew inside her. Jules hovered at its edge; she could feel the thread that connected her to the Fate Cipher for the first time.

Wandering without seeing.

Fading from this world.

She could see through her hands when she looked down. An unbound fae, forgotten by her people, by herself. She could not remember where she came from, who she was, what she was. Her fate was burned away.

"Hey, are you lost?" A human girl. What could she possibly do? No point in running. No point in hiding. She would fade away before the girl's eyes, their encounter a waking dream, a bizarre memory that would eventually fade as well.

Her form began to unravel. She pitched forward into the girl's arms.

"Whoa! Hang on. I got you."

Hands wrapped around her wrists. She could feel her dispersing body solidify beneath the girl's touch. Grounded to reality. The unraveling threads of her person wove back into her as the bond between them snapped into place. For an instant she saw it, braided livewire, glowing golden bright, threaded through the core of her unbound soul.

She could see it now, that brilliant thread pulled taut between them. The Fate Cipher held her to this reality still, and she refused to let her float away.

"Jules!"

Hel's face loomed over Jules's, the duality of beauty and death. The skull side of her face leered down, her single green eye stark and wide. Her human side was streaked with blood and soot. She cradled Jules's face between her hands, the brush of bone fingers against her cheek. "Hang on. I got you." Hel sobbed the words, her eye flitting between Jules and her fallen brother.

"Go to him," said Jules, her voice nothing but a cracked whisper. "Save him."

Hel exhaled a shaky breath and gently set her head on the sand. Through the trembling ground, Jules could feel the battle still raging around them. They were losing. They had already lost. The great serpent remained unmoving. How long could Hel hold the field before the giants over-whelmed her army of rot and bone? Jules's consciousness began to drift.

The warning caw of the raven jolted her awake. Hel's cry was cut short. Jules struggled to move.

Surt's ghastly visage loomed above her.

Her knife still protruded from his eye. Liquid fire trickled from the ugly wound. A drop hit her face and sizzled against her cheek. The fresh bloom of pain chased away the fog in her mind with a surge of adrenaline. Surt reached for her with a mad grin that promised horrors.

The roar hummed in her bones. A wave of scaled flesh rose around her. It encompassed the world. Jules had never seen anything so beautiful as that endless rise of white and dappled black snakeskin. The coil slammed into Surt, lifted the giant up and away from her. Jules found the strength to roll over.

She glimpsed her ruined hands, so charred it was a miracle they resembled hands at all. Gritting her teeth, she looked away. There was time for pain and loss later. There was *time*. She watched as Jormungand rose above the battlefield, coil upon coil, as he curled around the strug-gling figure of Surt. She recognized this maneuver, the same one she and Ives had narrowly escaped, but this time, Jules wasn't going to glamour him before the squeeze.

Grimly, she kept her gaze trained on Surt's struggling

form until the coils pulled tight. Jules slumped on her side as the giant's broken body fell to the sand. The great serpent was alive, and the vertically challenged little pisser got his ass squished. She'd laugh if she had the energy. She was viciously tired, so tired she couldn't remember why it was important to stay awake. The ground still trembled beneath her. Surt might be down, but there were plenty of giants to take his place.

"Jules, stay with me," said Jormungand. He was close.

She could smell him, that scent of sea salt and cool darkness, only slightly tainted by char. *She would have danced with him in the circle of sunlight with her sisters...*

Where did that thought come from?

Jules didn't have any sisters, right? Was her bond with Ives fraying at last? Her body was so weak.

"Mother Angerboda, no." Jormungand's fingers were cool against the fevered skin of her arms. They stopped just below her elbow. She could feel the tremor in his hands. Hands? He was human again?

Her gaze focused. Human indeed—one eye a burnt ruin, his features drawn and scared, but still beautiful. She gave him a tired smile. "You changed back on your own," she whispered.

"Yes," he said. He gently shifted her head in his lap. "Please stay." His shaking fingers brushed the burn on her cheek, a kiss of frost on the wound.

"Can I stay?"

He looked stricken by her question. She was certain she would have faded already if not for her bond to Ives. She closed her eyes, searching for it, as Jormungand called her name over and over.

"Jorm, we're in trouble." Hel's strained voice sounded distant. "I lost control for too long. The dead are falling."

The trembling ground beneath them settled into the

thunderous pound of approaching footsteps. The giants were coming for them. Jorm was still huddled over her. Why wasn't he fighting? Or running?

There, glimmering deep within, she could feel the golden wire—Ives anchoring her soul. It was not faded but brighter than before. It blazed with light. The thread expanded, doubled, tripled in size until an answering jolt of energy shot through her and filled her with that rich golden light. It leaked from her pores and rippled over her. Her hands tingled with the sensation of a thousand insects crawling over her skin.

Jules opened her eyes to behold the horde of fire giants bearing down on them. A ball of power rolled and crackled in her belly, fueled by the golden strength that poured from her bond to the Fate Cipher. Anchored to who she used to be. How dare they set foot into her realm? She dug her stinging hands into the sand and called to the earth.

The earth answered.

"Odin's Balls," Hel yelped as the rumbling ground took on a different cadence, a song of tumbling rock and soil. Giants stumbled to a halt as the earth cracked open around them. The rifts spread in yawning cavernous mouths and swallowed them up. Those with any sense fled, desperate to outrun the hungry earth, but the sand sucked at their legs, pulling them down into the suffocating depths of the desert. The roiling ground did not stop until every last giant sank into the earth below, leaving the remnants of Hel's army.

Jules stood as she released the earth. The desert wind blew through her curls, teased her memory. She could feel the satisfied harmony of the earth beneath her soles.

"It was you," breathed Hel.

Jules looked up at the flabbergasted goddess of death.

"That gout of steam from the earth in those snowy

woods. I thought Ives somehow drew on Pele, but it was you." Hel's single eye roamed Jules's face, full of awe and curiosity. "You're no brownie."

"Nope," said Jules, unwilling to elaborate on the painful subject. She braced herself and turned to Jormungand.

His expression was unreadable. Only his widened pupil gave away the depth of his emotional turmoil. "You're okay?" He asked in a strained whisper.

Jules held up her hands, the skin glazed with new scar tissue, but healed. She smiled, ready to offer a reassuring quip when he seized her, crushed her to his chest. She squeaked as he enveloped in sea salt and cool dark places. No, she wasn't done with him in the slightest.

Hel sighed. "Adorable."

Jules reached around Jorm's broad shoulders and flipped off the goddess of death.

Hel snickered. "As sweet as that is, darling, we still have an apocalypse to stop. Or did you think that was all the giants?"

That got Jules's attention. "Sweet Mab, how many more are there?"

Hel blinked at her. "Did you just say *Mab?*"

Jules ignored her question. "How many more, Hel?"

"Too many," said Jormungand.

"They'll be drawn to Dad like a beacon," said Hel with a grimace.

"Ives should have called for me by now," said Jules. She wondered what Ives sensed on her side of the bond. Had she drained her friend further? The thought terrified her.

"Are you sure you didn't miss it? We were all a tad preoccupied." Hel shrugged, the skeletal side of her body fading into tattooed skin with ease.

Neither of Loki's children needed her to glamour them again. *What did that mean?*

"I would have felt it," said Jules as she absently rubbed her chest. "We should go to them." She wouldn't let those snobby jerks turn her away again if she had to bring the realm down around their ears.

Hel glanced at her brother. "You up for kicking the Fates in the ass?"

Jorm raised the brow of his good eye. "You have the oddest turns of phrase, sister."

"Let's ROFL-stomp those noobs," said Hel and fist-pumped the air.

Jules grinned as she wrapped her arms around the siblings and hauled them into the In-between.

☖☖☖

Keawe held her daughter tight against her as if trying to regain the lost embraces between them. Ives could feel the differences, the new fragility in her mother's frame.

What you find in that dungeon is beyond our doing.

"You're mortal. How are you mortal?" Ives murmured, shell-shocked.

Her mother stiffened, drawing back to peer hard in her face. Anger bled into her expression. "So are you," she said, the anger faded as fast as it appeared, replaced by a worry that drew deeper lines around her mouth. She cupped her daughter's face. Her jaw quivered as she spoke. "They promised me. They promised they'd give it to you."

"Give me what?" Though Ives suspected the answer, she needed to hear it. The hope of answers, of help from the woman who'd served as Fate Cipher for millennia, sank to the pit of her stomach. She felt sick as her mother's face crumpled.

"My immortality," said Keawe. "They promised to save you."

Ives swallowed hard, keenly aware of her godly audience. "Who promised you, Mom?"

Keawe shook her head, tears streaked down her face. Ives resisted the urge to shake her. How could she fix this? She couldn't. There was no fixing this. Her mother shoved this impossible calling into her lap and left her mortal daughter at the mercy of a power she couldn't control or... or...

Ives stared at her mother, stared at the lines, and creases on her face—older, but still the same face her father loved despite decades apart. What would have happened to Ives if her mother hadn't willingly gone? Her mother, who gave up her *immortality* to save her baby girl.

The hurt she'd held for so long drained away with a sob. She leaned forward, touched foreheads with her mother. Their tears mingled with one another's.

"Who took it, Mom?"

"She can't say," said Loki, his tone subdued. "Likely from a geas."

Her mother went still, she tilted her face toward the Trickster as if she noticed him for the first time. "Loki Laufison," said Keawe with a surprising amount of venom. "You should not be here."

"That's not his doing," said Ives as she pulled away. "You might not be aware of this, but Ragnarök is in full swing upstairs—"

Keawe whirled on Loki. "You cannot ask her to undo it," she snapped, her voice laced with panic.

"Mom!"

"I know," said Loki. He leaned casually against the wall with his arms crossed.

"I'm standing right here!" Ives glared at him, irate at the both of them for making choices for her. "When did you come to that decision?"

"Do you think I couldn't sense your struggle to open this prison?" There was a quiet resignation in Loki's voice. "When the fates gave their leave to free your mother, I believed they saw no reason to keep a *mortal* under lock and key."

Ouch. She fought to keep her temper. "This wasn't her fault either," said Ives. Her mother couldn't have known how disastrous losing her immortality would be or that the mystery third party would filch on their end of the bargain. The whole situation left her furious and helpless. Her words tipped the Trickster over the edge.

Loki pushed off the wall. His anger scorched the air. "No, of course not. Instead of releasing the real Fate Cipher to do her job, we're left with a useless mortal," he snapped.

Ives's clenched her jaw so hard her teeth whined in protest. "Are you referring to her or me?"

Loki stormed out of the room. Ives watched him go, not sure if she wanted to cry or scream at him. As much as she understood it, she hated that he lashed out. Her mother was supposed to be their Hail Mary pass—immortal, powerful, able to take on the burden. Instead, they were looking at another shit scenario. Ragnarök would kill Ives if she tackled it. Even if she tapped into another god's immortal strength, it would blow her apart. Or Loki would choose to sacrifice himself after being imprisoned and manipulated for centuries, after finally finding his family again.

"I can see the conflict on your face, my heart. I missed your childhood, but I have shared your burden," said Keawe. She gripped Ives's chin. She met her mother's gaze, eyes the same color as the sea.

Her mother was mortal, but while she couldn't take over the Fate Cipher responsibilities, Keawe could be the teacher she desperately needed.

"How do I survive this, Mom? Please, I don't know what to do," Ives pleaded. "It's so exhausting."

Keawe's expression was bleak. "An immortal Fate Cipher's power replenishes on its own. They draw from the well of endless energy that comes with infinite life. As a mortal, you are burning the wick of your life hot and fast each time you access your power." She sighed and worried her lip as she studied Ives's face. "If I drained myself in the line of duty, I could tap into another immortal's energy to replenish."

Ives fidgeted. "I tried that. It didn't end well."

"Mortals weren't designed to channel such energy. I take it your *dear Auntie* kept you from blowing yourself up?"

"Yes, Pele stopped it." Ives made a face. "I can't imagine ever calling her Auntie anything."

"She has been the steward of your father's family for generations, the direct descendants of her mortal sibling," said Keawe. She sighed through her nose. "Never approved of me, either." Her expression turned thoughtful. "You are also a child of her line."

The middle Fate, the Mother, mentioned the very same thing. "Maybe, but I don't know how to tap into it either," said Ives.

"Then it is time we ask Auntie why," said Keawe.

Ives sucked on her teeth. It felt like she just experienced a celestial run-around. All these immortal and godly bloodlines sure looked fancy on paper, but in practice, she got the stubby end of the stick on both sides. If this was a possible solution, why hadn't Pele mentioned it in their previous encounter?

"I could have been playing with lava this whole time? I feel cheated," said Ives.

Her mother eyed the exit the Trickster stormed out. "I can't, in good conscience, let you pursue my path." She smiled, it erased the age from her lovely face. "But if you're anything like me, you will follow my path because you choose to, warnings and consequences be damned."

Ives's smile wobbled but held. "Guess I take after you more than I thought."

"Oh, don't worry," Keawe said and tweaked her nose. "I see plenty of your father's stubbornness, too." Her eyes crinkled at the mention of Lavi, the warmth and affection were genuine.

"He waited for you," Ives blurted. "He never looked at another woman."

This time, Keawe's smile trembled. "I don't deserve him."

"He deserves to be happy," said Ives. She bit her lip. She could understand her mother's hesitation, kept from the ones she loved for so long. She'd spent a lifetime angry at this woman simply for saddling her with her existence. "Mom, let's go home."

TWENTY-SEVEN

NOBODY THROWS A TANTRUM
LIKE A PISSED OFF DIETY

With Keawe on her arm, now was as good a time as any to get the 4-1-1 on the irritable Trickster.

"Mom, what do you know of Loki?"

Her mother squeezed her arm. "The All-Father once called him brother—not by blood, but by choice. They swore their oath to one another using the oldest of words, the wise king and the son of Laufi, the brute. Loki never accepted the limitations of his birth. That wit and charm caught Odin's eye. He wasn't simply a trickster but a master storyteller, and no matter what ruckus he caused, everyone loved him." Keawe frowned. "Though there was one…"

"One what?"

"One of the gods. They didn't like him, a hatred bordering on obsession."

Ives skin tingled. "Yes, I know."

They found Loki pacing in front of Ragnarök's tapestry. If he glared at it any harder, it would likely burst into flame. That would set the whole place on fire, not to mention earn the wrath of the Fates. Good luck getting them to bear witness if the Trickster torched their studio.

Ives worried her lip as she watched him. Loki wasn't long for this world. The moment he stepped foot outside this realm, the bonds of Ragnarök would tighten on him until he broke. All because some god had a personal beef with him.

He turned toward them as Ives and her mother walked arm in arm through the murky halls of the Fates. The haunted shadows around Loki's eyes strengthened Ives's resolve. She had to find a way around this pesky mortality problem.

Loki finally tore himself away from his masochistic musings and joined them, sheepishly bobbing his head to her. "I apologize for my outburst."

Ives snorted. "It's okay. We've been dealt a shitastic hand, and we have to make the best of it." She gave him a tight, wary smile. "It's time for plan B."

Loki raised a brow. "We have a plan B? I thought this *was* plan B."

Ives squinted at him. "Did I ask for more sass? Come on. We need to go speak to Auntie."

"*Auntie?*"

"I don't see those feet moving," called Ives.

Loki followed her, looking bemused. "You know, it's been a long time since I had the opportunity to banter with a mortal. I shall miss it."

"You'll have another chance," Ives murmured. She ground to a halt and detached herself from her mother, staring at the tapestry with the circle of the dancing fae, the center of the image destroyed by something deeper and darker than any flame. Ives stared into that melted mess of fibers and reached out to touch a small section that had escaped destruction.

"Ives?"

"Nothing. It's nothing," she said.

Loki didn't press her. Ives couldn't help but glance back, once, twice, at the destroyed tapestry. There were more pressing issues to deal with, for one, but she needed to commit it to memory.

There neared the end of the hall when the antechamber erupted in a shouting match.

"You can't be here, not with these...these miscreants."

"Buddy, I will make you eat that headdress if you don't get out of my way." Hel's snarl spurred them forward.

"Nobody calls my spawn miscreants but me," said Loki.

Ives caught sight of Hel and Jorm, worse for wear but alive, as they loomed over the same harried kahuna who'd met them coming in. Her heart squeezed with relief when she saw Jules's diminutive form weaving between them.

That feeling fled as Ives took stock of their injuries. Hel boasted several small scorch marks on her clothes and arms, but Jormungand fared much worse. His single good eye stared listlessly at the ground, the other a charred ruin. He clung to Jules's hand like a delicate lifeline.

"Holy shit. What happened?" Ives rushed toward the trio.

Loki brushed past her and caught Jorm as he rocked back on his feet. The kahuna squeaked and jumped away.

Ives ignored him and gasped as she caught sight of Jules's fresh scars. "Jules, your hands!"

"You should see the other guys," said Hel. She wiped a smear of ash off her cheek. Tears blurred Ives's vision.

Ives snagged the goddess and pulled her into a fierce hug, shocked by Hel's wet sniffle against her collar bone.

"You monstrous lot will not set foot in this realm," the kahuna shouted over them.

"Uh-oh," said Ives.

The air around Loki began to boil.

"On whose authority?" Keawe's voice was a cold snap that had the kahuna sinking to the floor.

He bowed to the older woman. "Sine Nomine—"

"It's Keawe Ives," she snapped, "wife of Lavi Ives."

The kahuna paled. "His wife?"

"Whoa, Mama Ives," said Hel. She lifted her head to watch the interaction as the kahuna's swarthy face turned an unhealthy mottled purple.

Keawe scowled at him; Ives was shocked by how much they looked alike. "Those bitches never bother to tell you? Typical."

"And it's time to go," said Ives. She hesitated as she eyed the bedraggled trio. "Er, think you're up for all of us, Jules?"

"No need," said Keawe, imperious as she bore down on the cowed kahuna. "Open the way home."

"Please," said Ives. She glared at her mother.

"I-I-don't think I'm allowed," the kahuna stammered.

Loki ignored the lot of them as he slipped an arm around Jormungand's shoulder. Jorm gratefully leaned his weight on his father. His wounded eye was already healing, but Ives would bet money he would still have a wicked scar. She slid a look at Jules, who watched the big guy with an intent expression on her face. *Apparently, fae chicks dug scars.*

"I might be able to take us," said Jules, clearly as exhausted as the rest of them.

Loki snorted. "Don't burden yourself, fae. We aren't utterly useless. I'll take us."

Jules stared at him through eyes like slits. "Do you know where we're going?"

Smoke curled off his shoulders. "The Fate Cipher will inform me of the location."

"I miss my horse," said Hel.

As if on cue, Helhest burst through the barrier between worlds. His hooves skittered as he tried to gain purchase on the smooth stone. Hildr clung to his back for dear life while the bloodied and unconscious Fenrir rolled free and slid across the floor.

Hel let out a short keening gasp as she rushed forward. "No, no, no, no."

"What happened?" Loki barked at the Valkyrie as she tumbled gracelessly off Helhest's back.

The three-legged creature ambled around, fascinated by his surroundings.

The appearance of Helhest was too much for the kahuna. "Blasphemy! I demand you leave this realm at once."

Loki sneered at him. The man's headdress caught fire. The kahuna fled as he batted at the flames. Loki's satisfaction was short-lived.

"The Lady Sigyn is dead," muttered Hildr. She knelt on the floor where she'd fallen.

The expression on the Valkyrie's face sent a shot of ice down Ives's spine. Her spirit was broken.

"My sisters were betrayed by one they trusted."

"They weren't the only ones fooled," said Loki. The news of Sigyn's death seemed to weigh heavily on him. "She fled from under the mountain long before I was set loose. Not that I blame her. She was as much a victim of Ragnarök as the rest of us."

"He killed them," Hildr whispered. "Lady Sigyn, my sisters, and who knows how many others?" Sorrow tinged the wrath that blazed from her ice-blue eyes. "The All-Father must learn the truth."

"Are you certain he doesn't know already?" Loki stared at her as her wrath faded and the golden glow of her skin dimmed.

Ives quietly slid down beside the blonde and wrapped an arm around the blonde's shoulders. She prayed the distressed Valkyrie wouldn't sock her for the gesture, but Hildr allowed it. Her shoulder's sagged under Ives's hold.

"He attacked you when you found Sigyn." Loki examined the fletching of the bolt still embedded in Fenrir's shoulder. "Centuries later, and the arrogant bastard still uses the same arrows. We can't stay here. He might follow us to this realm like Helhest, but he's gunning for the Fate Cipher. He'll go where he can inflict the most damage to draw you out."

He looked up as Ives realized what he meant. She knew exactly where the shining god would attack.

"Lavi," gasped her mother.

Loki snapped his fingers. Helhest trotted to him, his body already stretching to accommodate their sizeable company.

"That is damn unnerving," said Ives.

"But useful," said Loki as he gently slipped his arms under his son's arrow riddled body. Fenrir was large as a human, but the god handled his bulk with ease. None of his numerous wounds was healing.

Hel suddenly gripped Ives's hand, her face stricken. Ives wished she could tell the goddess it would be okay, but it was never good when an immortal couldn't heal from their wounds.

"Everyone, hop on," said Loki.

It was an odd assembly of mortals, immortals, and gods, but Helhest appeared to sense the gravity of the situation and held still as they mounted up.

"Helhest, bring us to the home of Lavi Ives," Hel said from her seat at the rear.

Their transition between realms was surprisingly smooth. Helhest emerged onto sands far different than the

Nevada desert. The air was sultry and intoxicating, a mix of floral scents mingled with the sea.

The picture of paradise was marred by the signs of battle—deep gouges that rent the beachfront, felled palm trees and crushed vegetation, scorch marks and slowly thawing swaths of ice.

Pele emerged from a patch of burning palms. Flames danced along her skin. Her thick curls trailed black smoke. When she came close enough, they could see the flaring coals of her eyes. She stopped a few yards from them and stomped her foot. The ground cracked open to ooze molten rock.

She glared at them and planted her feet in a clear fighting stance. "You better be in your right mind, Loki Laufison, or I will sink you into the molten earth."

"My children are injured, Goddess. Allow us to pass."

Ives poked her head out from behind him. "Easy there, Auntie."

Loki stilled. "*This* is your Auntie?"

"We have bigger fish to punch in the face," said Hel as she slid off her horse to help her brothers down.

Pele raised an eyebrow before she kicked sand over the lava to stomp it out. "I suppose you have a good explanation for coming back here with that lightning rod of the apocalypse, Ikepela."

"She does," said Keawe as she slid down to the sand.

Pele stared at the mortal former Fate Cipher. "Oh, he'll be insufferable now," she snarled.

⚄ ⚄ ⚄

If Keawe wasn't convinced Lavi Ives would welcome his long-lost wife with open arms, that doubt dissipated as the group limped their way to his battered home. The Hound

229

announced their presence with booming barks that made the walls shiver. Ives was mildly amused to see the divine beast bouncing around her father like a joyful pup.

Lavi turned from sorting through a pile of logs, his expression one of naked relief when he saw Ives. His gaze shifted to the woman she had on her arm.

A range of emotions paraded across his face, from shock, to sorrow, to sheer joy as he beheld the woman he'd lost over twenty years ago. Ives stepped back and let her father sweep Keawe up in his arms. He clutched her to him with such beautiful desperation Ives had to look away. Feeling like an intruder, Ives let her parents have their private reunion as her god squad filed into Lavi's living room. The feeling doubled as she saw Loki commiserating with his three wounded children.

She swallowed as she looked around the living room. "What happened here?"

The house was far more destroyed than it had been before she'd left for Vegas.

Pele, who'd entered behind her, flapped a hand at the caved-in roof and obliterated furniture. "Minor run-in with some frost giants. They weren't partial to sticking around in the desert, so they came back here for a tussle."

She grinned, which was terrifying. Fire backlit her teeth, and there was a feral glee in her gaze that made Ives slightly uncomfortable about confronting her.

Hildr huddled in a corner away from the others and her expression vacant. She stared at nothing, her internal glow somehow dimmed. Jules was curled up against Jormungand's side. Her encounter in the desert had changed her—physically and mentally. Ives desperately wanted to take her friend aside and ask what happened to her out there, but there had been no time. There was never enough time. Hel held her brothers' hands with a sort of helplessness that hurt to watch.

The Trickster knelt by their heads, staring down at his injured children with a bleak expression. Weak as her power was, Ives could see the thick ropes of Ragnarök slowly tightening around him. It wound tighter and tighter from the moment they shifted out of the Fates' realm. How long could he continue to resist it? Days? Hours? Or worse, the mastermind behind it, the shining god, could show up to spoil the party. Her anger simmered as she remembered her encounter with that creepy, gold-toothed deity. She looked outside, worried about leaving her parents alone when he could very well show up any minute now.

She swallowed and turned to her divine aunt. "What do you know of Heimdallr?"

Pele's burning gaze flared bright. She glanced at the other godly occupants of the room with a thoughtful expression. Her sigh sent gouts of sulfurous steam from her nostrils. "A spoiled prick, but clever, too clever by half. The minor gods gossip across continents, you know, and they have nothing pleasant to say of that one. Let me guess," said Pele as she folded her arms. "A certain golden weasel has been pulling strings behind the scenes?"

"Worse," said Ives. She watched Loki's family catch their collective breaths before the final act. A respite before the end, almost cruel when they'd come so close to a true reunion after centuries of isolation and torture. "Heimdallr made Ragnarök."

What Ives couldn't understand was *why*.

Pele was silent.

Ives frowned at her, surprised by the ambiguous expression on her face. "Did you know?"

Steam flowed from Pele's nostrils. She reached between

the folds of her simple dress into an unseen pocket and held up a now-familiar piece of black and gold thread.

Ives parted her lips as a frisson of heat passed through her nerve endings. She felt the oily darkness sliding against her senses. "Where did you find it?"

"When you snapped the prophecy's hold on the great serpent," said Pele as she pinched the scrap between her fingers.

Ives could see the thread struggling. It coiled and uncoiled like a snared worm.

"Hard to pin down, and tricky," Pele said. "If I released it, it would dissolve to nothing." She looked up and met Ives's gaze with the full force of her terrible beauty. "There are only so many deities on this plane of existence, and most have been around long enough for us to recognize each other's divine signature."

Ives frowned. "When you put it like that, it sounds so bloody simple." Her frown deepened as she mulled over Pele's words. "How did he hide it so long?"

Pele sneered. "By flattering three idiots who should have known better."

The Fates. Of course. Ives's nostrils flared. "They don't have the best hindsight, do they?"

A smile twitched on Pele's lips. She tucked the thread carefully back into her unseen pockets. "To play this game for so long, Heimdallr would have been thorough in his deception. The Fates might have helped to pull the wool over the All-Father's eyes, but he's playing the long con. To create a prophecy?" Pele shook her head. "That is a rare and dangerous feat." Her molten gaze flickered to a darker umber. "Stooping to that level of hatred and treachery takes commitment. The shining god will see this to its end, one way or another."

Ives swallowed against the tightness in her throat. Her

parents hadn't let one another go, huddled together in the hall. They savored their first moment of contact in over twenty years. Twenty years they'd waited to see one another again. To be a family again.

And behind her was a family that waited centuries.

"I—" Ives took a strained breath. She wished for more time. Except time wasn't the issue. All the training in the world wouldn't save her. "I can't beat him like this."

"I told you that," said Pele. There was no smugness in her voice. "If you attempt to use your gifts once more, you will consume your lifeline."

"Could I channel another god's energy like before? Or could you lend me some of your energy to replenish mine?" Ives could hear the waver in her voice, the first crack of her strangling fear.

Pele closed her eyes, her jaw set.

Ives pressed on. "The Fates told me to remember my bloodlines—"

Pele's eyes snapped open, full of fury that made her words falter. "Did they now? What about your supposed bloodlines? You were certainly blessed by your mother's side."

The scorn in the goddess's tone made her take a step back. "What do I get from my father? He's mortal, but he has godly power—"

"He does not have the power of a god," Pele snapped. Her pupils glowed like coals in a gust of wind. "Your father's family carries a blessing, an affinity for forge and flame. That is all. It's a drop of divinity in the mortal pool."

Ives's last shred of hope evaporated. "Then why would they tell me it was important?"

"Because the Fates are malicious and cruel and easily manipulated by a silver tongue," said Pele. She stalked outside and left Ives dangling from her internal ledge.

"So much for plan B," she said. Perhaps if she'd done things differently, she could have spent all her energy on freeing Loki first, given him the power to undo the rest, except she hadn't been able to find the Trickster until Heimdallr wanted her to.

Between the tender reunion of her parents and the divine family suffering at her back, Ives keenly felt the noose of her future. She wanted to be alone. She wandered through the house and exited via her father's workshop. This was where she first encountered Heimdallr, and if he was coming for her, well, she was ready for him now.

In the end, there was no choice. Ragnarök would destroy everything in its wake. Honestly, how could she hesitate at all? What was one life against the world? This stalling, trying to find a way to survive was selfish. The Fate Cipher would go on after her death. The power would either reassert itself with her mother or pass to some other poor being. The universe would balance itself.

An 'alalā landed on the ground, half concealed by the dense, low growth. It cocked its sleek, black, head to the side and cackled at her as only crows could. The sight of it surprised her out of her morose mindset. The native crows were extinct in the wild. This had to be someone's escaped pet. Unless…

"Oh," said Ives softly. She might not be fully versed in her Norse mythology, but she grew up on the myths of her home. "Have you come to guide my soul to the cliffs of Ka Lae?" Her smile was brittle as the crow hopped around at her feet. It stared up at her with bright brown eyes. "You're a little early, but probably not by much."

"Early for what? Why in the nine realms are you out here alone?" Loki stalked toward her, his green eyes full of that breathtaking rage as he eyed the surrounding trees.

The crow shifted out of sight.

"It's all right. I'm ready," said Ives. She rubbed her arms.

Loki paused. The anger banked as his brows drew together. "Did your 'Auntie' come through with something helpful?"

Ives hesitated. Her expression must have given her away. He was in front of her in a blink.

She jerked out his reach. "I know what I have to do."

He curled his hands into fists like he resisted the urge to shake her. "No," he said, his voice low and fierce, "there has to be—"

"There isn't," said Ives. She stared down at the ground rather, unable to meet his gaze. "Why do you even care? You don't know me from Eve. We barely know each other."

"You saved my children from a horrifying fate. You risked your life repeatedly to help us. Of course, I care what happens to you. Also, my daughter would kill me." Loki released her. His brows knit. "Who is Eve?"

Ives pursed her lips. "I don't get it. What apocalypse-worthy beef does Heimdallr have with you?" She rubbed her face, slightly overwhelmed by the proximity of the Trickster thanks to the prophecy that clung to him. Without the distraction of the others, it was an angry hum against her nerves, like standing too close to a live wire. She swore she could hear it, malevolent whispers that promised her pain. She shivered, trying to shut it out.

"I wish I knew," said Loki. "He was never thrilled by my presence among the host of Asgard, but this... I never thought him capable of constructing such widespread destruction, especially to get at me."

"Well, apparently, he has a hard hate-on for you, and according to the Fates and my lovely auntie, the other gods are as bound as you are," said Ives as she let her hands fall.

She stared at the ground as another crow landed in the bushes beside the first. It cawed loudly, making her jump.

"That's weird."

A chorus of caws surrounded them.

Ives whipped around. The trees overflowed with black, feathered bodies. "What the—"

The crows launched into the air; black feathers rained as they fled. Ives caught one and twirled it in her fingers as she turned to show Loki.

The Trickster knelt on the ground, his face paler than ever. Sweat ran down his temples. He looked up at her, eyes glassy and backlit by an eerie absinthe green. "Run."

Ives blinked as Loki jerked, his body bent at painfully odd angles. The coils of Ragnarök went taut.

"You just couldn't let it take you," snarled a familiar haughty voice.

Heimdallr stepped through the trees. Oily black threads streaked with gold dangled from his pale fingers like puppet strings. Ives could see where the black bled into the slick red cords of the prophecy.

"I had everything —*everything* —under control," he seethed as he approached, pale eyes like moonstones, cracked by madness.

His gaze snapped to Ives. She froze, pinned in place. Panic made her heartbeat like a hummingbird, battered against her ribs.

Heimdallr sneered, his gold teeth sharp and feral. "And you, you should be dead by now. Too scared to die for the greater good?"

He twisted his fingers. Loki screamed, full of agony, as his skin caught fire. The earth cracked and bubbled beneath him. Ives could feel the tremors beneath her feet. *Oh, no. It was starting.* The bastard was forcing the damn apocalypse into motion. Shouting came from the house. Ives yelped as the ground lurched upward and a flat-topped spike jutted upward into Heimdallr's chest.

He flew back and slammed into the closest tree hard enough to snap the thick trunk in half. Loki sagged. He clutched the ground as he shuddered. The threads wrapped around him tighter and tighter with each passing second. The tremors continued, just as intense as before.

The workshop door slammed open as Pele stormed out, Hel and Jules on her heels. She flicked her hands and snapped the door shut behind her, right in Hel's face. Rivulets of lava coiled around her arms as she raised her hands. She shrieked in fury as she sent another rock spike at the insane god.

"Ikepela, get your mother," said Pele, her voice hoarse.

"What, now?" Ives hissed, utterly wigged-out when Heimdallr staggered to his feet. Golden blood dripped down his chin from the corner of his mouth.

"He can't stay here," spat Pele.

Ives could see the strain on Pele's face and realized she must be keeping the tremors from tearing the island apart. Heimdallr bore down on them.

But what was her mother, fresh in mortality, going to do about it?

"I don't understand. Mom can't do anything—"

Pele stomped her foot, the earth rolled in a wave and knocked Heimdallr down. The shaking grew worse for a second while her attention wavered. Even a goddess couldn't keep this up for long.

"I'll force a transference," said Pele through gritted teeth. "She already said yes."

Ives froze. The horror of the situation bowled over her. She'd just accepted the whole dying crap, and here was her mother, prepared to take the bullet for her.

Leaving her dad alone. Again.

"No," whispered Ives.

"Ikepela, go," shouted Pele.

The goddess clapped her hands together. The surrounding palm trees crashed down on Heimdallr. Not to be out done, he shouted and snatched at the air. Loki jerked to his feet with the knock-knee movements of a living marionette. Fire dripped from his slackened hands, blackening the ground and burning the surrounding plants to ash.

It was now or never. Ives reached for her power, ignoring the watery tremor that invaded her limbs as she called it forth. Her life force guttered and wavered.

"Ike, no," Pele shouted at her.

The ground bucked beneath their feet. Ives staggered, her concentration broken. She swung her arms for balance. The crow's feather was still clutched in one hand, trailing wisps of rainbow-colored light.

What the hell?

Despite the surrounding chaos, Ives looked closer at the feather. The wisps of rainbow grew thicker as she watched, trailing upward. A caw sounded in the air, drawing her gaze to the circling crow, so peacefully at odds with the unfolding events on the ground. Higher above, she saw a spark, like a falling star descending to earth. No, not falling. The spark was on a collision course and approaching fast.

"Remember my heritage," Ives whispered. *An affinity for fire and flame.* She clutched the feather tight and flung herself at the burning Trickster.

She seized him around the waist as the air fizzed. Streams of kaleidoscopic color, every shade of the rainbow, surrounded them. Loki's flames licked her skin. It was a strangely gentle warmth to the electric sizzle of energy that enveloped them. She yelped as their feet lifted off the ground. Heimdallr's roar of rage echoed in her ears. Ives's stomach sank to her feet as the rainbow pulled them into the sky.

TWENTY-EIGHT

NOW OR NEVER

THEY SPUN through the sky for a small eternity before the rainbow spat them onto a polished stone floor in an unceremonious heap. Ives sprawled on Loki's chest, far to exposed for her liking.

She raised her head to cautiously take in their surroundings. Not that it did much good since she couldn't see beyond a few feet in any direction. They could be in a dungeon or a cave for all she knew. She never wanted to travel via that particular method again; Her head spun, and her internal organs protested with enough violence to make her long for the days of Jules's methods. After a few compulsive swallows, Ives met Loki's gaze, surprised to find him aware and watchful. The horrible madness of Ragnarök was muted here, but she could sense it hovering, like an ax waiting to fall.

"How long have you been awake?" she whispered. She stayed crouched over his prone form, unable to enjoy their moment of reprieve. Danger tickled her nerve endings, the hairs rose on the back of her neck. She was being watched, and it wasn't simply her leering companion.

"Long enough to find I rather enjoy this," said Loki.

Ives barely stifled the urge to slap him. He must have been an insufferable horndog before the prophecy. Divine looks aside, she knew better than to stray into that territory, again. This so wasn't the time to mull over immortal flirting.

"What happened?" he asked.

"Heimdallr decided he was tired of waiting for you to crack. Auntie tried to fight him off, but she couldn't do that *and* keep the island from shaking apart." Ives looked up into the surrounding gloom, unwilling to see his expression as she explained what she'd done. She knew he was unhappy with her when he lifted her off him, his good mood gone.

"How did we get away?"

She frowned, unsure of how to explain. "Would you believe the rainbow connection?"

"The Bifrost," said Loki, his voice higher as he spoke.

"Um, sure, I guess. The 'alalā's feather opened the way," said Ives.

Loki grabbed her wrist, fingers biting into her skin until she gasped. He loosened them immediately, his voice strained. "Ives, what's an 'alalā?"

She glanced at him, stunned by his fear. "A crow."

"Shit," Loki said. He sprang into action.

The Trickster spun her beneath him moments before a whistling shriek sang overhead. He grunted as something embedded in the stone floor by her thigh, carefully rolling off her. Light flooded the room, brilliant and blinding. Ives yelped at the invasion, squinting against the brightness, her eyes slow to adjust. Through half-blurred vision, she registered the pain on Loki's face. Clarity came with a terrible sight. A spear protruded through his shoulder, where it pinned him to the floor.

Details filtered through her shock and fear, the vast size of the ornate decorated Great Hall, the scent of roasted meats, smoky hearth fires, and warm mead, and the certainty they had an audience. Ives shook as she looked behind them. Her stomach sank as she caught sight of the watching group on the raised dais across the hall. Gods, all of them. The aura of their power would have given them away if the golden glow didn't. She only recognized a few of them, including the central figure, thanks to a healthy infusion of comic books and movies, though they looked nothing like their superheroes interpretations. Mostly they looked pissed off. Most gods didn't possess physical imperfections or long-lasting scars, a boon of divine stamina. This god did, but equating the All-Father's ancient scars to weakness would be a grand mistake. Ives fought not to quail under Odin's imperious stare but lost the battle as his voice rolled through the hall.

"Loki Laufison," said Odin, "Come meet your final justice."

"Brother," said Loki through his teeth, hands wrapped around the gilded runes etched in the shaft of the spear. "Brother, please, listen—"

"You lost the right to that distinction long ago," a woman snapped. She broke the line as she stepped forward. Another spear appeared in her hands. The warrior woman bared her teeth in a fierce snarl and brought her arm back to let the second one fly.

"No," Ives shrieked. She scrambled out from under Loki before he could stop her, ignoring his curses as she held up her arms to shield him. It was a useless gesture. The goddess would steamroll her in seconds. Incredibly, her appearance caused the warrior woman to falter with a frown. Confusion crossed the goddess's face as if she didn't know what to make of Ives. "A mortal?"

Mortal, indeed. Ives's heart slammed against her ribs as she faced the dais and the incredibly intimidating figures on it. "Please, you can't do this."

An incredulous murmur echoed among the assembled gods. The only one who didn't speak was Odin. His single eye stared at her with searing intensity.

"How did you get here, girl?" the warrior goddess demanded. She squinted at Ives with a superiority that made her grind her teeth.

"The magic feather," said Ives. She steadied herself as she prepared to dig her hole deeper. She hadn't dealt with so many gods at once before. Humility seemed a surefire tactic for handling divine beings. One she was going to throw right out the window. "Please, sirs, ladies, please listen to me. You've been played, manipulated. This whole Ragnarök business is one giant sham—"

"Silence," roared a blond giant of a god, a least a head and shoulders taller than the others. Thunder chased his booming voice. It made her bones shake. As if that wasn't enough of a clue to his identity, the skull-cracking hammer hanging from a leather strap at his wrist sealed the deal.

"Wow, Thor. It's almost like meeting a celebrity," Ives muttered.

"Ives, what the hell are you doing?" Loki hissed at her.

She gnawed her lip and wished she had a good answer. "Stalling," she said.

"What?"

She inhaled for strength and tried addressing their assembled audience again. "Ragnarök is a lie, nothing but a plot to villainize the Trickster and his family." Of course, the Fates were nowhere to be seen. So much for their promised boon.

"Foolish human," said the warrior goddess.

Ives was decidedly not a fan of that one.

"You are defending a murderer, one who killed the Beloved out of spite. His children are monsters."

"No," said Ives. "That was another manipulation, orchestrated by the same god who created the prophecy."

They were all looking at her now with a weighted silence that nearly broke her courage. Through all her prior encounters with Loki and his children, she hadn't felt her mortality as acutely as she did now.

Odin leaned forward. "Who do you believe responsible, Ikepela Ives?"

She startled at her name. It shouldn't have been a surprise, but as the other gods hadn't deigned to address her, its use by the All-Father jarred her.

The warrior goddess spoke before Ives could. "Why are we listening to this drivel? Where is Heimdallr? He will shine a light on what is happening."

"Yes, Heimdallr," the other gods echoed.

Ives's skin prickled as the air around the divine assembly shifted. Their collective golden glow dimmed as their eyes glazed over, a web of black and gold thread shimmered between them. The All-Father was no exception. Threads of influence circled him, but his lone eye remained sharp and focused on Ives.

"He's coming," said Odin.

Ives jerked around as Heimdallr's voice slithered into the hall. "Brothers, sisters, our time of glory is nigh."

"You," said Ives. She glared as the shining god beamed at her with gleaming gold teeth. "You did this."

Loki was too quiet behind her. With Heimdallr so close, he'd likely lost his resistance. But she couldn't look away from the shining god, not yet.

"You created Ragnarök," she said. "You tricked the

Fates, the other gods, even the Trickster himself. You set all of this into motion."

Her voice was loud enough for the gods on the dais to hear, but the declaration was met with silence. Despite her resolve, Ives's gaze slid to the other gods, whose slack expressions displayed how deeply Heimdallr's influence ran. His hooks were in too deep.

"What lies you speak, little mortal. Her words hold no merit," said Heimdallr, his voice calm and the complete opposite of her wavering one.

The other gods vacantly nodded in agreement.

The Fates had tried to warn her.

"Son of a bitch," Ives said. Here she was, stranded on Heimdallr's home turf, with no backup and no escape, because she trusted a freaking magic feather, a rather rash decision in retrospect.

Way to go, Dumbo.

Sure, it probably saved her mother's life and her home island. But this was Loki's realm, Heimdallr's realm, far outside the reach of Pele and Ives's mortal and divine family. She'd left Jules and the trio of siblings behind. There would be no more last-minute interventions. Her only present ally was pinned to the floor like an insect on display, slipping under the prophecy's grip. She was going to die here, defenseless, as Heimdallr killed everyone. Even if she threw everything she had left at Ragnarök, it wouldn't be enough, Heimdallr's influence was too strong. Ives could see now, clear as day, that he had the other gods as tangled in his web as Loki. He'd played the Fates, made the other gods into puppets, and all for what? She made a disgusted sound.

"What is your beef with Loki?" Her curiosity was genuine. Through everything, she still had no idea why this god was pissed off enough to incite an apocalypse.

And if she was going to die, she deserved to know, dammit.

Heimdallr blinked at her, clearly taken aback by the question. "He killed the Beloved One. His monstrous children spread chaos and misery. He—"

"Yeah, yeah, I heard the stories, but I saw that tapestry. *You* started it," said Ives.

Heimdallr sputtered, and his calm facade slipped. The rage burning in his pale eyes stole her breath. "Liar. He did. This is all his doing," he spat, his whole frame vibrated from the strength of his anger.

Ives licked her lips, her muscles tense against the instinct to flee as she pressed the unstable god. "How so?"

He didn't answer, too busy seething. She opened her mouth to say more when he snarled, drawing up like a cobra ready to strike.

"He stole everything from me," Heimdallr roared. His overbright gaze burned with a deep-seated insanity that took her breath away. "That—that *creature*, welcomed into our ranks like an equal. He had them all in his thrall, the fools, charmed by little more than a beast." His lips curled in a disgusted sneer. "Odin was the biggest fool of the lot. Fawning over him, doting on him like a treasured sibling. Calling him blood brother. The All-Father's favorite."

Ives stilled. Her jaw dropped as she processed what he said. "You... You were jealous? That's it? That's your world-ending grudge, that they liked him better than you?"

"Better than me?" Heimdallr snapped forward, inches from her face. Flecks of spittle hit her cheek as he spat his grievances. "Better than me? They allowed that filth to taint our pure Asgardian line. Condemned the pure Lady Sigyn to his marriage bed. Allowed his despicable children to roam the realm. I am a pure Asgardian. I should have had the All-Father's favor. It should have been me, not some filthy Jotunn half-breed." He reached for her, grabbing a handful of her shirt before she could scramble away from him. "And you, Fate Cipher, you nearly cost me everything. I've worked so long towards one goal, one end, and your damn meddling almost brought it toppling down. I never expected you to involve the gods of your homeland in our affairs."

His words tickled the edge of her awareness. Heimdallr didn't know her true connection to Pele? How could he not? He called himself the Sight of the gods, Ives thought that meant he knew all the pieces on the playing field. Or did her very mortal father not merit enough notice compared to her mother? She held her breath as she tried to puzzle together the importance of that ignorance.

Remember your other heritage. The Mother Fate's warning echoed through her mind now, anchoring her to the moment. She was the only mortal Fate Cipher to exist. She possessed an immortal power that consumed her life with each use. But it wasn't the only *blessing* she possessed. It shouldn't work, Pele told her it wouldn't work. She'd been surprisingly lucky so far.

In the confines of her mind, distinct even with a god sneering in her face, Ives heard the sound of a thread snap.

There was no such thing as luck.

"Despite your interference, the prophecy will come to fruition." Heimdallr's voice snared her to the present. "However, you won't be here to witness the end."

Ives jolted under his hold, the neckline of her shirt cutting into her skin. The shining god loomed over her as a very real, imminent threat. She stared up, drowning in the madness of his gaze when an animal's guttural roar sounded behind her. A blur of red shot over her head and tackled Heimdallr. The impact tore her shirt from his grasp. Ives fell backward, landing hard, as a bear the color of flame took Heimdallr to the ground in a rolling ball of fury and fur. A massive paw swung out from the fray, three-inch claws that raked deep gouges in the shining god's chest that bled golden ichor.

Where the hell had the bear come from? Ives shot Loki a panicked glance only to find a bloody spear on the floor. The lightbulb went off in her brain as she saw the open wound on the bear's shoulder. Shapeshifting was one of the Trickster's well-known talents, but it was one she hadn't seen him use until this moment.

Heimdallr wasn't out for the count yet. He shoved the bear off. A crossbow appeared in his hands as he struggled to his feet, panting, and bleeding. Wrathful determination blazed in his gaze. He leveled the crossbow as Loki charged. The cords of Ragnarök thickened, the threads twanged a discordant song that jangled inside her mind. She gasped, the tapestry flashed through her mind. Loki against Heimdallr. This was the showdown he wanted, felling the Trickster in battle, while the other gods stood witness.

"No," Ives shouted.

The crossbow fired. Time seemed to slow as the bolt moved through the air. Her gaze fixated on its path, everything else frozen in place. Her cry startled Loki. Green eyes stared at her from the bear's face, filled with confusion. He twisted away at the last moment. The bolt grazed his side as he rolled. A human Loki landed on his hands and knees only a few feet from her.

Ragnarok keened, the moment thwarted. The prophecy's displeasure scraped along her nerve endings. It wasn't over, not with the crossbow still in Heimdallr's hands.

A caw snagged her attention, pulling her gaze to the ensnared Odin. A crow perched on his shoulder, bright black eyes staring at her with equal intensity, expectant.

Waiting for her to act.

"It is time, brothers and sisters," Heimdallr cried out. A maniacal grin twisted his divine beauty into a grotesque mask as he aimed his reloaded crossbow at the kneeling Trickster. "Time for the end."

Loki shouted and burst into flames. The stone beneath them trembled as Ragnarök snapped its leash. Between nerves and the shifting ground, Ives didn't trust her balance. She dropped to the floor, crawling toward Loki as the stone split and blackened from the heat of his flames. Heimdallr ignored her. She didn't matter now. Ragnarök was unfolding around them. Dust and grit rained from the ceiling as the foundations of Asgard rocked beneath the prophecy's hold.

Ives kept crawling.

I am the Fate Cipher. A mortal fate cipher, with an imperfect power. I am also a child of Pele.

Her hands touched the molten stone surrounding Loki —warm, a heat like her father's workshop, comfortable and familiar. She embraced the heat and let it sing through her veins, welcomed it in like an old friend. She remembered long hours, cozy in the sweltering heat of the forge as her father worked metal. Forgotten memories of his hands plunged deep into the flame as she watched, eyes half-closed as she dozed off. An affinity for forge and fire, the blessing of her family line.

Ives crouched beside Loki. Flames harmlessly brushed her skin. She reached deep and summoned the exhausted power of the Fate Cipher. Cords of red, black, and gold filtered through her vision, they choked the air, an impossible tangle to unravel, but not to burn.

Ives couldn't wield divine power without destroying herself, but playing with fire? That was a family matter. Uncertain, she made to cup the flames rolling off the Trickster like molten water. The fire flowed into her hands, vibrant and alive, eager to answer her call. Loki jerked, eyes wide with realization. The flames spread, encasing them in a cocoon of fire.

Heimdallr's look of triumph slipped as he realized Ives wasn't burning to a crisp. "What are you doing?" he screamed at them. He swung the crossbow, aiming at her chest.

Now or never. Operating on a barely formed instinct, Ives used the guttering flicker of her power to seize the threads of prophecy binding Loki. His fire danced along her skin, burning hotter as she wrapped her hands around the cords. Her weakened power did the one thing it needed to, giving the prophecy a physical presence for the fire to latch on to. The threads of Ragnarök popped and sizzled, burned more like meat than thread. They writhed like a living creature as the fire ate them away. The keening hiss of the dying prophecy was amplified by the massive stone hall, but over it all, she could hear Heimdallr's incredulous screams. Her concentration nearly broke when the crossbow fired, but Loki knocked the bolt off course with a casual flick of his wrist, turning it to ash. He steadied her with a hand on her shoulder as she coaxed the fire in a wider, finer arc, directing the flames to the massive web of Heimdallr's devious threads. Ash rained over the polish stone. The gods sagged as their strings dissolved. Vacant gazes switched to sharp, dangerous focus, but Ives didn't stop. Sweat coated her skin. Exhaustion sent every muscle trembling. She swayed, but she didn't stop, not until every last scrap and fiber of Ragnarök was burnt away.

Ashes, the only evidence left of the prophecy and Heimdallr's insidious influence, swirled across the floor. Ives sucked in a gasp, the awful pressure finally gone as her body gave out. She collapsed, barely cognizant of the god who caught her. Loki shielded her as they watched the gods awaken on the dais.

Ives could barely keep her eyes open, but her blurry gaze eventually found Odin. Was it possible for a one-eyed god to wink at you? A forming revelation stole over her as the deities glanced between Loki and the unhinged Heimdallr.

The warrior goddess was the first to react, emitting a shriek of fury like an ice pick to Ives's eardrums. "What is the meaning of this, Heimdallr?" Her hands tightened on her spear, wrath etched in her features.

Ives was grateful all that venom wasn't directed at her.

"You've ruined everything," said Heimdallr.

Ives felt Loki tense. She looked at Heimdallr, whose luster was severely diminished. His crossbow lay at his feet in a smoking ruin. Ash streaked his skin, coated his clothes and hair. Golden blood still oozed from the slashes across his chest and the corner of his mouth. His pale eyes glowed with hatred as he stared her down.

"After all these centuries, you're still a spoiled little pounce," said Loki, dismissal dripping from his tone.

An ugly sneer twisted Heimdallr's face. "You." A dagger appeared in his hand as he charged them, snarling like a wounded bull.

Ives's exhausted body refused to move. She would have laughed if a homicidal god wasn't barreling down on her. She'd found her loophole, survived Ragnarök, only to get gutted by an insane immortal with a superiority complex.

A caw rang in her ears like a harsh laugh. The crow landed beside her and cawed again as if it shared in her internal joke. She'd be damned if it wasn't the same one who'd given her the magic feather that brought her here.

Heimdallr's steps staggered, thrown by the sudden appearance of the bird. He was so focused on the crow he didn't see the goddess of death until she grabbed him and flipped him in a perfectly executed suplex.

Hel straightened and planted her booted foot on Heimdallr's stomach, leering down at him. "You so much as twitch, and I'll elbow-drop you into the next century." She glanced up at them. Her smile turned genuine. "Ives! You're alive! Now Jules will let me live."

Tears blurred Ives's vision. Crying compounded her exhaustion, but she couldn't help it. "Your timing is perfect," she sniffed. "I had no idea you were a WWE fan."

"I am a woman of varied tastes," said Hel. She drove her heel into Heimdallr's gut to punctuate her statement.

The warrior goddess appeared next to Hel, glaring at Heimdallr with disgust. "I shall take charge of the bastard, daughter of Loki."

"Skadi!" Hel squealed, wrapping the goddess in an exuberant hug that Skadi bore with stoic stiffness.

Skadi gave Hel an awkward pat on the head before viciously driving the butt of her spear against Heimdallr's chest.

Ives's grin faded as she realized the warrior goddess wasn't the only one to leave the dais. The entire Norse pantheon surrounded them. The confluence of divine energy was suffocating.

"Back it up. Back it up," said Hel. She planted herself in front of her father and Ives, shooing the collective gods from coming too close.

"Hel, your face," said one of them, a note of awe in their tone.

"I know right? Tattoo chic," said Hel. She fluffed her hair.

Ives hid her face against Loki's chest. She wished the lot of them would go away so she could sleep.

"Not yet, little one."

She couldn't help but respond to the command in that voice. She turned to find the All-Father crouched beside her, probably too close, judging by the tension in Loki's frame, though the Trickster was oddly subdued in Odin's presence.

Skadi glared at Loki while keeping Heimdallr pinned to the floor. "Anyone care to explain what the sniveling dog has done? Are we not taking the Trickster and his whelp to task for their part in this plot?"

Ives hated her, totally hated her. "Touch them, and I'll burn your hair off," she said.

Skadi raised an eyebrow, either surprised a mortal would dare threaten her or mildly impressed by Ives's spunk. Possibly both.

"We can explain. And we can attest to the Trickster's innocence," the eldest Fate said.

Ives made a face. Her head lolled as she swung a glare at the Fates. "*Now* you show up?"

They looked the same and different from how they had in their realm, the bottom half of their faces visible under their hoods.

She swore the Mother's blood-red lips lifted in a small, subtle smile. "I am afraid we were as bound by the prophecy as the other occupants of this room. Its hold on us collapsed when you succeeded in burning it out. Well done, Fate Cipher."

Silence fell as the collective of gods and goddesses stopped to give her a long scrutinizing stare.

"That's the Fate Cipher? Isn't she rather....puny?" Skadi said. Of course, it was Skadi.

When Ives got up from her week-long nap, the first thing she was going to do was find the goddess and punch her right in her smug, punchable mouth.

"That puny mortal just saved your ass," Hel snapped.

"She saved the world," said the Maiden.

"She undid our great mistake," said the Crone.

"She fought impossible odds to right an ancient wrong," said the Mother.

"Take it away, ladies," muttered Ives.

The gods listened with rapt attention as the Fates filled in the gaps. Ives, too tired to care, let them. She was perfectly content to fall asleep while the gods sorted themselves out. Ives started to drift, feeling relatively safe guarded by Loki and Hel when she realized Odin was still watching her.

She debated telling him off for being creepy when the crow nudged against her hand.

"I dare say Muninn likes you," said Odin. Another crow perched on the All-Father's shoulder.

"Mortals are easy to like when you give them a chance," said Loki. His tone held remnants of anger.

Odin sighed.

Ives watched him, her exhausted brain slowly putting a few pieces in place. "You knew about Heimdallr," she said. There was no accusation in her voice, but the lines in the elder god's face etched deeper, world-weary.

"It is impossible not to be aware of the noose around your neck," said Odin. "You do not know the depth of our debt to you, Ikepela Ives, the prison you have freed us from." A dangerous glint entered his single eye. "Heimdallr will pay for everything he's done, for everyone he has wronged." His gaze flickered over her head for a moment. "I promise you, brother."

The tension drained from Loki. The rift between Trickster and All-Father ran deep due to Heimdallr's machinations, but maybe it wasn't an insurmountable one.

Ives smiled in relief. "You sent the crow to bring us here?"

Odin nodded. "And a Valkyrie too young for Ragnarök to have complete control of her actions."

"Hildr," said Ives, remembering the poor Valkyrie's broken expression after her gruesome discovery. "She found Lady Sigyn."

The gods closest to them looked shocked by her words.

Odin bowed his head, his grief was evident. "Heimdallr has much to answer for, as do I for not seeing the signs sooner."

"Don't be too hard on yourself. He managed to trick the Fates, and they're supposed to see more than you," said Ives.

Odin's cough sounded suspiciously like a chuckle. Loki's shoulders were shaking with suppressed laughter. Ives rolled her eyes. *Gods.*

She bit her lip. "Thank you for helping where you could," she said.

Odin smiled, an odd expression for such an intense man. "A trifling. Thank you for saving the world, Fate Cipher."

"All in a night's work," she said as she finally lost the fight to exhaustion. Ives conked out, oblivious to the gods who watched over her.

☗☗☗

Loki eased the Fate Cipher into a comfortable position, allowing her head to rest on his knee. She reminded him so much of his daughter, his heart hurt at the risks she took for his family. Speaking of…

Hel plopped down next to them and leaned against his side. Her tattooed fingers gently smoothed Ives's hair from her face. "So cute when she's sleeping," she sighed. Loki's ears perked at the wistful tone in her voice. He studied his daughter, who'd never managed to form a close attachment to anyone other than family in his long memory.

Odin shook his head. "Mortals, so very easy to get attached to, but it is a transient attachment."

Loki scowled. "Not another word on the subject, brother." But he didn't miss the somber shift in his daughter's expression as she watched the sleeping mortal.

TWENTY-NINE

UNRAVELING

IVES WOKE up to her childhood ceiling, still dotted with the same old glow-in-the-dark stars plus a few new cracks from tussling with frost giants. Odd how normal that sounded in her head. She lay there, in the quiet, as she slowly gained her bearings. Ives tried to discern if waking in her old room was disappointing or a relief. She'd passed out surrounded by gods, a somewhat frightening and thrilling situation.

She sighed and looked to her left. Her mother was asleep next to her. The sight did strange things to her heart. In her sleep, the effects of Keawe's new mortality were not so obvious, her face comprised of the same smooth angles that were etched into Ives's memory. There was so much time lost between them, so many unspoken words and missed moments. Her presence should have been awkward or uncomfortable. But Ives's chin trembled as tears slid across her face. This was the first perfect moment she shared with her mother. She watched Keawe for several minutes, content. She'd survived her first big apocalypse. She'd lived! Pele could suck it!

The thought chased away her high. She survived but she was still the Fate Cipher, and still an inadequate one.

What would happen next time? Would there be a next time in her lifetime? How long would her life be when her power had used up her 'mortal wick?' She couldn't shake the feeling she was on borrowed time.

A small sound behind Ives distracted her morbid train of thought. She rolled her head to the other side to find Jules nestled against her other side. With a watery smile, she shifted and gently tugged on one of the fae's curls.

Warm brown eyes shot open, widening when she saw Ives's awake. Jules's face crumpled as she wrapped her arms around her roomie. Her small frame shook with quiet sobs.

"Oh, you're awake," Keawe murmured. She stretched as she sat up. Her mother ran a tired hand through her hair. She smiled. "Why don't I let your father know you're awake and let you two catch up?"

"Thanks...Mom," said Ives.

Keawe's smile widened. "I'm so proud of you, Ikepela." She reached over to cup Ives's cheek, the one not obstructed by a sobbing fae.

For once, Ives didn't mind hearing her first name. It wasn't so bad. Her mother slipped off the bed and quietly shut the door behind her.

Jules pulled back, checking Ives over. "I thought you were a goner," she whispered.

Ives swallowed past the tightness in her throat and pushed the tangled curls off her friend's face. "I thought I was, too. Figuring out how to use Loki's fire was a lucky break."

Jules fidgeted. "If it had been anyone else—"

"It wouldn't have worked," Ives admitted. Maybe if she'd finished her confrontation with Heimdallr with Pele at her side, she could have figured out how to use the goddess's fire, but it might have been too little too late, especially with Ragnarök inducing earthquakes. That would have led to a body count she didn't want on her conscience. The fact that Loki was also a god of fire didn't escape her. It wasn't a coincidence and Ives's thought, at last, she had an idea what or who was responsible for her streak of luck.

"Does this mean you're retiring from the Fate Cipher business?" Jules's tone was neutral, but her gaze remained watchful.

Ives paused, as the idea tumbled over and over in her thoughts. "I don't know."

"You're still mortal," said Jules. "Those limitations are still there, worse than before."

Ives nodded. "I think the first order of business is to find out who bargained away my mother's immortality."

Jules frowned, worry tempering her relief at Ives's survival. "You're going for it, aren't you? Not that long ago, you wanted nothing to do with being the Fate Cipher."

"I admit—it felt pretty good playing hero," said Ives.

Jules nudged her. "You weren't playing, silly. You *are* a hero. You stopped a crazy god and cleared the name of a mythical villain. That is going to look amazing on your resume."

Ives laughed and wiped the tears off her face. Her heart twinged a little at the mention of Loki. Where were the Trickster and his family now? Between long overdue reunions, cleaning up Heimdallr's mess, and getting reacquainted with their divine brethren, her new divine friends had their plate full. She twisted her blanket between her fingers, surprised by the line of her thoughts. Did she really consider the god of mischief and his children friends? She didn't even get the chance to tell Hel goodbye, or thank her for everything. She found she missed the goddess and her brothers, but time moved differently for divine beings. By the time the straightened things in Asgard, Ives could be decades older, if she was fortunate enough to live that long.

Right, first she had to tackle her little mortality problem. She pushed aside her morose thoughts and observed Jules. Her friend was holding something back. "What happened to you guys while I was chasing Fates?"

"Oh, you know, the usual—smacking around giants, raising the dead, et cetera," said Jules. "We took care of Heimdallr's nasty little Jotunn army while you broke Mama Ives out of jail."

Ives shook her head. "Considering how much of a purist he was, I'm amazed he deigned to work with them."

Jules shrugged. "The enemy of my enemy is my unsavory ally." She paused and fidgeted again. "I'm really glad you're okay."

Ives gently flicked Jules's nose. "Me, too. Now spit it out."

Jules's smile trembled a little. "You know me too well." She took a steadying breath. "I'm leaving."

"I know," said Ives. She pulled Jules into another hug.

"How?" Jules's bewildered muffle made Ives grin.

"When I went into the realm of the Fates to rescue mom, I saw your tapestry, the circle of dancing fae who looked just like you and the burnt-out center." Ives pulled back to see her friend's expression. "We passed it on the way out, too. The threads in the middle were healing, weaving back together."

Jules scrubbed her face. "Out in the desert, I remembered who I was, who I used to be before you found me. You saved me too, Ives," she said. "Now, it's time to find my fate again."

"And if you need me, you know where to find me," said Ives. She raised an eyebrow. "Are you tackling this alone?"

Jules made a face, and a blush crept up her cheeks. "Actually, uh, Jorm asked to come with me."

"You two are adorable!" Ives squealed before Jules knocked her off the bed with a pillow to the face.

☺☺☺

It wasn't until Jules left her alone that Ives dared voice her theory out loud, convinced she sounded like an idiot, but half certain there was another party listening.

"I know it was you." She held her breath. She wasn't one hundred percent certain until she heard the now-familiar snap of thread in her mind. One of the hooded Fates sat at the end of her bed as if she'd been there all along.

The Mother sighed. "It was that reminder about your heritage, wasn't it?"

Ives nodded, mulling over the hundreds of questions she wanted to ask the Fate. "Did you...were you directing my fate?"

The Mother's hood tilted upward. Only the bottom half of her face was visible beneath the gauzy gray cloth, but Ives felt the weight of her gaze. She squirmed under the Fate's stare. "Your education has been severely lacking. The Fate Cipher is immune to the influence of Fate. Have you never noticed you have no fate line?" She reached over to lift Ives's hand to the light, comparing their palms side by side. Ives's never noticed the missing crease until now.

"Well, that's freaky," she muttered. She frowned. "But you kept me alive?"

"Yes, I manipulated events in your favor, twisting and pulling the fates of those around you to subvert your mortality," said the Mother. She dropped Ives's hand, bowing her head. "I didn't fully succeed. Your lifeline is far shorter as a result, and I cannot interfere in such a manner again."

"You mean your sisters won't let you?" Ives couldn't keep the bitterness out of her voice.

"They don't know I helped you," said the Mother.

Ives shook her head at the admittance. "Why help me at all? Why expend the energy to keep me alive? Aren't we on opposite sides here?"

The Mother was silent so long Ives thought she wouldn't answer. "There must be a balance, Fate Cipher. We do function as we should without a countering force to keep us in check. Life requires Death, Light requires Darkness, and the Fates require Free Will. You represent that balance."

Ives crossed her arms. "That doesn't explain why *you* helped me."

A smile tugged at the corner of the Mother's mouth. "I had a child once. I could not witness another mother's pain and do nothing." The Mother rose, smoothing a hand down her robes. "Fix your mortal problem, Ikepela Ives, because we will meet again."

Ives opened her mouth to ask another question, but the Mother was already gone.

☗ ☗ ☗

Things weren't perfect.

Jules left within a week, hand in hand with Jorm, who sported a rather dashing eyepatch. Their battle with giants left the World Snake with a few new scars. Considering how breathless Jules got every time she looked at him, he didn't seem to mind.

Lavi Ives's house was still overcrowded. Between her

parents, uncomfortably touchy-feely after so long apart, and the rather violent bickering between her mother and the recovering Valkyrie, Ives quickly found she couldn't stand the company. Fenrir had joined his divine family in Asgard before Ives woke up, Hildr had stayed, still shaken by her encounter with Heimdallr. There was a lot of healing happening in her father's house, mentally, emotionally, and physically. Ives, desperately, didn't want to spoil the mood.

It wasn't their fault Ives felt lonely and rudderless. Luckily, there was one other individual who felt a little out of place. Chester the Hound was all too happy to jump into Ives's Jeep and keep her company in her now-too-empty apartment.

Two weeks. From Hildr tracking her down at Johnny Ho's to the two days she spent sleeping after. That was how long her little adventure took in real-time. It felt like a lifetime ago. Her parents were experiencing a near blissful reunion with one another. Jules was reclaiming her destiny with Jormungand at her side. Other than the World Snake, Ives hadn't seen hide nor hair of the Norse Pantheon since her roommate left, though she did take the opportunity to brush up on her mythology. There were some eyebrow-raising stories of a certain red-headed god and his children. Ives was curled up in bed. She spoiled Chester with belly rubs as he cuddled up next to her while she read a book of Norse Fairy Tales.

"Keep spoiling him like that, and you'll never get him out of your bed."

Ives shrieked and threw her book at the god perched on her dresser. Loki effortlessly caught it. She clutched her blanket to her chest as she tried to banish the rush of adrenaline at his sudden appearance.

"Most people call first," she snapped, though, between

Loki and the Mother Fate, she should be used to the instantaneous comings and goings of the gods.

"This is far more entertaining," said Loki, an eyebrow rose at the book in his hands. "Interesting choice of reading material."

Ives huffed her hair out of her face. "Did you really give birth to an eight-legged horse?"

Loki's eye twitched. "That was one time. I was young and stupid and full of mead."

Ives laughed. The sound tapered off as Loki sat on the foot of her bed, his expression somber. Was he here to deliver bad news? Chester rolled over and offered his belly, which the Trickster obliged with gentle scratches.

"Not many people would keep a Hound as a pet," Loki remarked.

Ives shrugged. "We had a few hiccups. He has a straight-up vendetta with sports cars. The other day, he ripped the bumper of this dude's cherry-red Porsche. Thought the guy was going to have an aneurysm, but he didn't press charges. I think Chester made him nervous."

Loki grinned. "I suspect so."

Ives nibbled the inside of her cheek. "So, I take it Heimdallr is receiving his just desserts?"

Loki was silent as he pet the Hound. Ives wished she could have stayed awake longer during her brief time in Asgard. She missed pretty much everything. Without the influence of Ragnarök, Loki seemed so at peace, it was hard to compare him to the god she met a few days ago.

"After much discussion, we have relinquished him to the Norns," Loki said.

"The Fates? But why? Out of everyone he wronged, you suffered the worst," said Ives, surprised by her anger.

"Do you think he deserved to die for what he did?" Loki watched her. Those green eyes were unnerving.

She snorted. "Maybe. I don't know. He might have had a hand in stealing my mom's immortality, not to mention all those attempts on my life." She frowned down at Chester. "I don't know if I could have killed him, even in the heat of the moment."

For some reason, her answer made Loki smile. "Trust me when I say his punishment from the Fates will be just." He sighed. "Before they took him, he revealed something that has many of the gods... upset."

Ives could tell Loki was holding back. Her lips twitched at the thought of how similar he and Jules were in their habits. "Spit it out."

He snorted. "Fine. He revealed Baldr's death was not what it seemed."

Her eyebrows shot up. "What does that mean?"

"The Beloved One is possibly alive," said Loki. He rolled his shoulder in a half shrug. "And for my role in his fate, I have volunteered to find him."

The news left her surprisingly disappointed. He was leaving on a personal quest like Jules. She itched to ask him about the others. Where was Hel? Did they send her back to the Underworld? Did he have her email address? Why deliver the news personally?

"I can't thank you enough for what you did for my family, for me," said Loki. He halted over the words. Ah, so that was it. He wanted to thank her for—

He leaned over and pressed his lips to her forehead. Ives's froze, her veins fizzed at the point of contact as a spark of something that passed between them. She tingled down to her toes.

"What—What was that?" Ives furiously rubbed the spot, goosebumps dotting her arms. Did the Trickster just whammy her?

Loki bowed. "A blessing. Or perhaps it would be better

to call it a divine favor? If you ever require my aid, Ikepela Ives, I will answer your call ."

She blinked at him, flustered and a bit overwhelmed. "A trickster at my beck and call? That's a mighty gesture of trust. What if I want you to do my laundry or something?"

He chuckled. "You've earned that and more." His gaze sobered. "Take care of yourself, Ives, and uh, be gentle with her."

Ives frowned, wondering if the Trickster left a visible 'mark' on her forehead. "Be gentle with who?"

Loki was already gone. "Gods," Ives muttered.

It didn't take long for Hildr to take her leave. Intending to return to Valhalla and rebuild the ranks of Valkyrie that Heimdallr had destroyed, Hildr officially left Chester under Ives's care, decreeing both Hound and Fate Cipher would keep an eye on each other. Despite Chester's company, Ives felt lonelier than ever until she stumbled out of her bedroom one morning to find Hel making scrambled eggs.

"Ah, you're up," said the goddess of death. She set a fresh cup of coffee in front of Ives. Hel wore cutoff jeans and a ratty Bon Jovi t-shirt and looked utterly at home in Ives's kitchen.

Ives didn't trust herself to speak until she gulped down half her cup. "Would changing the locks do anything to keep gods from randomly showing up in my apartment?"

"No, we don't pay much attention to personal boundaries," said Hel as she placed two plates of cheesy scrambled eggs on the table. "However, a divine roommate might make more use of the front door." Her tone was nonchalant.

Ives nearly choked on her coffee. "What happened to your duties in the Underworld?"

Hel took a bite of her eggs and moaned softly. "So good," she said. She savored the mouthful before answering. "Here's the situation. With Heimdallr's nefarious plot revealed, there has been a bit of restructuring in management."

"Is that your fancy way of saying you're a free agent now?"

Hel tilted her head, thoughtful as she chewed. "Not quite. I've decided to keep my duties as the lady of the dead, but my job is no longer my life. More freedom, more choices." She closed her eyes and smiled as sunlight from the window played over her tattooed skin. "A chance to soak in the sun."

Ives sipped her coffee. "There is an awful lot of sunlight in Hawaii."

Hel opened her eyes. "I'll pay half the rent as long as you don't mind a roommate who keeps odd hours and raids twice a week."

"Are you okay with a roommate in her twenties who has mommy-and-me time?"

Hel grinned. "I love your mom. Can I come along once in a while?"

"Totally. I think she'll love you, too," said Ives. She grinned at her new roomie. The eggs were delicious.

Epilogue

THREE MONTHS LATER

Ives wiped the sweat from her forehead as she unlocked the door to her apartment and staggered inside. Chester the Hound bounded ahead of her, still brimming with energy after their two-mile run. She felt like crawling.

"I hate you," she whispered to the Hound, who took the opportunity to lick her sweaty face without mercy as she tried to catch her breath.

"Yo, roomie, that you?" Hel called from the other room. Laughter and chatter from her guildmates on vent poured from her computer speakers. "Quit griping, you sissy bitches. I'll be right back. Fine! Pull without me! Don't stand in fire!"

The goddess of death emerged from her room a moment later, hair in a high ponytail. She wore yoga pants and a t-shirt with a picture of a cartoon unicorn with a knife attached to its horn that said, *I'll cut you*. They'd been living together for months and her apparel still made Ives smile. Hel grinned at her. "Have a good run?"

Chester bounced up to her. Hel crouched down to pet him. "Oh, who's a good boy? Yes, you are."

Ives winced as she stretched. "It was good. I need a shower. Any, um, calls while I was out?"

"Your mom called to confirm Tuesday brunch, but other than that, no," Hel said softly. She peered up at Ives through her brand-new bangs. "I'm sure if anyone runs into trouble, you'll be the first to know, sweets."

"Right," said Ives. She shoved her disappointment down. "Off to the shower then."

She limped down the hall and passed the dining room table overflowing with 'research.' These last few months, she'd spent making up for years of slacking and had read every myth in every religion she could get her hands on. She would be ready in case someone came looking for help. Not that she could do much considering she was still very mortal. With Keawe's and Hel's help, they'd chased a few leads on the missing immortality of the Fate Cipher, but nothing had paid off. Ives hovered in a sort of limbo. She hadn't heard from Jules in months, or Hildr, or Loki. Not that she would be much help to them. She hadn't even seen her divine auntie since departing over the rainbow bridge. She suspected Pele might be sulking.

Ives sighed as she finished her shower. "Stop feeling sorry for yourself, idiot."

The doorbell rang.

She heard Hel yell, "I'll get it," as she grabbed her towel and wrapped it around herself.

"Ives?"

Ives frowned at the strangled note in Hel's voice and rushed out of the bathroom without thinking. She froze in the hall. Water dripped all over her floor as she stared at the figure on her doorstep. She hadn't thought about him in months, but there he was in all his gothic glory, dark eyes apologetic as they peered at her from over Hel's shoulder.

"Mordred," said Ives. "You're the last person I expected to see."

He rubbed the back of his neck, clearly uncomfortable. Good, the smug jerk deserved a little discomfort.

"I know we didn't end things on a high note," he said.

Ives glared at her ex. "What do you want?"

"I need your help," said Mordred le Fey.

ACKNOWLEDGMENTS

The act of writing might be a solo enterprise, but the creation of a book, like raising a child, takes a village. This book baby came to fruition thanks to many amazing people and serendipitous moments.

First, thank you to Elle and the Midnight Tide Publishing crew for giving another chance to Ikepela Ives and her gang of divine misfits. Here's to many more divine chances.

Thank you to my parents, especially my father for that first summer, freshman year of college, where you gave me the chance to write a novel. I learned a lot about myself during those late hours.

Thank you to my Wattchicks, Debbie, Keri, Gaby, Leigh, Tammy, and Darly. You ladies saved my sanity, lifted my heart, and enriched my life. To all the late night and early morning conversations, the celebrations, the venting. To coming up with bad romance titles and why vegetables should never be used as romantic descriptors.

To my Wattpad readers, who loved these characters and this story, who harassed and pleaded and nagged, and gave me everything I needed. You guys kept me coming back to this story, kept me working on it until I finished. Thank you for loving this story as much as I do.

ABOUT THE AUTHOR

Kristin Jacques is a science fiction, horror, and fantasy author based out of New England. She holds a B.A. in Creative Writing from Wells College. She's had several short stories published in and written for multiple digital platforms.

On the digital writing platform Wattpad, she was selected to be part of the Wattpad Stars program. She has written for Warner Bros, National Geographic, and her stories, *Marrow Charm* and *Edgewise* won two consecutive Wattys in 2015 and 2016 for excellence in digital story-telling.

Her award-winning dark fantasy *Marrow Charm* was picked up for publication by Parliament House Press for Fall 2019. The sequel, *Skin Curse*, releases November 2020.

When not writing, she is juggling two rambunctious boys, spoiling her cats, and catching up on a massive TBR pile. She is currently working on projects full of magic, mystery, and delight.

www.kristinjacques.com

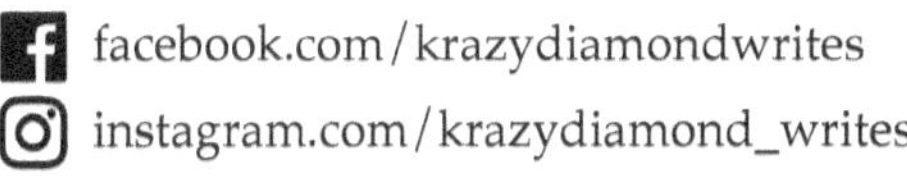

facebook.com/krazydiamondwrites

instagram.com/krazydiamond_writes

MORE BOOKS YOU'LL LOVE

If you enjoyed this story, please consider leaving a review!

Then check out more books from Midnight Tide Publishing!

Hex Next Door by Lou Wilham

For the Crow Witch, Icarus "Rus" Ashthorne, Moondale seemed the perfect hiding place. But like they always say, you can't go home again, and Rus finds out quickly that nothing is how she remembered, while at the same time very little has changed. Then she comes face to face with the only woman she's ever loved, Az Elwood, and... well, things get messier than she thought they ever could.

The Elwoods are a staple of Moondale, respected, feared, powerful, and Azure Elwood was always happy with her place amongst them. Happy to play the part of the good little witch, until Rus Ashthorne. Eleven years ago, Rus got on a bus and left Azure behind, but she's back, with two little girls trailing her like ducklings, and enough unspoken things between them to drown the town.

Now witch hunters are knocking at their proverbial door, the council of magic is being a real pain in the ass, and Rus wonders how much magic it'll take to protect the people she loves from herself and the danger following her.

Available Now

Seeds of Sorrow by Elle Beaumont & Christis Christie

Wishing for more adventure in her life, and hoping to escape from under her overprotective mother's thumb even for just a night, Eden accepts an invitation to a ball in another king's court. Despite her mother's ire, it all seems worth it as their travels take Eden away from home for the first time and into the middle realm.

Draven, known as the king of nightmares and ruler of the dark realm, Andhera, desires only to remain in his kingdom and maintain control and order over the ravenous creatures that lurk in the shadows. However, he finds himself drawn away by the mysterious summons of his brother, who appears to need his aid desperately.

As politics and death intermingle, can two entirely different fae learn to rely on one another? Or will the dark realm destroy all that is held most innocent and precious within the realms, and Eden herself?

Available Now